What readers are saying about *Broken Acres*, book one in the Jacob's Bend series:

Wonderful read! This book takes you on a journey full of heartfelt self-realizations from a woman coming into her own self-awareness. Can't wait for the next book!

—KS

Broken Acres is a powerful story of a woman overcoming the loss of her husband and growing stronger in the process of moving into the next season of her life. The author describes Maddie's struggles and self-doubt while also showing how one choice to push through the hard things makes the next right choice a little easier. The book was not only entertaining but also inspiring (without even coming close to preaching). I had a hard time putting it down and can't wait for the next book in the series!

—JZ

I just finished the book. Wow. When is the next one? I need more. I feel like I know all these people now. I definitely want to know what happens.

—HF

This book hooked me from the beginning paragraph and kept me engaged to the last sentence.

The writer has a unique gift to touch every human emotion throughout Maddie's journey of life after tragedy makes its mark. I'm making this book a Christmas gift to family members and friends.

—BP

My sister gave me your book for Christmas. I just got to it last week and gobbled it up. Wonderful. I, of course, love Maddie's farm. She needs sheep. Thank you. Can't wait for *Splintered Lives*.

—LMH

I loved this book. It kept me intrigued the whole time I was reading it. I can't wait to see what happens in the next book!

—SV

Excellent read that draws you in so the characters feel like friends. This is a wonderful story of loss, love, and faith. The characters were wonderful, and the descriptions of the areas and people made me feel like I knew them personally. I highly recommend this book!

—TT

Love the intrigue that never slows down. This book is a gem! I connected with Maddie as her story of self-discovery after tragedy unfolded. There are twists, tears, chuckles, and there is love. I found myself cheering Maddie on, as she is determined not to be a victim of widowhood but to overcome and have the life she has always dreamed of but never truly knew existed. I read it too fast and cannot wait for book two. *Broken Acres* is a must read!

—SM

I read your book in two days. Couldn't put it down. It was excellent! I loved it! Great job, Anne. You're a wonderful writer! Please get the next book out *soon*. I'm eagerly waiting!

—JH

Jacob's Bend · Book 2

SPLINTERED LIVES

A NOVEL

ANNE WATSON

Splintered Lives
©2020 Anne Watson
watsononline1711@gmail.com
AnneWatsonAuthor.com

Published by Fitting Words
www.fittingwords.net

All Scripture quotations, unless otherwise indicated, are taken from the New American Standard Bible® (NASB), Copyright © 1960, 1962, 1963, 1968, 1971, 1972, 1973, 1975, 1977, 1995 by The Lockman Foundation. Used by permission. www.Lockman.org.

Amplified Bible, Classic Edition (AMPC) Copyright © 1954, 1958, 1962, 1964, 1965, 1987 by The Lockman Foundation.

Library of Congress Cataloging-in-Publication Data

ISBN 978-1-7322391-8-0

Cover photos by Janis Rubus
Cover design by Sarah O'Neal/Eve Custom Artwork
Pen & ink illustration of Broken Acres by Kristi VanDuker

ALWAYS FOR THE KING

BROKEN
ACRES

"You can't go back and change the beginning, but you can start where you are and change the ending."

—C. S. Lewis

ONE

Silence shelters fear.

Lydia wrung her hands. The taunting voices and small rocks hitting her house did not scare her. The light of day did.

One last glance in the mirror. Disguised perfectly. Gray wig in place. Heavy makeup, a concealing mask. She hunched her back and grabbed the broom housed just inside the front door.

"Witch Hazel, get out of our town. You are not one of us. We don't want you here." Each boy took a turn screaming his own taunting barb.

She had heard these jeers before. Leaning her forehead against the front door she closed her eyes and breathed deep.

Lydia opened the door and hobbled toward the road, thrusting her broom like a sharp spear. "You boys get out of here or I'll cast one of my spells on you," she cackled.

The young wannabe tough guys sprinted down the sidewalk full bore.

As she slowly moved toward her shack, Lydia caught sight of a woman out of the corner of her eye holding tight to one of the out-of-breath hecklers.

Was she a mom to one of the boys? Lydia had never seen her before.

The boy escaped the woman's grasp when she looked in Lydia's direction.

Lydia slipped into the house and slammed the door behind her. Peeking around the edge of the drawn curtains, terror threatened to close her windpipe.

1

She's coming this way. Lydia's hands trembled. Wide-eyed, she prayed to some unknown being who had yet to answer her pleas for help. "No, not again."

The attractive middle-aged redhead stopped outside the gate.

"Don't come in. Don't come in," Lydia whispered.

With her hand on the gate, the woman shook her head and Lydia blew out the breath she had been holding. *What does she want? Is she looking for me? No, that's impossible. Everyone thinks I'm Witch Hazel. She couldn't know.*

Not daring to move, Lydia peered back through the gap in the curtains as the woman walked away.

Lydia fell into the lumpy, sheet-covered armchair. She was so tired of running. Tired of hiding. Would this never end?

TWO

M addie sipped coffee and gave Rusty, who shared the porch swing with her, a loving pat. His silky, russet coat was soft, his body warm against the crisp March morning. She looked across the orchard. "What do you think, buddy? Will we be able to finish the outside of that house before the last snowfall of the season?" They had been fortunate to have light snow this year. With the exception of that first blizzard. Maddie shivered at the thought of the blinding whiteout and Nathan's horrifying accident.

Rusty panted, cocked his head, and let out a weak bark that sounded more like a sad whine.

"Yeah. I agree. Finishing is probably not gonna happen, is it?"

The image of Nathan Carter, her building contractor, unconscious in the hospital still caused her heart to ache. Madison Crane had lived and breathed Nathan's every move for three days and nights at the foot of his hospital bed, not knowing whether he would live or die. Fear throbbed deep inside her whenever the machine attached to Nathan's heart flatlined.

Maddie had desperately wanted Nathan to wake up. To see his cobalt-blue eyes light up when she shared her feelings with him. Love hadn't always been the case with the two of them. As a matter of fact, loathing had often been a better description of their relationship, with anger and flaring tempers almost a daily occurrence. It wasn't until she became conscious of the fact that Nathan could die that the reality of her feelings for him hit her heart with intense force.

Nathan stirred something in her womanhood she had never known before. Even with Jeff, her deceased husband, Maddie had not experienced the passion she felt when Nathan kissed her—his strong arms holding her, his hands clutching her auburn hair as he pulled her into an intimate embrace.

Enough of this. She needed to stop thinking about Nathan Carter. A flash of Nathan's wavy brown hair beneath the bandage around his head caused her breath to deflate. *Enough, Maddie.* Pastor Ben said he was recuperating well in that rehab place. No doubt with the beautiful Ms. What's-Her-Name right by his side.

Maddie shook her head. "You know, Rusty, I've kinda lost the drive to finish this project."

The solemn golden retriever looked up at the mention of his name.

"Still, I know finishing the big house and welcoming those who are hurting and broken is what Broken Acres is all about." She gave a deep sigh.

Movement on the other side of the apple orchard that connected her cottage to the big house caught Maddie's eye, and her sigh gave way to a smile. Billy Chambers, a young man with a painful past, had been putting in long hours to finish the outside work on the two-story vintage dwelling that would house those who were looking for a safe refuge. Since they had already had one unexpected blizzard, Billy was working at a fast pace to accomplish all Nathan had planned to get done in case snow fell again. Which it often unexpectedly did in the Pacific Northwest. As Nathan's helper, Billy was the best. But as construction foreman? Maddie had her doubts.

Maddie looked over her shoulder when the rusty hinge on the screen door squeaked open and slapped shut. She always left the heavy wood door of the cottage cracked so Rusty and Sarg could slip out by pawing the screen open, but they had yet to figure out how to get back in without her help. Sarg, her misfit black cat, stretched his front legs and arched his back. Rusty opened one eye, his head unmoving between his paws, and glanced at his pal.

"Hey there." Maddie stroked the white stripe that ran down the cat's soft back as he threaded her legs. "You finally wake up? I thought military personnel were up at the crack of dawn."

The cat yawned.

"Yeah, I know you were never a military cat." She smoothed his fur. "I'd sorely love to know your background."

Maddie smiled at her two companions. "You know, guys, I had the strangest dream the other night. I can't imagine what it meant."

Carolyn always called Maddie's dreams the product of an overactive imagination. Still, some of them stayed strong in her memory. Sipping her coffee, she squinted at the sun. "Dreams and imagination are different, though, aren't they?" Sarg flicked his tail in her direction and curled up beside her, ignoring her questions as usual.

Carolyn. Maddie closed her eyes and considered her friend. Carolyn Moreno had been Maddie's best friend since they were five years old. Now a tall, beautiful, and slender aerobics instructor, Carolyn's thick, unruly brown hair and sparkling blue eyes reminded Maddie of her need to get in shape and work on her appearance. She had really let herself go since moving into and renovating the cottage.

Even with the miles between them, Carolyn was still her best friend. How was house hunting going for her and Alex back East? And what about Alex's new job? Maddie tilted her head and looked out over her land as if looking for answers from all those miles away.

Rusty nuzzled the back of her hand with his nose and Maddie smiled. She never would have moved clear across the country to Jacob's Bend if she'd known the Morenos were going to be transferred to New York. She would have stayed in Chicago. "But then I wouldn't have you and Sarg, would I?" And she wouldn't have Broken Acres either. She shaded her eyes and scanned the acres of farmland and grazing cattle.

Broken . . . Broken background. Background checks. Oh yeah, the dream.

Who was the other person in the dream? Maybe Ben. She smiled.

It's funny the things that are in your subconscious and how they come out while you're sleeping. In the dream she and this other person had been doing background checks on the people who would be living at Broken Acres. Maddie took another sip of coffee.

But she hadn't done background checks on Billy or Shauna. Honestly, she really didn't care about their pasts. And why was Witch Hazel in her dream? She had only seen her once or twice out front of that broken-down old shack she called home. She hated that people called her Witch Hazel. Was Hazel her real name? Good grief, she hadn't given her a thought in months. Not since the day several months ago at church when she asked Madelyn Simpson, the woman who knew everything about everybody in Jacob's Bend, why North Hills Chapel hadn't done anything to help her.

"Oh, honey, we have tried, believe me," Madelyn had said. "We've invited her to church, to special functions, Bible studies. She just waves us off and slams the door in our faces."

"Maybe we ought to just show up with rakes and wheelbarrows and clean up the lot next to her house."

"Oh, I wouldn't advise that. She doesn't like anyone coming within twenty feet of her place." Madelyn had pulled in closer and whispered in Maddie's ear, "Besides, she's been known to put a hex on people."

Maddie remembered the disgust she'd felt at that statement.

Those background checks in her dream had her running all over kingdom come. She checked on people from the East Coast to Texas to the Northwest.

The uncertainty she felt in her dream made her wonder if she should check out the people who came to Broken Acres to live. "What do you think, buddy?" Rusty breathed deep and let his breath out slowly.

Maddie squinted into the distance and rubbed her chin. Would the woman known as Witch Hazel be coming to Broken Acres? Hmm, now that was one she'd never thought of.

Maybe the next time she was in Carterville she'd stop in and see Elias Jones at the county offices, ask about the name on the property. After all, she didn't want to call the woman "Hazel" if that was not her name. "Hey, this sleuth stuff is fun." Sarg glanced up at her with his *you-talkin'-to-me?* look, meowed, and jumped from the swing to saunter into the apple orchard.

Billy waved from the big house across the orchard and Maddie waved back. She needed to get busy and finish pruning those trees. She ruffled Rusty's coat. "Okay, back to work."

*   *   *

Billy knew the contractor's licensing exam was no slam dunk. He had worked on several construction sites and felt like he knew the ropes. Still, having considered taking the class and exam for months, he had never followed through. But with Nathan Carter, the general on Maddie's renovation project, being in rehab, it gave him the nudge he needed. Nathan encouraged him to go for it, even though he assured Billy he'd be back on the job soon. Nathan also promised any help Billy might need with his studies for the exam.

The class started in two weeks. He'd have to work under Nathan's license until he could get his own. He hoped Maddie would let him stay in the studio apartment in the big house until the project was completed.

Billy knew without a doubt Shauna Flanagan was the reason he'd finally decided to do whatever it would take to get his contractor's license. He closed his eyes, thinking about the first kiss he gave Maddie's beautiful houseguest. It was Shauna's eighteenth birthday, and his intention was to give her a peck on the cheek. But when he held her shoulders and bent to say happy birthday, her beautiful heart-shaped lips drew his there. She flushed and didn't say a word, which wasn't unusual since she hadn't spoken since her aunt and uncle's traumatic car accident. Yet her eyes said the kiss not only made her happy; she was also . . . what? Embarrassed? Interested? Grateful? Relieved. She was relieved. Some day he would ask her about that.

Back to work, Billy. He pounded a couple of nails into the siding and smiled, remembering Nathan holding the other end of sheet after sheet of siding. Billy had been shocked when he heard Nathan Carter was co-owner of a multimillion-dollar construction company in Portsmouth. He had a hard time seeing Nathan with all that money and power. It just didn't fit the jeans-and-work-boots guy he'd been working with. He'd thought Nathan was a good ole boy with a story he didn't want told. The story part was true enough. Did Maddie know Nathan was rich? He rubbed the stubble on his chin. Naw.

Billy had heard through the rumor mill that Nathan had taken a leave of absence to get over a broken relationship with his ex-fiancée. Who, somehow or another, was once again his fiancée.

Billy ran his hands through shaggy jet-black hair. Funny, he'd always thought Nathan and Maddie had a thing for each other. Even though they fought like they couldn't stand each other, the looks he'd seen them exchange sometimes said otherwise. He shrugged.

Having fallen in love himself with a silent girl with no family, Billy shook his head at the remarkable circumstances that had brought them all together.

Shauna had been living with Maddie since October. Shauna's father took off with another woman long ago, and sometime later Shauna's mom died. Her only other relatives, an aunt and uncle, were killed in an auto accident five months ago, and she hadn't spoken a word since that day. "Trauma," the shrink said. Billy was determined to get Shauna to talk.

He wanted her to say the words, "I do." But he wasn't telling her that . . . yet.

Billy hoisted his tool belt up to his waist where it immediately slipped back down to his hips. Wiping his forehead with the back of his hand, he looked up at the big house. One more section of siding and the outside would be done. *I wonder if I could get Shauna to come over and hold the ladder.* He grinned as he climbed up.

"Billy, you really need someone down here holding the ladder when you're up there." Maddie hung tight to the sides of the ladder below him, shielding her eyes with her hand.

"Huh?" Billy looked down wondering when Maddie had arrived. "Oh, yeah. Thanks. That's probably a good idea."

THREE

Nathan Carter played the scene over and over in his mind. Maddie, sitting on her couch in the cottage, before a cozy fire, kissing Pastor Ben.

Concerned about the Jeep parked out front, Nathan had quietly tramped through the falling snow to peek in the window. The scene caused his temperature to rise and his anger to blaze. Nathan had barely held himself in check, wanting nothing more than to smash the window and Ben's face.

After that, the accident was his own stupid fault. Speeding, under the influence, in a blizzard. Thankfully no one else had been injured.

Nathan, on the other hand, had not been expected to live. After days in a coma and weeks of brutal rehab, he was determined to strengthen every muscle to get back in shape so he could finish what Madison Crane had hired him to do.

Would she still want him to complete the renovation on the big house after she found out about the cause of the accident and what he'd done? Nathan had no idea.

They had a contract. He was going to live up to the terms of that contract, whether she liked it or not, and finish the project.

Nathan closed his eyes and imagined the feisty redhead who, for some unknown reason, desperately tried to conceal her tender heart. Emotional bricks around Nathan's heart created a safe barrier until he remembered the passion he'd felt radiate from Maddie's body when he kissed her.

Stop it, Nathan. Let it go. Let her go.

What did it matter? With constant memories of Ben kissing Maddie, the emotional mortar between the bricks around Nathan's heart would soon be thick and solid.

Still, the ache inside was like nothing he had ever felt before. The emptiness he had suffered when Chelsea, his blonde siren fiancée, jilted him for a real estate baron had been nothing more than a slam to his ego. This was different. Every time he thought about his life without Maddie, desperation swelled up from deep inside, threatening to close off his air supply.

Tears fought to emerge. Only once had Nathan let the tears fall full force. Once was enough. The heavy brick wall around his heart would remain a sure protection. It had to.

FOUR

Billy knocked on Maddie's cottage door, stepped inside, and wiped his feet. Shauna waved her arm, inviting him to come sit at the table. A warm tingle ran through all of Billy's lean, muscular six-foot body. He smiled and swiped his fingers over the scar that ran across his forehead.

Always asking questions that needed responses, Billy asked, "Hey, Shauna, how was your day?"

Shauna smiled and wagged a finger at him.

"Can't blame a guy for trying."

The three sat down for the evening meal of spaghetti and meatballs, one of his favorites. The first meal Maddie had served him after he'd arrived at Broken Acres.

Broken Acres. Maddie's farm would ultimately offer a quiet place for people to heal from the emotional pain inflicted on their lives. Billy had to wonder what kind of people would end up here. Maddie continually talked about how she wanted the big house to be a comfortable home for broken people. Broken, like Shauna.

Pastor Ben said that God had His hand on Broken Acres. Billy wasn't so sure about the God thing, although he did attend North Hills Chapel on Sundays with Shauna and Maddie. He liked Pastor Ben a lot. And Shauna, of course. But God?

Well, Billy had to admit there were some pretty broken individuals healing from splintered lives living at Broken Acres already. He glanced over at the two animals, Rusty, Maddie's gentle, protective golden retriever and Sarg, her stray cat, both brutally beaten castoffs. And Shauna, alone since she was seventeen, silent. Maddie would say she, too, an insecure widow, was part of the misfit community. Billy remembered his previous life of petty crime and no hope for a better future. The life he would have liked to forget. He also fit right in with the other residents of Broken Acres.

I hope Broken Acres will be everything Maddie envisions.

"Maddie, I was thinking about Nathan again today."

Maddie shifted, clearly uneasy, in her chair. "Yeah?"

"Did you know he owns that big construction company in Portsmouth?"

"Co-owns. Although from what I've pieced together he started it himself and it grew far beyond what he ever dreamed or wanted. But I had no idea until I met his partner when Nathan was in the hospital." Maddie looked at Billy, then glanced down at her plate. "Nor did I know he had a *fiancée*," she said under her breath, just loud enough for Billy and Shauna to hear.

She shrugged. "I just thought he was an out-of-work contractor with a history."

Billy frowned. "A history?"

"It's a long story, Billy."

"I'm all ears."

Shauna smiled and nodded her head, her eyes asking to hear Maddie's story.

Maddie sat back in her chair, crossed her arms, looked past Billy and Shauna, and groaned.

"The first time I met Nathan Carter was in a bar."

Billy sat up straight. "A what?"

Maddie held up her hands. "No, no. A bar and *grill*. I was on the last leg of my trip driving out here from Chicago."

Billy and Shauna sat silent, no doubt waiting for the meat of the story.

"It was late, I hadn't eaten, and I was showing signs of it . . . light-headed, dizzy. Not many places to eat on that particular stretch of highway, so I stopped at Sam's Bar and Grill. To make a long story short—"

"Don't make it short on our account." Billy grinned.

Maddie rolled her eyes and smiled at the two. "To make a long story short, while I was eating a sandwich the bartender had made for me, I smiled at the bartender, and the guy at the other end of the bar thought I was smiling at him."

"That guy was Nathan?"

"That *very drunk* guy was Nathan."

Billy frowned and gave a sideways glance. "Drunk? I thought Nathan said he didn't drink because his dad was a miserable alcoholic?"

"Hmm. Yeah, that's the story I heard too. I can tell you firsthand, he was drunk. Nathan tried to pick me up. Even pinned me to the bar between his arms."

Billy shook his head. "That doesn't sound like the Nathan I know."

Shauna's eyes grew wide.

"Mind you, I had never been in a bar before. I was already uncomfortable. Nathan actually asked me to follow him back to his place. My anger escalated so quickly I literally screamed in his face."

Billy nodded. "Ah, yeah. I have to say I've experienced that anger."

Maddie shrunk. "I know. I'm sorry, Billy. I'm still learning how to keep it under control."

He smiled and waved her off. "So?"

"I confronted him several months later when we were discussing the possibility of him renovating the big house. He couldn't even remember that night at the bar." Her face flushed, a frown between her eyes.

Maddie stood abruptly, grabbed their empty plates, and deposited them in the sink. "Still infuriates me when I think about it."

Shauna nodded.

"Anyway," Maddie leaned against the counter and continued, "When I found out he was the only available contractor within two hundred miles, I had no choice *but* to hire him." Maddie shook her head and headed back to the table. "Despite my doubts, Nathan has done an excellent job. You too, Billy."

"I wonder why he never told you about his business and being a millionaire?"

"Who knows what motivates a man like Nathan Carter? Carterville was named after his great-great-great grandfather, you know. Maybe that's too many 'greats' and maybe he just needed to get away. It can't be easy being heir to the city's founder."

Maddie pushed her chair in, squeezing her hands hard around the wood ladder-back frame. "Well, he'll be back in Portsmouth with his famous fiancée soon, I'm sure."

"Oh, no. He's staying in the Thompson place so he can finish this project as soon as he's strong enough."

Maddie put her hand over her heart. "He is?"

"Yeah. And he's going to help me study for the contractor's exam so I can get my license." He glanced over at Shauna.

Shauna ducked her head.

"Really? I wonder what Ms. Cover Model has to say about that."

"I wouldn't know. But I'm really glad he's hanging in there with this project."

"One thing about Nathan Carter, he's reliable. And he's also good at what he does. Never thought I'd hear myself say that."

"He's a good guy, Maddie."

"Hmm."

FIVE

Pastor Ben left the church office early and headed to Sunset Stables where his two saddle horses, Tomas and Teri, were boarded. The only living creatures he had ever really loved. Until . . .

Ben had brought Tomas and Teri with him when he left his Uncle Terry's ranch in Idaho. Jaunts on Tomas gave him a sense of freedom. Riding in the country air cleared his head and helped him see life as it really was.

Grabbing a saddle, Ben headed to Tomas's stall. Tonight the two would sleep under the stars, one of Ben's favorite places to have a heart-to-heart with God. Even though it would be cold, the sky was clear and there wouldn't be any new snow. The campfire and his goose down sleeping bag would keep him warm. It was in a setting just like this on his uncle's horse ranch where Ben realized his calling as a pastor.

Calling it to mind as if it were yesterday, Ben scratched Tomas's ear. "Do you remember, Tomas? We were out on the range herding strays and had set up camp for the night. After settling in near the fire, I laid my head against the saddle and marveled at the stars." Tomas shook his mane and snorted as if in reply.

Ben stroked Tomas's flank. "I remember lying there with my hands clasped behind my head thinking about the host of stars, knowing this earth was just a speck in the billions of galaxies God had created. I thought about how insignificant my life was, how I was just a puff, a breath. As far as I could see, my life held little value." Ben looked up at the sky.

"You know, buddy, God told Abraham that He would multiply Abraham's descendants as the stars of the heavens." Ben patted Tomas's neck affectionately and swung his six-foot-three frame into the saddle. "God as my witness, I heard God say—not in an audible voice, of course, but it sure sounded like His voice in my spirit—*"Tend My sheep. Abraham's seed. My Son's beloved. Shepherd My sheep."*

Ben pulled his cowboy hat from his head and ran a hand through his curly brown hair that snagged his collar. He led Tomas out of the barn and settled the black, broad-brimmed hat back on his head. Thankfully cowboys were permitted to wear sunglasses when they rode the range here. That would definitely never happen in Idaho on a horse ranch. The sun's rays were now directly in his line of sight. He pulled the brim of his hat lower.

Less than an hour later they trotted up the trail to the meadow where he had taken Maddie on their first ride together. "What do you think, pal? This meadow make for a good campsite? A heap better than your stall, huh?"

Ben set up camp and started a fire. He let Tomas roam and feed while he leaned his back against his saddle, finishing off the bread and chili he had warmed over the campfire. The coffeepot perked until the glass top evidenced the soothing black brew.

Ahhh. There was nothing like coffee under the stars.

Ben rested against the saddle and counted stars, which had become his habit to get the smallest grasp of how immense God really was. Even though He was the sovereign God of the universe, He was also an intimate God who had created humans to have a relationship with Him. Ben loved the conversations he had with God. Although some would say they were one-sided, Ben knew different.

"Lord, life is complicated." He shook his head. "You already know that."

"When You brought me to North Hills Chapel . . ." Ben threw another log on the fire and paused. Had it been six years already? "When You brought me here there was an awful lot of damage control in the church. I was on my knees constantly asking for the Holy Spirit's insight and help. There was no way I could have known all the pain and heartache these precious people hid from everyone else. Little by little the truth is coming out, healing marriages, friendships, families, people. Making them, one person at a time, new creations through Your love and forgiveness."

Forgiveness.

Ben shook his head, bowing low. "Lord, where would I be without Your forgiveness? I *so* screwed up my life. Yet You forgave me."

He wondered where Samantha was. Had she accepted God's forgiveness?

Ben pushed back the pain. It was all his fault. He should have taken control and stopped before it went too far. He didn't.

"One might think seminary would be the safest place to stay pure. But it's not where you are, it's where your focus is. And then my focus shifted from You, God, to my physical needs and flesh. Purity was the furthest thing from my mind."

Tears made their way to Ben's chin.

"I know, Lord. I know. I'm still so overwhelmed with the truth of Your forgiveness; it humbles me every time I remember."

He looked up at the myriad stars. "You know I never wanted Samantha to have an abortion. I did everything I could to talk her out of it, but she wouldn't listen. I pleaded with her. You know I did. Even offered to marry her. But she said she had her whole life ahead of her and she was not ready for a kid. I even suggested adoption. I begged her to let me raise the baby myself." Ben swiped the tears with his forearm.

"When she told me the abortion had been done, something in my soul snapped. I knew my sins were beyond forgiving. There was no way I could finish seminary and be a pastor."

Ben smiled into the vast darkness. "But, God, You brought Charles into my life, at the very moment I was ready to quit."

Ben stared into the fire. Charles, a black man with a heart for young people. A man with wisdom, godly character, unbound love, and patience. That man had such patience with him. Charles had walked him through so many scriptures about forgiveness, yet his heart didn't get it. Until Charles showed him Hebrews 10:10 and 12. "By this will we have been sanctified through the offering of the body of Jesus Christ once for all. . . . But He, having offered one sacrifice for sins for all time, SAT DOWN AT THE RIGHT HAND OF GOD."

Charles had said that humanity disregarded the great sacrifice Christ made for them and gave little or no significance to His atoning blood when they knowingly disobeyed and refused His forgiveness.

Ben shook his head and then grinned, thinking of his tall, lanky, gray-haired mentor. He remembered his words like he had spoken them yesterday. *"Either Jesus died for all sins or He didn't. What do you believe, Ben?"*

Charles had called it Ben's crisis of faith. He was right. Back then, Ben had to come to terms with what he really believed, not just what he had been taught in school. "Thank You, Lord, for Your sacrifice and forgiveness for *all* my sins."

He was grateful Charles encouraged him after graduating from seminary to live a God-honoring life. He'd told Charles he would do just that. What he hadn't told him was that marriage would not be a part of that life. Ben wanted to pour everything he had into serving the Lord and the sheep He'd given him to tend. Not to mention meeting the needs of the poor, both here in Jacob's Bend and in Carterville.

Having tied Tomas to a nearby tree and blanketed him for the night, Ben stood tall and looked toward heaven. He spread his arms wide, closed his eyes, and praised God until shivers from the cold night air drove him back to the embers of the dwindling fire. Ben added logs, stoked the fire, and settled between the layers of his sleeping bag. His head resting on his saddle, he looked up to heaven again. "Then Madison Crane came along."

SIX

"Hey, sis. How's life in the good-ole-boy state of Texas?"

"David. What's up?"

"Boy, you get straight to it, don't you?"

"Well, I can count on one hand the times my big brother has called me in the last year. Everything okay? Is Mom all right?" David heard the panic in Ruth's voice.

"Ruth, you are such a worrywart, always thinking something terrible has happened."

"I know. I'm working on that."

"Mom is doing great. That's kind of why I wanted to talk to you. You know how much I've always wanted to be a veterinarian?"

"Yes. And I still don't understand why you dropped out of school."

"Yeah, well, I've been taking as many basic education classes online as they offer, which aren't many. Most of the courses are hands-on—"

"And?"

"Let me finish, Ruth."

Her heavy sigh on the other end of the phone caused him to cut to the chase.

"When I went to see Mom last summer to help her on the farm—you need to go see her, by the way, her farm is incredible—"

"David, I just haven't had a chance—"

"That's not it and you know it."

She let loose another heavy sigh.

"Anyway, I only got to stay for a couple of weeks. There are farms everywhere out there. I'm thinking too many for the few vets they have. I didn't get to meet Dr. Adams, but she and Mom are friends and—"

"David, you're beating around the bush. What are you trying to tell me?"

"Do you think I ought to ask Dr. Adams if I could do my training there in Jacob's Bend under her and maybe join her practice someday?"

Ruth chuckled. "I should have known. When you set your mind on something you don't let go. I'm proud of you for keeping up your studies, David. You and Bracy, always ready to take a class, get a degree." Ruth cleared her throat. Twice.

David waited, thinking she had something else to say. "Ruth, everything okay?"

"Well, actually, I've been taking some classes myself."

"Really? What kind of classes? I thought you hated school."

"No, I don't hate school. Just never thought I'd go to college."

"But . . . ?"

"But, I'd like to work in a doctor's office."

"Really?"

"David, you already said that."

"I know. I'm just shocked. I never knew—"

"Okay, enough about me. Right now, I'm just Matt's wife."

"There's more to you then just being a wife, sis. You are the most organized, detailed, intelligent woman I know. Even if you are my sister." He laughed.

"So, you'd rather be a farm vet then a city vet?"

"In a heartbeat. My plan was always to move out of the city and have a country practice. Jacob's Bend and the surrounding area is way beyond what I ever could have imagined. And I'd be near Mom."

"Well then, I say go for it."

"Really? You think I should?"

"Absolutely. There's nothing to keep you in Chicago, is there?"

"No. This was too easy. You were supposed to be my test run. Someone to talk me out of doing something stupid."

"Sorry, bro. You dialed the wrong number."

"Well, aren't we loosening up in our old age?"

Ruth laughed. "I'm happy to admit I am learning to let go of control these days. And trying to see things from the perspective of others."

"Whoa. Who is this woman I'm talking to? It doesn't sound like my sister."

"Oh, stop it."

"Okay, well, I'll give Mom a call, see what she thinks about my idea and if she'll give me a job and a place to sleep on the farm while I do the vet thing."

"You're kidding, right? Mom would drive clear across the country to bring you and all you own to her farm."

"I know. And I love that I'll be there to help her."

SEVEN

Maddie walked hand in hand with Michael down Main Street. "Look at that funny cake in the window. Should we go inside and get a cookie?"

Michael's eyes grew big. "Cookie?"

Maddie smiled. "I hope your mom is okay with a little sugar."

The scent of coffee and cinnamon welcomed them when they stepped inside the Maison la Patisserie bakery.

"Hey, Maddie. Hey, Michael. What can I get for you?" Starla's smile was as warm as the bakery.

"This one." The excited boy pointed to a large chocolate chip, his nose pressed against the glass display counter.

"A chocolate chip cookie for Michael and a cinnamon roll and medium French roast for me."

"With room?"

"Absolutely. What's French roast without a touch of real cream?"

Starla grinned as they collected their treats and left.

Maddie strolled behind Michael as he skipped through downtown glancing in windows, giggling. After making the loop on Main they found themselves sitting on a bench in front of Harper's Hardware finishing up their goodies, waiting for Dr. Adams.

"Mama, Mama, I got a cookie." The little guy held up what was left of his giant chocolate chip cookie.

Jennifer looked down at her son's chocolate-smeared face and over at Maddie. "You spoil him rotten."

"Aw, what's one cookie?"

"And one dump truck and one three-wheel bike and—"

"Okay, okay, so I spoil him. It's fun to have a little one to spoil. Jenny, you look a little tired. Everything okay?"

"Adding another day to my schedule has meant less time with this guy. I hate that." Jenny ruffled Michael's thick black hair.

"Why don't you hire a helper?"

"We need more than a helper. We've got Patti who answers the phone and Diane who takes care of the accounting. What we need is a third vet. Bryan and I can't cover all the needs here in this little valley. We are stretched to the max. I thought the two of us could handle Doc Sawyer's growing business, but it's impossible for us to keep up. How Doc did it on his own, I have no idea."

Maddie cocked her head. "Know anyone in the area?"

"Yeah, there's a vet out on Highway 47 who works out of his house. Well, actually his barn. But I'm not so sure we'd be compatible. He's kind of arrogant and has an answer for every question, even the questions no one asks. He talks nonstop. Not sure Bryan's and my nerves could take that."

Maddie thought about David and his dream to become a veterinarian. For some reason David had quit at the end of his first year of vet school with little or no explanation. *David and Jenny would make a great team. Yeah, right. Like that's gonna happen. Let it go. Don't be an interfering mom.* Maddie closed her eyes and released her plans and ideas.

Besides, David has three jobs in Chicago, and I think he might even have a girlfriend. She took a deep breath. *Let. It. Go, Maddie.* "I'll sure keep my eyes and ears open. And I'm happy to have Michael out at the farm any time you and your sister have to work. He's a great little helper."

Michael smiled up at Maddie.

"Rusty and Sarg love him."

"I wanna ride Rusty."

Jenny shook her head. "Michael, Rusty is not a pony, he's a golden retriever."

"But I want to."

Maddie laughed. "Rusty plays the pony for a while and when he's had enough he plops down on the floor and pretends he's asleep. Michael will lie down next to him and then Sarg joins them. Sometimes his purring lulls

Michael to sleep. As you well know, Sarg is not fond of many people. The only other two he tolerates, well, actually likes, are Billy and Nathan . . . and now Michael."

Nathan.

"Have you heard from Nathan since he was released from the hospital?"

"No, but Billy sees him regularly. Nathan is helping him prepare for his contractor's license exam."

"Good for Billy. I guess he found a reason to stick around."

Maddie lifted an eyebrow. "Yeah, all five feet of her. It didn't take Billy long to see how beautiful Shauna is on the inside as well as the outside. I don't doubt for a minute Billy was taken with that gorgeous curly blonde hair, but once he got to know the gentle, kind woman she is, he didn't stand a chance. And I think all those hours helping her with her studies made him decide to study for the contractor's exam."

"Not to mention, that sweet little woman can't take her eyes off him when they are in the same room." Jenny smiled big.

"I know, they are so cute together. Who would have thought those two would learn to care for one another so quickly? Billy is determined to help Shauna talk again. The trauma that poor girl has been through."

"Yes, poor thing. She's been through a lot. But you and Billy and Broken Acres have been good for her."

"Thanks, Jenny. I often wonder who else will come to our door."

"That's what Broken Acres is all about. Helping and caring for others, right?"

"Right."

EIGHT

B illy sat at Nathan's kitchen table poring over the contractor licensing course materials. "There's so much to learn. How do they cram this into a three-hour test?"

"I know what you mean. There's more to it now than when I took it years ago." Nathan smiled. "You know, Billy, you could work under my license and not mess with all this."

"Yeah, I could." He looked at the man twenty years his senior. "But what if something happens to you . . . again?" Billy pointed to the cane that hung on the back of Nathan's chair.

Nathan stroked the bristles on his chin. "Good point. They almost lost me twice in that hospital. Still, I'm determined to get this leg back in shape." He rubbed his left knee.

Billy shook his head. "That freak snowstorm did you in."

"Yeah, well, I didn't help the situation with that bottle of wine."

"Speaking of that, what happened? I thought you never drank alcohol."

Nathan stayed silent, but his guilt-ridden eyes caused Billy to turn the subject to another question that had been bothering him.

"Nathan, do you remember what happened? I mean, you had so many broken bones and so much damage to your body we weren't sure you were going to make it. You couldn't even breathe on you own. You kept mumbling something while you were in the coma. The only word anyone could understand was 'Maddie.'"

Nathan groaned. "All I remember is lights. Glaring lights. Squealing tires. Metal crunching. Breaking glass. And beeping. Then crying. A woman crying."

"That must be hard, trying to piece it all together. I'm really glad you survived. You're recuperating well."

"Yeah, well, I'd rather come back stronger than before instead of just recuperating well."

Billy nodded.

"So, Billy, my turn. It looks to me like you've got a thing for that cute little Shauna."

Billy rubbed his fingers over the scar that ran across his forehead. "She is cute, isn't she?"

Nathan raised his eyebrows.

"Yeah, I can't help it. She's so helpless, but not. Shauna is really smart. But boy, don't get her angry. She may not be able to give you what for with words, but those hazel eyes can zap you with anger bombs if you push her too far."

"Is that the voice of experience talking?"

"Well, I was only teasing her, trying to get her to talk."

"And?"

Billy took a deep breath. "And if I had been in closer proximity, those eyes probably could have turned me to toast."

"I understand. Do you think she learned that from Maddie?"

Billy laughed. "I think it is just part of the package Shauna came with. Like the rest of us with things we'd like to be rid of."

"Uh-huh. I'm with you on that one."

Billy stuck the eraser end of the yellow pencil in his mouth and looked down at the paper in front of him. "Okay, so give me the next scenario that might be on the test."

*   *   *

Nathan leaned heavily on his cane as he brought lunch to the table.

"Chili and corn bread. My favorite." Billy pushed his studies aside.

"Me too."

"Where did you learn to cook, Nathan? This is really good."

"Living alone I've had lots of time to learn. Restaurants get old real fast. Besides, Tim and I have this, what you might call, competition going on. On a dare, my sophomore year of high school, I took a home economics cooking class. Lots of cute girls in that class." He winked.

Billy grinned.

"I got pretty good at trying out new recipes. The girls loved that." Nathan raised an eyebrow. "Tim couldn't stand that I was in there with all those girls every day while he sat in a shop class with a bunch of sweaty guys." Nathan gave a half grin. "So the next semester he took cooking, too, and the competition began. Believe it or not, we've even taken gourmet cooking classes just so we could outdo each other."

Billy took a spoonful of chili. "I gotta say I'm glad you did."

"Yeah, well, don't tell anybody. It's not very macho."

Billy laughed when he saw Nathan's white apron with black script that read, "Real men cook quiche."

"I won't say anything if you don't tell Maddie your chili wins hands down over hers. She's a good cook, and I like the food she makes, but gourmet it's not."

A shadow of pain settled over Nathan's face.

"What's wrong, Nathan? Are you okay?" Billy glanced at Nathan's knee.

Nathan gave his head a slight shake. He breathed deep and closed his eyes.

"Did I say something wrong?"

Nathan rubbed his forehead. "Maddie—"

"Yeah, she's pretty amazing. Like the way she sat at your bedside in the hospital. It's a good thing she kept watch or you might not be here."

Nathan's head shot up. "What are you talking about?"

"You didn't know? They had to defibrillate your heart. Twice. I think she might have called the doctors in both times. Maddie refused to leave your bedside for three days and only left for a short time after you were stable. She even made Pastor Ben stay in the room until she returned."

"What?" Nathan jumped to his feet and paced across the living room, limping without his cane's support. "But Chelsea said—"

"I don't mean to put your fiancée down, but I'd seriously check anything that woman has to say if I were you."

Nathan's house phone rang. He glanced over. "The machine can pick it up. Why do you say that, Billy?" Nathan frowned.

"Are you sure you want to hear this?"

"Yes, I do."

"Well, once she got to the hospital, Chelsea all but banned any of us from visiting you. She had your doctor order that only she, Tim, and family could enter your room. I'm not even sure she *told* your family."

Nathan shook his head. "I don't really have any family. Are you telling me it wasn't Chelsea I saw at the foot of my bed when I was slipping in and out of consciousness?"

"Chelsea wasn't even there then. That was Maddie. Ben couldn't get her to leave until he promised to let her know if there was any change while she went home, cleaned up, and slept for a few hours. When she returned to the hospital there was a surprise visit from Tim and your *fiancée*."

"Why did Maddie stay? Why would she do that? She and Pastor Ben——"

"Your guess is as good as mine. Ben said she apparently had something to tell you."

"What? What did she need to tell me?" Nathan grabbed Billy's shoulder.

Billy held up both hands. "Whoa. Nobody knows. After Tim and Chelsea showed up, no one was allowed in. And you came out of the coma the next day, so I guess whatever Maddie had to say wasn't important anymore."

Nathan stopped pacing and dropped down on the couch, his head in his hands.

Billy looked at him concerned. "Nathan? What's wrong?"

Nathan shook his head. "Nothing. I, uh . . ." He waved off the question with a frustrated gesture.

Billy closed his contractor training books. "Okay. Guess I'll head home and do a little more studying. Thanks for your help and thanks for the chili. Make sure to let Tim know I gave it five stars." Billy gave Nathan a thumbs-up with his free hand.

"I have made a terrible mistake," Nathan mumbled under his breath.

"What? I couldn't hear what you said."

Nathan walked Billy out to his car. "Oh, nothing. See you tomorrow, Billy."

*   *   *

Long after Billy left, Nathan fumed while listening to Chelsea's message for the second time. Why was she calling the house phone anyway? She probably hoped he wasn't home so he wouldn't argue with her about the change of plans. Everything was always about Chelsea.

"Sweetie, I know you won't mind, but we'll need to change the location for the wedding. I'm afraid my agent booked a photo shoot in New York the week before. Remember you said it didn't matter to you where we got married? Give me a call."

Nathan clutched his fists tight and swore through a clenched jaw. Eyes flashing, he turned to the table, picked up the plate that held the corn bread, and threw it across the room, hitting the wall, crumbling pieces of corn bread and ceramic onto the message machine.

*   *   *

Billy left the exam room after three grueling hours of testing. He was sure he answered most of the questions correctly. But what if he messed up? What if he didn't pass? The guy sitting next to him kept glancing over at Billy like he might know him. Billy couldn't think of anywhere he'd seen him before. *Oh well, I've met a lot of people through work. Maybe he's one of those guys.*

Before he even had a chance to put his books down back in his room in the big house at Broken Acres, his cell pinged. He didn't recognize the number. "Hello?" he answered cautiously.

"It this William Chambers?"

"This is Billy. Who is this?"

"Mr. Chambers, this is one of the examiners with PSI Exam Services."

"Yeah? I didn't think you called with the test results. I thought it took twenty-four hours to find out if we passed."

"You did not pass, Mr. Chambers."

"What? What was my score?"

"I wouldn't know."

"Wait. What is this about?"

"You were observed cheating—"

"Cheating? I did not cheat. Who said I was cheating?"

"We have proctors who are in the room and others who watch through a two-way mirror during the exam. One of them said you repeatedly looked over at the paper of the young man to your left."

"That's not true. I looked at him once or twice because he kept clearing his throat and sitting up in his chair looking my way."

"Be that as it may, one of the proctors feels sure you were scanning his paper for answers."

"I did not." Billy shouted the words through his phone. "Did you watch him? I think he was the one who was cheating."

"We are checking into his answers, matching them with yours to see if there are resemblances between your answers."

"Can I contest this? It's not true."

"Of course you have the option of contesting our decision, but should we find conclusively that you cheated on the test, you will be unable to take the exam again. However, if it is determined that you did not cheat on the test, you will have the opportunity to take it again."

Billy rubbed his eyes and shook his head.

"The matter is under investigation and you will receive a call when your guilt—"

"Or innocence," Billy chimed in.

"Yes, or innocence has been established."

Billy clicked his cell off, running his fingers across the scar on his forehead. Why did people always assume guilt before innocence? This wasn't fair. He'd done everything according to the rules and look what happened. He got busted for something he didn't even do. His anger building, Billy checked the time on his phone, jumped in his truck, and skidded out over the knoll. "Time to break prohibition."

NINE

Maddie grinned watching Ben gallop across the grass at Beauregard Taylor Park in the middle of downtown Jacob's Bend with six-year-old Brian Metzger sitting atop his broad shoulders, giggling and shouting, "Giddy-up."

Ben waved to Maddie. She smiled and waved back. He was so good with kids. Brian and Michael both loved him. He'd never had kids of his own. Did he want them? Her kids were grown. Did she want to start all over?

The all-church picnic brought parishioners from every church in town. Food glutted the tables set up for salads, main dishes, and desserts. Even with her advanced planning, Madelyn Simpson, chairwoman of the All-Church Picnic Committee, had to add two additional tables to handle the varied delectable desserts.

Maddie watched Angela Metzger unsaddle Brian from Ben's shoulders. Was she imagining it, or was the fleeting glance Angela gave Ben not one of adoration for her pastor but love for the man? Funny, it didn't send pangs of jealousy through her as meeting Chelsea, Nathan's secret fiancée, had.

Angela was too young to stay single. When her husband died in a farming accident she couldn't have been more than thirty. She needed to find a nice man and fall in love.

Love? Is that what I feel for Ben? What about the horseback rides, the dinner, the kiss? Maddie's thoughts tumbled rapidly as Ben ruffled the boy's dark hair before moving away. *Surely I love Ben. He must be the one God has for me. At least that's what I hear from everyone.* Maddie sighed. *What do I know of God? I wish I could say I love God like Ben does. Maybe that's what makes him so special.*

Maddie watched the tall, handsome cowboy pastor walk toward her, stopping only long enough to say a few words to those who shook his hand along the way.

He is everything I could ever want in a husband.

When Ben sat next to her on the blanket and gave her a quick peck on the cheek, she smiled into his gentle brown eyes.

Yep, he's the one.

*   *   *

When Maddie arrived home her thoughts were no longer that confident. Did she love Ben? Did she even want to get married again? *A pastor? Good grief. And this God thing . . .*

Why was everyone so intent on telling her how great God was? That pastor in Chicago told a pretty good story, but had that helped her? No. God had never done anything for her. Especially when it came to Jeff and their marriage.

Maddie grabbed Gram's Bible and pulled out Jeff's confession.

Maddie,

If you are reading this letter two things have taken place. One, I've run out of time to muster up enough courage to share face-to-face what I'm about to tell you. God knows I've tried.

And two, you've finally realized what a treasure you hold in your hands. Not just because it belonged to your sweet Gram, more because the words in this book are alive and have the power to change even the most disgraceful sinner—me.

I know you've seen a change in me, you have said it more than once, but you never asked how that change came about. I could not live with the tremendous guilt I felt over my affair and the disrespectful way I treated you for so many years. Prestige, money, fancy cars, property, none of it relieved the anguishing pain of betraying you and disappointing the kids, should they ever find out.

One night, not too long ago, while you and Bracy were at the movies, I held a bottle of prescribed sleeping pills in one hand and a bottle of wine in the other. I figured if I drank half the wine, I'd have enough guts to take the pills. Then I realized it was only right that I leave a note for you and the kids, so I rummaged through the junk drawer for a pen and some paper. Lots of pens, no paper. When I looked up, there among your cookbooks, I saw some papers sticking out of one of the books. I pulled one out and it had a Bible verse on it. When I looked back at the book it came from, I realized it was your Gram's Bible. The verse on the paper was Jeremiah 31:3: "The LORD appeared to him from afar, saying, 'I have loved you with an everlasting love; therefore I have drawn you with loving kindness.'" I thought, yeah, right.

I couldn't write my suicide note on that paper. It seemed too sacred. I opened the Bible to look for another piece of paper and there before me was Jeremiah 31:3. Your Gram had written in the margin Romans 6:23 and Romans 10:9–10. I couldn't help myself. When I found and read those verses, I knew deep inside me I had found the one thing, Person, rather, who could take away my guilt. I cried like a baby and told God every sin I could remember and desperately asked Him to forgive me. Now here is the unbelievable part, within a few minutes the guilt was completely gone, and I felt loved, truly loved, for the first time in my life.

Maddie, I can only hope you have found this incredible love, too, and that you can find it in your heart to forgive me.

I love you,

Jeff

As she read Jeff's letter for the umpteenth time, Maddie's anger swelled inside. Her temper exploded. Again. *All those years of abuse and pain and all it took was a couple of Bible verses to change him?* Disgust and resentment filled the room. She wadded up the page and tossed the ball of paper in the trash beneath the kitchen sink.

Taking Gram's Bible to the chair in the living room, she looked up. "Gram, I can't love your God. He didn't help me when I needed it most. Living in fear for years when Jeff couldn't control his temper. And then your God supposedly changes this man and gives him a new lease on life. What about my life?" Maddie held her arms out wide, questioning her Gram in heaven.

Nothing.

"Give me something, Gram. Anything. Please."

Maddie looked down at the Bible in her lap. She opened the book to a place that looked like Gram had visited it many times. Worn pages, coffee-stained and wrinkled. Gram's handwriting covered all the previously empty spaces. One line was highlighted in yellow. "'For I know the plans that I have for you,' declares the LORD, 'plans for welfare and not for calamity to give you a future and a hope.'" Gram had written in the margin, "Because of God's great love for us."

Maddie slammed the book shut. Well, if He loved everyone so much, why had He let her go through so much heartache and pain?

Walking over to the kitchen sink, she pulled the letter out of the trash. She smoothed out the wrinkles, and a tear fell on Jeff's handwriting. It was the last thing Jeff ever said to her. Maybe she needed this to remind her that there was a time when things were good and Jeff felt loved. Why couldn't she get over the bad memories from the past and just remember the good things that happened during the last year of his life?

TEN

Maddie knew Billy would continue as best he could with the interior renovation of the big house. Yet one barely experienced man doing the job would take forever. Now, after he'd gotten arrested and spent two days in jail for being drunk and disorderly in that bar in Carterville, she wondered if he was the right one for the job. *What was he thinking? I thought he was done with all that.*

Maddie watched as Billy took a sip of hot coffee and grabbed his forehead tight with his fingers. He seemed to be trying to release a tight clamp on his head. "Billy, are you okay?"

He squinted up at Maddie and rubbed his fingers over the scar that ran across his forehead. "Yeah, I'm fine."

"Are you sure? You don't look fine."

"Maddie, I'm fine. What did you want?"

Hmm, just a bit tense, huh?

"Well, you said Nathan plans to come back and finish the work on the big house. Any idea when that might be? How is he doing, anyway? Healing?"

Billy shook his head.

"What? Is he okay? What?"

"He's doing really good, Maddie."

She let out a long sigh.

"But the doctor won't release him to work construction until he can walk without his cane, with only a slight limp. He's got an appointment to see his doctor this week."

Suddenly the memory of Nathan's passionate kisses flooded her mind. The overpowering emotions hit her again. *No, that was just a reaction to being scared by a bat.* She inhaled sharply.

"Oh, good. That's good."

"Maddie, Nathan said prices on materials keep rising and this project may cost a lot more than originally expected."

"I was afraid of that. How much more?"

"I don't know exactly. You'll have to ask Nathan."

"Okay."

*   *   *

"Hello?"

"Hello, Nathan. You have certainly learned to be more pleasant when you answer the phone. Much better than the first time I called you."

"Yeah, well, I've done some changing since then."

"Have you?"

"What's that supposed to mean?"

"Nothing, Nathan." He heard Maddie's screen door slap shut and the noises of the countryside pick up behind her voice. A faint squeak, and he could picture her settling onto the swing before she continued.

"Billy said material prices for the renovation project are rising and you think the cost to finish the job will go beyond your bid. How much beyond?"

Nathan rubbed the back of his neck. "Well, if prices continue to rise at the same rate, we're looking at about . . . forty thousand dollars more."

"What?"

"Now, don't get all cockeyed on me. We can work this out. Remember I have a very successful construction business in Portsmouth. I can help you out."

"No. No you cannot. If I can't do this on my own then . . . well then, I'll just have to put it on hold and earn some money somehow."

"Really? How?"

"Are you insinuating I wouldn't be able to find a job?"

Nathan could imagine those sea-green eyes igniting. "No, Maddie." His grip on the phone tightened. "I'm not saying that at all. Why won't you just let me help you?"

"Absolutely not."

"Why do you always have to be so da—darn stubborn?" Nathan started to pace. *Why can't we have a civil conversation?*

"Me stubborn? Ha. Isn't that like the pot calling the kettle black?"

"What's that supposed to mean?" He heard a deep breath released through the phone line and knew Madison Crane well enough to know her eyes were closed while she organized her thoughts.

"Listen, Nathan. I know you are just trying to help, but I've got investments my husband made and they should be enough to finish the job. I'll check with Isaac, my investment counselor—"

"Maddie, will you at least consider some help from me?"

"No. I need to finish something myself."

The next words came as a whisper, barely loud enough for him to hear.

"I've never really done that before."

Nathan jumped on that. "What are you talking about?"

"Didn't you hear what I said? I need to finish something myself."

"I heard that and the other part too. You have done it. You sold your house in the city, moved clear across the country, bought the property, fixed up the cottage, not to mention took Billy and Shauna in. You help the farmers and cattle owners by leasing your land to them. You're managing 427 acres by yourself. You've already accomplished a lot."

Silence. Then a faint squeak. "It is beautiful, isn't it?"

"What's beautiful?"

"My property. I never would have thought—"

"Maddie, you are an amazing woman." Nathan looked out the window, curious to hear what her reaction would be. Anger?

"I am?"

Surprise? Shock? Well, that's better than anger, Nathan thought.

"Really? You think I'm amazing?"

"Yeah, well, ah, that's what Billy said the other day." *Playing it safe, are you, Nathan?*

Her voice recalled him to the conversation. "Nathan, I need to do this myself. Let's change the subject. Billy said you had a doctor's appointment last week. What did he say? How are you healing?"

Nathan blew out a mass of air. "Why do you do that? Whenever you aren't getting your own way—"

"Nathan. What did the doctor say?"

"He released me to go back to work after I complete a couple of weeks of PT. I'm thinking of coming by on Monday just to check out how much Billy has accomplished and see where I need to start when I come back to work."

"Oh, that's . . . that's wonderful news."

She didn't sound sure. It would be the first time she'd seen him since he'd gotten out of the hospital. Was she worried he wasn't up to the job?

Her voice sounded oddly noncommittal. "That's great. I'll see you on Monday, then."

ELEVEN

Nathan rummaged through his closet looking for his work boots. Even though he had a couple of weeks of physical therapy before the doctor would release him, he was ready to get back to work. At least he could go take a look at the progress on the big house.

There in the back of the closet, pushed down inside the black cowboy boots he had worn the night of the accident, was something wrapped in brown paper.

What the . . .

Sitting on the edge of the bed he removed the paper. It was a book. When he turned it over, the heat rose to his face. He scowled. *Holy Bible.*

When he raised it above his head to give it a dump shot in the trash, an envelope fell to the floor.

Nathan,

I'm guessing you aren't much for spiritual things, but I bought this Bible hoping you'll read it during your recovery. I hope you find the peace only God can give.

Ben

Nathan sucked in air. He read the message again. Peace? The feeling rising in his chest certainly wasn't peace. Instead, he threw the Bible across the room, slamming it into the wall. He sank to the floor and screamed up to the ceiling, "Who are You?"

Nathan covered his eyes, his head touching his bent knees. To his own surprise, tears dripped between his fingers. "Who are You?" he whispered.

Nathan glanced at the Bible on the floor. "Are You the mean God who let my little sister die as soon as she took her first breath? Are You the angry God who killed my brother in boot camp? Maybe You're the God who let my dad ruin our family with his drinking because he was too weak to face life. Who are You?"

His tears turned to sobs of anger and bitterness and regret he had never allowed himself to feel before. A memory of Mrs. Severs, a Sunday school teacher at the church his mother had dragged him to, came to light. If Mrs. Severs was right, and it was God's will for them to die, he wanted nothing to do with God. He'd cursed any god that would allow or cause such pain and had spat the name of Jesus, the one Mrs. Severs said was to blame. So why was he talking to this God now?

Tears blurred the Bible that lay sprawled on the floor across the room. Nathan glanced at the crumpled note on the floor near his boot. "Peace! Yeah, right. Who is this God Pastor Ben believes gives peace? Is He even real?"

Nathan wiped his eyes with his shirtsleeve. He picked up the open Bible. The top of the page said "Job." He began to read.

He stretches out the north over empty space
And hangs the earth on nothing.
He wraps up the waters in His clouds,
And the cloud does not burst under them.
He obscures the face of the full moon
And spreads His cloud over it.
He has inscribed a circle on the surface of the waters
At the boundary of light and darkness.
The pillars of heaven tremble
And are amazed at His rebuke.
He quieted the sea with His power,
And by His understanding He shattered Rahab.
By His breath the heavens are cleared;
His hand has pierced the fleeing serpent.
Behold, these are the fringes of His ways;
And how faint a word we hear of Him!
But His mighty thunder, who can understand?

Nathan wasn't sure he understood or believed what he'd just read. "He stretches—and these are the *fringes* of His ways? What does the rest look like if these are just the fringes? I don't get it. If You are real, show me who You are."

Nathan read to the end of Job and noticed small notations on the side of the page. They looked like other addresses in the Bible, from what he could guess, having never actually taken time to read the book before. He only remembered his Sunday school teacher writing the words on the blackboard. He had never really paid much attention. He'd seen John 3:16 on signs while watching football on TV. These looked like that.

One said, "1 John 4:16." He had no idea how to find that book of John. He held his hands open and looked up.

Table of contents—yeah.

He found the page number for 1 John and thumbed through the Bible looking for the verse.

Nathan found chapter four and ran his finger down to the paragraph that began with the number sixteen. He began reading.

We have come to know and have believed the love which God has for us. God is love, and the one who abides in love abides in God, and God abides in him. By this, love is perfected with us, so that we may have confidence in the day of judgment; because as He is, so also are we in this world. There is no fear in love; but perfect love casts out fear, because fear involves punishment, and the one who fears is not perfected in love. We love, because He first loved us. If someone says, "I love God," and hates his brother, he is a liar; for the one who does not love his brother whom he has seen, cannot love God whom he has not seen. And this commandment we have from Him, that the one who loves God should love his brother also.

"'God is love.'" Nathan felt heat wash over his insides. It was like warm water running throughout his body. He breathed deep. "'Perfect love casts out fear.'" He looked up and whispered, "How do I get this love?"

A memory ran through his mind. Maddie in his arms, surrendering to his kisses, kissing him back. He knew she wanted him as much as he wanted her, yet she had pulled away.

"Nathan, I wish . . ."

His pleading eyes drew her in.

He lifted her, cradled her in his strong arms, and passionately kissed her lips.

She clung to his neck, then pushed away, her chest heaving with emotion.

"Nathan, as much as I want to . . . Everything in me is shouting yes. But I can't."

Her rejection was like a slap in the face. He set her feet back on the floor. "Listen, Maddie, I know you want me as much as I want you."

"You don't understand. Please try to understand. I can't."

The tender moment stopped, the memory gone.

"She wanted me." Suddenly anger flooded his heart. Nathan ran his hands through his thick, shaggy hair. "The truth is, she just doesn't want a jerk who practically mauled her in that bar when he was drunk."

But she wanted me.

A thought hit Nathan out of the blue.

She must have wanted something else more. Chelsea and Maddie both rose up in his mind, one who claimed to love him, and one who wanted something . . . more. Nathan's head dropped into his hands. "What's the truth?"

He longed to know the truth. His chest heaved with pain from years of wanting only his own truth—the realities he had formed from pain and disappointment. The bricks of frailty and falsehood kept him safe, unapproachable behind an impenetrable fortress.

If he opened up and let love in, he would be vulnerable and weak.

His tears fell on the next page of the Bible as he read 1 John 5:20: "And we know that the Son of God has come, and has given us understanding so that we may know Him who is true; and we are in Him who is true, in His Son Jesus Christ. This is the true God and eternal life."

"Who are You, Jesus?" he whispered. "These words say You'll give me understanding."

Nathan quickly checked the table of contents to see if there was a chapter or book about Jesus. Nothing.

Thumbing frantically through the book looking for something that would tell him about this Jesus, he remembered . . . John 3:16. "For God so loved the world, that He gave His only begotten Son, that whoever believes in Him shall not perish, but have eternal life."

"'Whoever believes in Him.' How do I do that?"

Nathan read all of John, and by the time he finished reading the book of Acts the sun was rising on the horizon. He looked at his watch. It was Sunday. Nathan smoothed Pastor Ben's crumbled note and used it to mark the page where he stopped reading.

He needed some answers. Maybe he'd try a church in Carterville. He sure as heck was not going to Pastor Ben's church.

TWELVE

L ydia peeked out her living room window. *What is* she *doing here?*

The woman's persistent knock on the door let Lydia know she would not leave without an audience. She cleared her throat, adopting her Witch Hazel voice. She checked her disguise in the mirror and straightened her gray wig. Hunching to make her height smaller and her features less apparent, she opened the inside door. Head bent, she glanced up at the pretty redhead.

"Hi. My name is Madison Crane. Maddie."

Lydia sneered through the screen door. "What do you want?"

Maddie smiled. "I was walking through town several months ago and noticed some boys throwing rocks and insults in the direction of your house."

"So?"

"Well . . . ah, have they been back?"

"Yeah. So?"

Maddie looked past the old woman into the dark house. One small lamp lit the old table it sat upon.

Lydia watched the woman's eyes. "What do you want?"

"I, ah, don't think it's right for those boys to treat you like that. They might hurt you."

"Those boys? They can't hurt me. As a matter of fact, they make me laugh. Not much does these days."

Maddie glanced at the side yard with junk stacked high, and Lydia's gaze followed. Cracked sinks lay against old tires. Chairs with shredded webbing. A refrigerator with a sign propped against it that read "Night

44

Crawlers—$2.00." Old newspapers and trash heaped in piles everywhere. An overgrowth of weeds and trees dominated the front yard of the little house.

"Um . . . okay." Maddie looked around again as if trying to figure out how to keep the conversation going. "I was wondering if you would like some help pruning your yard and maybe disposing of those things"— Maddie extended her hand to the lot next door—"at the dump?"

"No. Now leave me alone." Lydia slammed the door in the woman's face and leaned against the door, trying to listen over her pounding heart.

Silence. A shadow fell across the front window, but with the drapes drawn, Lydia didn't know what Maddie was doing.

Lydia held her breath, frantic to hear the sound of the woman walking away. *What if she asks the owner if she can clean up the place? What if she comes back with the sheriff? What if* . . . She wrung her hands. "Busybody."

Steps tapped away from the door, and Lydia dashed to a gap in the curtains to be sure Maddie was leaving. Lydia watched Maddie dodge a dead rose bush and open the half-attached gate. Maddie looked back over her shoulder and gave a small smile that slid from her face at the silent house.

I don't need your smile, thought Lydia.

*   *   *

Shoulders slumped, Maddie stopped at O'Donnell's Brier for some tea with her friend Gael O'Donnell. On her way to the back of the store she fingered through new dress arrivals. "Gael, are you back there?"

Gael, a fifty-something woman, was on her knees in the back of the store. When she leaned her head around a curtain, her beautiful curly red hair danced across the floor. She pushed herself up with her hands.

"Maddie, me girl. And how are ya doin' this fine mornin'?"

Maddie turned on the hot plate to heat a kettle of water.

"I stopped by Witch . . . I mean, the elderly woman's house the kids are always taunting. She doesn't want any help cleaning up the lot next door or help pruning her front yard."

"She talked to you?"

Maddie cocked her head. "Yeah. Why?"

"Since she moved here I haven't heard of her speakin' a word to a single person. Except maybe to threaten to cast a spell."

"Really? She has threatened to cast spells?"

"Well, that's what the boys would be sayin'."

"How long has she lived in Jacob's Bend?"

"I'd say nigh onto three years now."

"And nobody has befriended her or seen to her welfare?"

"Not that I know of."

Maddie clasped her hands together tight and pursed her lips. "Society's misfits," she whispered.

"I don't like the look on your face there, Maddie girl."

"Gael, I hate it when people are cruel or don't give a darn about those who have little or nothing. They cast them off and keep their distance like they have typhoid or something."

Gael moved to Maddie's side and took her by the crook of the elbow. "I know what ya mean. And you're doin' somethin' about that, now aren't ya?"

The kettle whistled. Gael poured steaming water over a strainer full of loose-leaf almond tea that rested on the lip of an Irish teapot.

Maddie shook her head. "It's taking so long to finish the renovation project on the big house at Broken Acres, and now Nathan says I need another forty thousand dollars because material prices keep rising. I need to talk to my financial guy and see what my money situation is."

"Oh my. That is a dilemma. And what will ya do if ya don't have the money?"

"Good question. I'm not sure. Probably talk to my son, David. He's good with money and ideas on how to earn it."

"Handsome young man, your David."

Maddie smiled at her friend. "He is that, and smart too. Strong, kind, loving . . ."

Gael lifted an eyebrow. "If I were a wee bit younger—"

"And coming here." Maddie's eyes sparkled as she waited for her friend's reaction.

"Really? You don't say. I'll have to iron me best dress."

Maddie laughed. "He is definitely a great catch. And I'm not saying that just because I'm his mother. Actually, I'd love to see him and Jennifer Adams meet and maybe make a connection. They have so much in common."

"Sure, and your boy wants to be a vet now, doesn't he?"

"That's been his dream since he was a little boy. Until a few years ago. I don't know what happened to change that. But"—she smiled big—"he has started talking about finishing school to get his veterinarian's license. And the best news yet, he wants to come out here to do it."

"Comin' to stay? Are me prayers bein' answered, now?"

Maddie tugged on her ear as she sipped her tea and took a bite of blueberry scone. "He's going to move to Broken Acres, help Billy finish the renovation, and take online classes at Forest Hills University. I am so excited I can hardly hold it in."

"Well now, I'm guessin' you'll be callin' your financial man soon then?"

"Yes. I'll give Isaac a call this week. I need to know exactly where I stand."

THIRTEEN

"Hey, Mom."

"David. How's it going? What's the plan? Are you ready to head out here? School all set?"

"Mom, which question do you want me to answer first?"

Maddie giggled. "Sorry, son. I'm just so excited."

"Me too. That short visit last summer was not nearly enough once I saw your farm and the surrounding area."

"And, of course, you miss your mom too?" Maddie's brows came up waiting for an answer.

"That's a given, Mom."

"Well, a mom likes to hear it now and then."

"I know. I'm really excited to put the past behind me and finally realize my dream."

"The past?"

"No way. We're not talking about it. It's done and over. I'm looking to the future."

"You sound like me when I made the decision to move out here. Okay, no more talk about what was, only what is to come."

"Thanks, Mom."

"So, do you have a timeline for when you'll be here?"

"I'm thinking in about three weeks. I should have everything wrapped up here by then."

"Then I am one happy woman. Until the renovation is finished, I'm afraid you'll be sharing a space with Billy in the studio apartment in the big house. Shauna will move into one of the rooms in the big house when it's finished, if—"

"If what?"

"Well, I wouldn't be at all surprised if Billy and Shauna get married."

"Really?"

"Yeah, they are quite the couple. So sweet."

"Glad I'll be there to see the romance blossom and attend the wedding."

"If there is a wedding."

"Yeah if—but you're pretty good at recognizing true love."

"I am?" Maddie glanced in the full-length mirror in her loft bedroom.

"Of course. You always knew the couples who would be going to prom together."

"That's different than spending your life with someone."

"Maybe so, but you knew Ruth and Matt were a match long before anyone else."

"I just always thought they would be good together." Maddie flashed back to Ruth and Matt's wedding. *They are a good match, aren't they?* "I'd love to see them move out here too."

"That's quite a stretch, Mom. Matt has a great job with Dad's company in Texas. I don't think that particular wish is going to come true."

"You're probably right. Besides, I've got plenty to keep me busy. No time to daydream about what might be. Guess I'd better get something done around here. I love you and can't wait to give you a tight squeeze."

"Love you too, Mom. I'll call before I head out."

*   *   *

Maddie looked up as she normally did when talking to her dearly departed Gram. "It's all coming together. The big house will be finished in no time. Right?"

Nothing.

"This is certainly not how I imagined things would go. Nathan's accident, Billy working alone on the project. But now David will be here to help him. Still, this is not how I planned it. In my mind that house should be filled with people by now. People who need a safe home. But then, what do I know?" She walked to the coffeepot and poured herself a fresh cup.

"Ben says God owns the cattle on a thousand hills. I hear your voice sometimes, Gram, when he quotes the Bible. Can I really give control of this farm to your God?"

More silence.

"If Ben has anything to say about it, the answer will be a resounding yes." Maddie rolled her eyes.

Gram used to have a lot more to say.

FOURTEEN

Maddie sat in the back-row pew of the church deliberating the conversation she would have tomorrow with Jasper Worthington III. Jasper wanted to negotiate more land to lease for his cattle to graze.

It seemed his land baron father, Jasper Worthington II, with over four thousand acres of land north of Portsmouth, sent his son packing after finishing college when he refused to bow down to his father's demand to work in his corporate office selling real estate to high-end businesses.

Jase, as Jasper III was called, had agreed to attend college only so he could one day ride the range and run a horse ranch like his grandfather from the back of a horse, not the seat of a swivel chair.

Jase's grandfather had left him a substantial inheritance to be received after he finished college, with the stipulation that Jase receive only a stipend until he earned, at his own hand, enough to buy a small ranch. Jase and his grandfather had talked at length, and Jase agreed wholeheartedly with his grandfather's wishes.

Maddie understood where Jase was coming from and what his ultimate plans were. One day when he came to the farm to discuss leasing more land, he gave her an overview of his family and his future plans. She could see by his expression when he spoke of his grandfather that he loved and respected the elder Worthington a great deal. Jase told Maddie that the two of them had thought so much alike they often finished each other's sentences. Jase also had the distinction of being the spitting image of his handsome grandfather at the age of twenty-five. Blonde hair, hazel eyes, rugged, solid cowboy stock with the strength needed to tame a bronc and hog-tie a steer.

From Jase's narrative Maddie gathered that, though rich from growing his cattle ranch, Jasper Worthington I was the salt of the earth and had been the one who practically raised Jase when his father spent every waking hour running his business. Half of the four-thousand-acre ranch, now in his father's hands, would belong to Jase when he met his grandfather's conditions according to the will. But Jase's father wanted to get rid of the land so Jase would have no choice but to work for him in his corporate office.

Maddie left her meandering thoughts and glanced up at the lull in Pastor Ben's message just as he sent a smile in her direction. She could feel the blush rise from her heart all the way to the top of her head. Maddie quickly glanced around to see if anyone was looking at her. No one seemed to notice Ben's attention thrown her way. They all seemed entranced by his sermon. She was having a little more trouble staying focused on it.

"Several businessmen have come to me recently asking about what it means to be unequally yoked and wondering if that command extends to the field of business. I'll let you decide for yourselves."

God talks about business? Maddie wondered.

Ben read the passage in 2 Corinthians 6, culminating in verse 14. "The apostle Paul is making the case in the fifth chapter that if anyone belongs to Christ, those who have received Jesus Christ as their Savior, this person is a new creature, having been reconciled to God through the sacrifice Jesus made. When we belong to Christ, His love overtakes us and we long to serve Him. That said, Paul also makes the point that we are not to be bound—yoked—together with unbelievers.

"He says in 2 Corinthians 6:14–15: 'Do not be bound together with unbelievers; for what partnership have righteousness and lawlessness, or what fellowship has light with darkness? Or what harmony has Christ with Belial, or what has a believer in common with an unbeliever?'"

Ben scanned the congregation. "So I ask you, how can one who has no understanding of or love for God enter into a union, whether marriage or business or any other, where important decisions must be agreed upon, with one who has totally surrendered his or her life to Jesus and His love? They don't start from the same understanding of what is important.

"The two are incompatible in another way as well. The believer has the Holy Spirit living within him or her to give wisdom and understanding of the Scriptures and life decisions. But the unbeliever does not. How can the two even speak the same spiritual language?"

Maddie could feel the gripping hollowness in her stomach reach up and strangle her racing heart.

FIFTEEN

When Nathan reached the top of the knoll that overlooked Broken Acres, he put the truck in park and gingerly stepped down from his new truck using the cane his partner, Tim, had given him. Removing his sunglasses, Nathan glanced at the cottage where his troubles began. He rubbed his left thigh to ease the throbbing that his therapist told him would be a reminder of his injuries for a while. He shook his head and scanned the farm, from the small cottage to the orchard and over to the renovated exterior of the big house.

He knew Billy would not be there today. He was in Portsmouth taking his contractor's exam for the second time. The investigation had been resolved after one of the proctors who watched over the participants the last time Billy took the test returned from an emergency trip out of town. He had assured the PSI examiners that Billy had not cheated, but he was extremely suspicious of the young man who had been sitting next to Billy. PSI allowed Billy to retake the test.

There was movement at the big house. Nathan frowned. Surely Maddie wouldn't have hired someone else to replace him. Not after he told Billy to make sure she knew he would be back to finish the job. And he'd told her himself on the phone. The heat traveled up his arms to his neck. He squinted at the cottage and brought his sunglasses back to his face. He told himself to calm down. This was no way to start back on the job. *Why not? Isn't that the way it all began?*

Nathan climbed in his truck, took a deep breath, and drove toward the cottage.

The unseasonably cool wind caused smoke to swirl above the chimney. Nathan opened the squeaky screen door and knocked on the heavy oak. He shook his head and grinned. *She's been talking about fixing that squeak since she moved in. Maybe I'll give it a WD-40 squirt tomorrow.*

Maddie swung the door open and seemed flustered as Nathan stood, sunglasses in hand, grinning.

"Hi, Maddie."

"Hello, Na . . . Mr. Carter."

"That's very formal." Nathan grimaced at her cool tone. "I thought I made it clear the last time we talked that I'd be back to work after my PT."

"You did." Maddie frowned.

Nathan glanced over his shoulder at the big house. "I know Billy is in Portsmouth today, but it looks like someone is over there." He threw a thumb over his shoulder.

"That's my son, David. He just moved here from Chicago. He's going to help with the renovation and finish his veterinary schooling at Forest Hills University."

A vet? "Hmm. Does he have any construction experience?" Nathan could tell his voice had turned brusque and saw the frustration begin to build on Maddie's face.

"Of course he does. Do you think I'd risk him hurting himself working on the big house if he didn't?"

Nathan chewed the inside of his mouth trying to squelch his reaction to her anger. *Just like old times.* He took a deep breath. "Would you mind introducing me to your son and letting him know I'm still the super on this job?"

Maddie caught her lip between her teeth. "Mr. Carter, you and I have a contract, and David knows that. Actually, he knows *all* about you." Maddie tapped her finger against her crossed forearm.

Nathan merely raised an eyebrow.

Maddie marched past him with Rusty, her protective golden retriever, at her side.

SIXTEEN

Billy stared at the back of the church. *I guess it's time to give up hope of Shauna speaking before our wedding*, he realized as he looked out over the people gathered to share this special day with them.

It amazed him that she hadn't needed to speak when he finally summoned the courage to propose to her. He knew the answer by her animated response. He would never give up on loving and encouraging her. Billy gazed at the door Shauna would walk through to begin her walk down the aisle toward him. He thought about the beautiful, kind woman she was and realized he didn't care if she ever said a single word. He would spend the rest of his life making her happy. No more sadness or death. She'd had enough of that to last a lifetime.

He didn't think Shauna could take another loved one dying, and he was really sorry she wouldn't have any family members at their wedding. But then, he acknowledged, he didn't have any family members there either.

Billy offered one of his infectious smiles as he saw Nathan glance at his watch.

Family wasn't always biological. Maddie had adopted both Shauna and him since they'd come to Broken Acres. Maybe not legally, but definitely in her heart. Maddie never once gave a single hint that he and Shauna were rushing into marriage after only knowing each other a few months. She simply loved and encouraged them.

Billy glanced over at Nathan standing next to him in a tux. "You clean up real nice."

Nathan grinned and punched Billy's shoulder. "This is the first time I've ever been a best man. I'm honored you asked me, Billy."

"There's no one else I'd rather have."

*   *   *

Nathan eyed the young man and wondered about his recent slip back into drinking. He'd been so drunk and disorderly the police had arrested him and kept him in jail for two days. The talk they had afterward gave Nathan insight into his actions, but just because things weren't going as Billy wanted them to with his exam was no reason to fall back into his old way of life. Billy agreed and realized he had to stay completely away not only from drugs, as he had since moving to Broken Acres, but from alcohol as well.

Billy mentioned that he and Shauna had discussed it . . . well, he talked while she gave him uncertain looks and wrote her thoughts on paper for him to read. Billy said he'd promised her he was done with all that. They decided to start going to premarital classes with Pastor Ben and attending one of his Bible studies.

Nathan fidgeted with his tie, trying to loosen the tight grip of the collar on his throat. *I hope the time with Pastor Ben makes a difference.*

The music started to play, calling Billy's and Nathan's attention to the back of the church.

*   *   *

It never fails, thought Ben. *Weddings give women an extra glow.*

Maddie, in a flowing knee-length, sage-green chiffon dress that gave her the look of an autumn rose against her red hair and creamy skin, walked arm in arm down the center aisle with Shauna. Shauna's white satin wedding gown sparkled and shone as she walked, scattering bits of light almost as bright as her smile. It didn't matter to her, Ben saw, that only about twenty friends were gathered for the day. Shauna's eyes were only on her groom.

Had Maddie told Shauna about the inheritance she would receive from her aunt and uncle's estate? When Shauna went to live with her aunt and uncle after her mother died, they changed their will so that all their assets would go to Shauna should anything happen to them. After their deaths in an automobile accident, Pastor Ben introduced Maddie to the deceased relatives' attorney. He gave her all the information about Shauna's inheritance.

Did Billy know about it? Ben shook his head. He doubted it. The last time he and Maddie talked about it, she intimated it would be his responsibility to tell Shauna when he thought the time was right. Maddie was Shauna's temporary legal guardian, but she felt Pastor Ben, as Shauna's religious mentor, ought to be the one to spell it out. Should he tell her now that she was getting married? Ben grinned to himself. *Probably not in the middle of her wedding ceremony.*

Pastor Ben smiled at the two women and looked over at Billy, who stood with his mouth hanging open, obviously captivated by his gorgeous bride. Just past Billy, Nathan was also gawking . . . at Maddie. Ben frowned and tried to control his own face as he saw Maddie's eyes on Nathan, her face flush.

Ben cleared his throat and broke their eye contact. "Dearly beloved . . ." Ben began. As he went through the ceremony, explaining the eternal commitment the two were making to one another before God, a split-second vision of Samantha and the baby Ben never saw passed before his eyes. He blinked several times to relieve the pain in his chest and glimpsed Maddie giving him a questioning look.

Ben focused on Billy. "Do you, Billy, take Shauna to be your lawful wedded wife, to love and to cherish, in sickness and in health, until death do you part?"

*   *   *

Maddie looked down at Shauna's bouquet, which Maddie held tight. She tried desperately to keep back the tears that threatened to reveal her true feelings. Maddie felt nothing but joy for Shauna's new life with Billy, whose love for his bride shone deeply from the smile in his glimmering eyes. But she realized she also felt envy as those disappointing words from Ben's sermon passed through her mind. *Unevenly yoked.* If Ben meant what he had said, she would have to live her life alone and unloved.

Stop it, Maddie. This is Shauna and Billy's day. Smile. Be happy for them.

Maddie watched as Billy and Shauna faced each other, holding hands. Billy's sapphire-blue eyes sparkled. "I do."

"The ring please."

Nathan handed Billy the band that encased three diamonds. Billy, tears still glistening in his eyes, placed the ring on Shauna's left ring finger.

"Do you, Shauna, take Billy as your lawful wedded husband, to love and to cherish, in sickness and in health, until death do you part?" Ben bent over and whispered to Shauna, "You can just nod your head, that will be fine."

Shauna gave Billy a brilliant smile. He smiled back and nodded slightly.
"I do."

A gasp ran through the church as Shauna's voice rang out clear and strong.

Not an eye in the room was dry as, wide-eyed and with tears running down his face, Billy pulled Shauna in a tight embrace. Through her own tear-muddled excitement, Maddie saw both Ben and Nathan reach to wipe the tears that threatened to flow heavy in response to Shauna's first words in almost a year.

Billy, overcome, leaned in to kiss Shauna but jumped back with a laugh when Ben cleared his throat.

Ben smiled at the two. "I'd better hurry this up. The ring, Shauna?"

Maddie handed Shauna the ring and smiled excitedly as Shauna placed it on Billy's left ring finger.

"I now pronounce you husband and wife. *Now* you can kiss your bride."

And kiss her he did, as both shed joyful tears.

SEVENTEEN

Granny Harper set the hot jars on the counter next to the pot of stewed tomatoes, all the while reminiscing out loud of days gone by.

"First time I met Jess Harper he got fresh." A slight grin crossed her face.

"Fresh? What happened?" Maddie asked as she ladled tomatoes into the jars.

"Oh, he says to me, 'I think you're pretty cute.'"

Maddie smiled at the disgusted expression on Granny's face.

"I told him, 'We'll have none of that.' And then he looks at my left hand and says, 'Oh, you're married.'

"'Widowed,' I told him. He grinned real big, and the grin got so big I had to inform him, 'But I'm not available.'

"'That's too bad,' he said. 'I thought I'd ask you out to River's Edge Market to sit in lawn chairs on the blacktop, get a tan, and share a peanut butter and jelly sandwich. But if you're unavailable, then the heck with ya.'

"With his dirt-crusted overalls and sweat-stained T-shirt he looked like an old reprobate who didn't have a pot to pee in or a window to throw it out. The nerve, asking me out on a silly date like that." Granny shook her head and smiled with her eyes.

Maddie held the ladle over one of the jars, waiting to hear the rest of the story. "What happened?"

"Oh, his ma and pa held a summer social here at the farm, and one of the young men at church invited me to attend. I didn't know it was Jess

Harper's farm we were going to. Didn't even know he had a farm or anything of value. I tell you, Maddie, the first time I met him he looked like a tramp who just jumped off a boxcar. And he had the nerve to go along with it and make me think it was true."

"How did he look at the social? Did you recognize him?"

Granny smiled and looked out to the farmyard into yesteryear. "I can see him as clear as if it were just the other day. He was standing right there." Granny pointed to where the well pump house stood.

"Two heads taller than Isaiah Bellows, who looked to be turning Jess's attention to a group of giggling girls over by the punch bowl."

Maddie set the ladle on the counter. Granny had her complete attention. "And?"

"And he scanned the girls and brought his handsome gaze around to me."

"Handsome. You said handsome, Granny."

"Yes, indeed. Jess cleaned up real nice. His jet-black hair was slicked back and those pale green eyes bore enough heat to melt my heart."

Maddie clapped her hands. "That is so romantic."

Granny came back to herself.

"Yep, I was a goner after that. Giddy and ridiculous every time he looked my way. And when he asked me to dance—well, let's just say fireworks ignited for both of us."

Maddie picked up the ladle and started spooning tomatoes into jars. "I remember a time when it was like that for Jeff and me until . . ." The spoon hung over the hot jars.

Maddie's imagined memories were flooding back for Granny.

Granny titled her head, and Maddie could read the older woman's concern in her gaze. She was one of the few people Maddie had confided in, sharing the whole story of her marriage to Jeff, his abuse and unfaithfulness, and her determination to start over after he died.

Granny put her hand on Maddie's arm in a comforting gesture and winked. "Well, Jess was thirty-five, ten years older than me, and he said he would know when the right girl came along, and he was bent on not wasting any more time alone once she appeared. It seems I was that girl."

Maddie laughed as Granny got up from the kitchen chair, pulled two muffins from the breadbox, and put the teakettle on to boil.

"What a great story, Granny." Maddie sighed. "And now, how many years later, you've got your sons and their families to care for you. Glenn with the hardware store, Peter's a sheriff, and John, who has taken over running the farm."

"Yes, God has certainly blessed me. I just try to stay out of the way in my little one-bedroom suite." She pointed to a closed door off the kitchen. "Except when it comes to baking and cooking. I guess you could say the kitchen is still my domain. John's wife is very kind. Although when I put myself in her place I'm sure she'd like to have the kitchen to do her own cooking."

George's face flashed through Maddie's mind. She remembered the good-natured bantering the two had shared back in Chicago. George, the cook at Southside Manor Retirement Home, made the best orange scones Maddie had ever tasted.

"So, do you ever get lonely? I know you have John and Nancy and their three boys to keep you company."

"Oh, yes, of course I do. When Jess died four years ago, I felt like the pain would never stop, and then when it did, everybody seemed to think I needed to go out and hog-tie another man so I wouldn't be lonely. I admit sometimes I think about it, but I'm fine with my little place off the kitchen and the family around. Although they are awfully busy folks with the farm and the kids' activities. We see each other just enough to say hi and goodbye." Granny sighed.

"I felt that way the first year after Jeff died. After the funeral and everybody went home, I was very lonely. The girls lived in other states and David had little time for me, what with working three jobs. And there were so many things I had to learn. All the things Jeff took care of. Finances, that huge house, keeping up with everything that needed attention."

Maddie breathed deep. "Then my best friend challenged me to sell the house and most of the furnishings—they were more to Jeff's liking than mine, very modern." She shook off the shivers of distaste from her shoulders. "I decided to take her challenge and move to Jacob's Bend. I'm glad I did."

"Me too. I so appreciate your friendship and your help." Granny pointed to the jars that lined the table.

Maddie nodded. "Well, I'm very thankful for your friendship. Why, look, here I am learning to can tomatoes. Who would have thought?"

Granny smiled. "Speaking of which, when we finish this batch we're done and it'll be a good time for some tea and muffins."

"Sounds great."

EIGHTEEN

"So, Nathan, what's next?" David fastened his tool belt together and settled it on his hips.

"Well, Maddie . . . your mother," Nathan corrected himself, "wants the kitchen finished first since she's got some guy about to show up any day from Chicago."

"Yeah, George. He was the cook at Southside Manor where my mom volunteered. He really knows his stuff."

"So she said. How many misfits—ah, people, does she expect to house here anyway? There are seven bedrooms and the servant's quarters off the kitchen. Is she planning on filling them all?"

"Honestly, I'm not sure even she knows what all this is gonna look like." David scanned the room and shook his head. "Sometimes my mom just jumps in without thinking things through. My dad was the detail thinker in the family."

Nathan grinned. "For some reason that doesn't surprise me."

"Look, I don't want to get too personal, but what is it between you and my mom, anyway? She told me how you met." David raised an eyebrow.

Nathan closed his eyes and ran his hand over the back of his neck.

"She also told me you were the only contractor around who had time to do the work. Why is that? With your mega contractor business, I'm surprised you had any time at all to do the renovation."

Nathan rubbed the two-day growth on his chin. *Start with the tough one.* "From what I understand, our meeting was not good. Don't remember too much about it. As a matter of fact, I don't remember it at all. I was drunk."

A long-forgotten memory of his father ran through his mind.

Nathan snatched the wine bottle from the floor where it lay after his father's drunken tirade. A red blotch had seeped into the carpet. Mom would have to move the furniture. Again.

A bitter sneer and flaring nostrils gave witness to the ten-year-old's disgust and anger while burning, cobalt-blue eyes glared at the man snoring on the couch, his arm out-stretched, a limp hand open where the empty bottle had been.

Nathan spoke from his past. "I swore I'd never drink."

"What happened?"

David's voice brought Nathan's thoughts back. Nathan slowly shook his head. "A woman."

David breathed deep. "I understand."

"You do?"

"Yeah. It's a long, sad story, not worth mentioning. What about you?"

"I let my temper get the best of me. I just wanted to feel nothing." Nathan wasn't sure he could look David in the eye. "So, I was at a bar, drunk, and I tried to pick your mom up when she came in to get something to eat. From what I gather, I was a real jerk."

"Mom did mention that."

"I never should have been in that bar. My dad—" Nathan's fists clenched, the veins in his neck tightened—"my dad was a drunk. All my life he was an angry man who couldn't find happiness anywhere but in a bottle. I swore I'd *never* drink. Can you believe that was the first time I had ever touched alcohol? And there I was no better than my dad, trying to drown my sorrows." Nathan shook his head.

"My dad would drink too much and get physical with my mom." David's nostrils flared.

Nathan's wide-eyed surprise obviously gave David pause.

"I take it Mom never told you about my dad's temper."

"No." Nathan could feel the heat move up his neck to his face, his protective instincts kicking in. Why did that always happen when it came to Maddie?

"No, I guess she wouldn't. It didn't happen often, and my mom tried to hide it from us kids. But I knew. We all knew. I actually walked in on him one time when he had her backed up against a wall and was screaming in her face." David closed his eyes and shook his head. "It still kills me that I didn't have enough guts to stand up to him."

Nathan's head shot up. He remembered Maddie's response as if it had happened yesterday instead of months ago. Inside her cottage to rescue her from a sleeping bat, he let his growing passion take over. He cradled Maddie in his arms against his chest and kissed her lips. Then . . . he *backed her up against the wall.*

Nathan groaned. "No wonder . . . Nathan, you are such a——" He hung his head and held his forehead in both hands.

"Nathan?" David shook his shoulder and moved closer. "Nathan, are you okay? Are you in pain?"

Nathan looked the young man in the eyes—Maddie's eyes. "No, I'm just really sorry to hear that about your dad. And doubly sorry your mom had to live through it." He shook his head, then looked up to catch David's gaze.

"David, let me tell you, I stood between my mom and my dad's violent temper many times, and it really didn't make any difference except to build up the same kind of anger deep inside me. Trust me, David, you don't want to live with that kind of bitterness."

David nodded. "You're right. I loved my dad, but I couldn't help him with whatever it was that was eating him up inside. Only God could do that. It makes me sad to think he never found peace."

Peace. There's that word again, thought Nathan.

He straightened up and grabbed his tool belt. "Yeah, well, what do you say we get this kitchen ready for George and make it everything your mom wants it to be?"

David smiled. "Let's do it."

NINETEEN

Jasper Worthington III was more like his father than he cared to admit. He knew what he wanted and was determined to get it. Maddie had told him all but about fifteen acres on Broken Acres were leased out to another cattle owner with a small herd and farmers who needed more land for their crops. The one hundred acres Jase already leased was all she had available.

"I'll give you twice what the other cattle owners are paying."

Maddie shook her head. "Jase, you are not hearing me. I cannot break the leases I have with the others just to please you. Why don't you take that money and buy your own grazing land?"

The last conversation Jase had with his father reeled through his mind. *"No one will sell you land once they know who you are. They know I have plans for you in my company, and they know I can make life very difficult for them should they even consider selling you land."*

"Mrs. Crane—"

"Maddie, please."

Jase smiled. "Okay, Maddie, my funding is being held up by my father in hopes I'll join him in his business. I'm not interested in sitting behind a desk growing my dad's business when I can be outside growing my own herd of horses."

"I remember you saying that was your dream for the future. You sound a lot like Ben Farrington. He spent much of his life on his aunt and uncle's horse ranch in Idaho. He would still be there if it weren't for the stars." Maddie grinned.

Jase tilted his head. "Stars?"

"It's a long story."

"Is he an astronomer then?"

"No, he's a pastor."

"Aha. A pastor. That explains it." Jase grinned.

"Jase. I wish I could help you with more land, but that's not going to happen any time soon. I will, however, put your name on the top of the list should any more land come available."

Jase extended his hand. "Thank you, Maddie."

She offered her hand and her own grin.

"Maddie. If you hear of anyone else with land to lease would you please let me know?" Jase handed her a business card with his cell phone number.

"Of course."

TWENTY

"Hey, Billy, how's the new place in Carterville? Is that 1940s bungalow the rental you thought it would be? And how's Shauna doing with her online college courses?"

Billy buckled his tool belt and grinned at Nathan. "It's great."

David and Nathan gave him a wary look.

"No, seriously, married life is the best. You two ought to find your own soul mates and try it."

Billy shook his head when Nathan looked down at the floor and David just gave him a grin.

"Yeah, yeah, I know, lovesick pup. I've heard you say it enough. But I'm telling you, my life has never been better. And Shauna is so smart. She is acing all her classes. Once she gets her AA degree in marketing, she's looking to find another online school where she can finish up and get her BA in business."

David gave Billy a thumbs-up. "That's great. No matter what kind of profession we choose, we all need those basics. I really struggled with the business classes. I'd rather dissect a frog any day."

Nathan wrinkled his nose. "Seriously? Better you than me. I can't believe you actually like all that blood and guts stuff."

Billy couldn't help but laugh when Nathan gave David a look that said, "I think I'm gonna be sick."

"So, Billy, have you heard anything from the contractor's licensing board?"

"No, nothing yet. They said it takes three to ten days to receive my license after the licensing office receives my test results and application.

That is, *if* all the paperwork has been filled out and signed correctly. If not, the application goes back to the applicant to correct and then back to the licensing office for another three to ten days."

"That's a lot of hoops to jump through." David ran his hand through his thick auburn hair, pushing it off his forehead where it promptly fell back down.

"Yeah."

"By the way, why did it take so long for you to take the contractor's licensing test after completing your training? I would have thought you'd be on the CCB office steps when their doors opened the next day."

Billy felt uneasy answering Nathan's question. He shrugged. *These guys have been good friends. I can be honest with them.*

"Honestly, I was scared."

"Scared?" Nathan and David chimed together.

"Scared that I would fail. So I went over and over all the lessons from the class and the twelve-inch-thick textbook—well, okay, it wasn't really twelve inches thick, but it sure felt like it—so that I would pass. It took several months to get up the courage. And then when Shauna spoke for the first time in almost a year at our wedding, I knew I had done the right thing, taking the test, whether I passed or not. If my wife could be so brave after all she has been through, who was I to be afraid of a stupid test?"

David nodded, and Nathan slapped Billy on the back. "Way to go. I'm proud of you."

Billy cleared his throat. "Okay, so how about we get some work done?"

Nathan agreed. "With the three of us working on the big house, we should be done in no time."

A couple of hours later Billy looked back over his shoulder from his position in the entry as Nathan and David tugged on the last piece of demolition in the kitchen, a counter that would not budge. Billy walked over and helped heave the stubborn piece from the wall.

Nathan rubbed the sweat from his forehead with his shirtsleeve. "Three definitely moves the process along. I hope Maddie can find the money to finish the job."

David had just landed the first blow to the wall between the dining room and the parlor with a sledgehammer when he turned to Nathan, a questioning frown on his face. "Really? I haven't heard anything about that from Mom. Are you sure?"

"Yeah, I'm sure. I offered to help with the finances when she gave me that now-what-do-I-do look your mom gets. But you know how stubborn and hard-headed—" Nathan took a deep breath and shrugged. "Sorry, David."

"No. I know what you mean. When Mom makes up her mind there's no changing it, no matter what the reality is."

Nathan rubbed the back of his neck. "You got that right."

"I have a little money saved. Maybe she would accept help from me."

"I thought that was for veterinary school. You have three more years, right?"

"Yeah. But this is important to Mom."

"And vet school isn't important to you?" Nathan sent a questioning glance at the young man.

David shrugged.

Billy picked up the crowbar. "Come on, you guys. At least we can finish tearing this wall down. That doesn't cost anything."

*   *   *

Maddie's cottage may have been small, but there was plenty of space to pace. She walked from her living room to the kitchen, waiting for someone at Isaac Birnbaum Financial to call. Having left a message with Isaac's secretary, she continued to pace.

Half an hour later, the phone finally rang. Pleasantries concluded, Isaac cleared his throat. "Maddie, I have some disconcerting news."

"What's that?"

"Your investments have been frozen."

"What?" Maddie gripped the phone.

"Your investments have—"

"I heard what you said. Why?"

"There seems to be some concerns about money Jeff invested for several of his clients."

"What concerns?"

"Concerns about their legality."

Maddie frowned, remembering Jeff sitting behind his large cherrywood desk in the sizable office down the hall from Isaac's office suite.

"Isaac, you know as well as I do that Jeff was a man of integrity, honest to a fault." At least that's what she had always believed until . . .

"Yes," he said, then added under his breath. "So we all thought."

"But?"

"It looks like the reason he stopped paying on his life insurance was because he cashed it in. He had invested a lot of money in a single-pay whole life insurance policy, pretty risky, actually. Not like Jeff at all. Anyway, he cashed it in to show his investors this scheme was sound by putting in his own money."

The word jumped out at Maddie. "Scheme? Come on, Isaac, that doesn't sound like Jeff."

"I know, I know. And none of us would have suspected indiscretion—"

"But?"

"But, Maddie, you of all people know Jeff had secrets. And I didn't want to have to bring her up, but Rachel is also under investigation."

Tears welled up in Maddie's eyes thinking of Jeff with the young, attractive associate from his office. And not just in his office . . .

"Maddie?"

She took a deep breath. *Breathe in, breathe out. Breathe in, breathe out.*

"Maddie? I'm sorry to bring up something so painful, but you need to know I can't send you any more money until this is cleared up. *If* it's cleared up. Are you going to be okay with your ranch and all?"

"Farm."

"What?"

"Broken Acres is a farm, Isaac, not a ranch."

"Ah, okay. Are you okay out there?"

"Yes, I'll be fine. We'll figure something out."

"I'll do my best to help. But the investigation is obviously out of my hands. It's going to take some time. The SEC is not known for their speedy investigations."

*   *   *

The screen door clapped shut, hinges squeaking as they had from the first day Maddie moved into the little cottage. "Good grief, I keep forgetting to find the WD-40."

"Maybe that should be the Broken Acres theme song." David grinned back over his shoulder at the door as he walked to the kitchen sink and filled a glass with cold water.

"Mom, what's this about not having the money to finish the renovation on the big house?"

"David, until I talked to Isaac I thought I had the money to finish."

"But Nathan said—"

"Mr. Carter doesn't know everything. He told me the cost of materials continues to increase, and so I planned to ask Isaac for more money." Maddie took a deep breath. "Isaac told me today my investments are frozen."

"Frozen?"

"Yes." It was hard to say this to her son. "They are investigating some of your dad's investment practices."

"Are you saying Dad did something dishonest?"

"That's what they're trying to find out."

"No way. Dad had some emotional stuff going on, but he was totally honest when it came to his business practices."

"I agree."

David set his glass in the sink, obviously thinking. "How long did Mr. Birnbaum say the investigation would take?"

"He didn't know. We'll just have to stop the renovations until the investigation is completed."

"But, Mom, that means Nathan and Billy will need to move on to other jobs."

"I know." Maddie walked out to the front porch. The screen door slapped back in place after David followed her. Glancing past the orchard to the big house, she couldn't help feeling sad. One more week and there would be no more hammers in sync, no more helping with the drywall, no more cinnamon rolls with apology notes. She breathed deep and released a heavy groan.

"Mom, we may not get them back."

"I know, sweetheart. I know."

"I have some money saved. Let's use that. This is your dream."

"Absolutely not. You are going back to get your degree and become a vet. That is *your* dream. And it has been on hold far too long."

"Mom," David pleaded.

"David, it will be fine. I'll just put the project on hold until I have the funds to finish it. Maybe I'll get a job."

"A job? Doing what?" Her face must have reflected her thoughts, because David rephrased his question. "I mean, are there any jobs available around Jacob's Bend?"

"I really don't know. I haven't had a chance to look. Maybe there's an opening at the library or one of the shops in town. I could see if they need a waitress at Lettie's."

David frowned.

"Whatever it is, I'll need to do something pretty quick. The money I receive from the leases on the property goes to pay the loan on the property with the rest put away for taxes."

"But what about Nathan and Billy? What if we never see them again?"

"If they're available when it's time to start up again, we'll welcome them back on the project. If not, we'll find someone else." Maddie's heart rate doubled. *Never see Nathan again.*

"David, this is the time for your dream of becoming a veterinarian to come true. Mine will still be there when the investigation is over. Have you talked to Jenny—Dr. Adams—about sponsoring you and doing your internship with her?"

"No, not yet. I figured there was plenty of time."

"No time like the present. The plan is still for you to stay here and commute to Forest Hills University, right?"

"Right."

"Great. Call Dr. Adams."

TWENTY-ONE

D avid dialed the number, not sure what to expect. He took a deep breath while listening to the recording.

"You have reached the College of Veterinary Medicine at Forest Hills University. Our normal business hours are eight to noon and one to five, Monday through Friday . . ." The voice droned on as David listened to the options.

"Our large animal clinic . . ."

David switched the phone to his other ear, surprised to see that his hands were feeling sweaty.

"For the dean's office, student services, admissions, or scheduling tours, press one."

David hit the one on his cell phone.

"Dean's office, how may I help you?"

"Hi, I'm interested in your veterinary program. I have a BS in animal science/pre-vet medicine from Southern Illinois University and one year at the University of Illinois College of Veterinary Medicine. If possible I'd like to finish the rest of my schooling at Forest Hills University. How can we make that happen?"

"Why don't I let you talk to the dean? He'd be the best person to tell you what will be necessary."

The phone clicked, and a few bars of tinny music rang across the line until a voice boomed out. "This is Dean James. I hear you're interested in vet med."

"Yes, sir." David ran through his background again.

"Impressive resume."

David shrugged. "I'm not trying to be impressive, just thought I'd cut through all the interview questions and get right to the heart of the matter. I'm anxious to get this going so I can finally practice medicine."

"Why didn't you finish up in Illinois?" The question caught David off guard.

"Well, ah, I took a couple of years off to—" David moved clear across the open living room and kitchen area of his mother's cottage and back to the two large picture windows in a matter of seconds. *What can I say that isn't a lie?*

"I needed to earn more money to help with the final three years."

That was true enough.

"Will you be living on campus?"

"No, I'll be commuting from Jacob's Bend—"

"That's a heck of a commute. Must be a couple of hours at least."

"I know. Any suggestions?"

"Do you live in Oregon? Are you an Oregon resident?"

"Yes, I live in Oregon with my mom. Why?"

"Nonresidents pay about three times more for tuition than residents. You must live in Oregon for a minimum of one year in order to be considered a resident."

David flopped down on the couch. "Oh brother, I totally forgot about the nonresident thing. I've only been here a couple of months." David shook his head. Another delay. "I guess I'll get a job while I wait to become a resident."

The dean's voice continued, not rough, but realistic. "If you've got a degree already behind you, I'm sure you remember that for every hour you spend in the classroom, there is at least that much time needed for homework. Not to mention practicum time with the animals. So, when you do decide to start school, you might want to consider moving a little closer to Forest Hills."

"No. I have to make this work for my mom. She needs my help with her farm."

"Be that as it may, when you are ready to enroll we will need your transcripts from the two schools you mentioned in order to proceed."

After the call David stared at his cell phone.

This isn't going to be as easy as I thought.

*   *   *

Maddie sat at the kitchen table with her budget book spread out before her. The first time Jeff mentioned living on a budget, she had no idea what he was talking about. After he walked her through the process, she flat out told him she didn't need to go to all that trouble. She confidently tapped her right temple and told him she could keep it all right there.

Three months later when she didn't have enough money left in the middle of the month to buy more groceries, she asked Jeff to teach her how to work with a budget. Over the years living by a budget became second nature. She wouldn't have known what to do without the monthly financial sheet telling her how much money was coming in and how much needed to go out. And if there was enough to meet her needs.

This was not looking good. She was right back where she started when Jeff died, with the exception of a lot less money.

*   *   *

Maddie picked at the food on her plate with her fork.

"What's wrong, Mom?"

"David, I'm not sure what we're going to do about George. He's looking forward to starting a new chapter in his life. And I'm excited to have him here."

"What do you mean? Didn't George say he was ready to quit his job as the cook at the retirement home in Chicago? He said he liked the idea of cooking for the people at Broken Acres. Does he know about the delay in the restoration of the big house?"

"No."

"Mom, didn't you say you thought he would be okay living in his fifth wheel until the big house is complete? He's probably old enough to get social security, right?"

"Yeah, I guess his social security and navy pension would hold him. I just feel bad asking him to uproot his life to come here and not have everything ready for him."

"Mom."

"Yeah?"

"George will be fine, and so will we. We'll figure out something."

"I agree. There is always a way to overcome obstacles; we just need to brainstorm to find it."

"And pray."

"Pray? David, when did you get so religious?"

"When did you turn your back on God?"

"Who said I turned my back on God? I still attend church. Good grief, David, I've dated Pastor Ben."

"Mom, attending church and dating a pastor does not make you a Christian."

"David, can we *please* change the subject?"

"Okay, but I have one more question I want to ask you."

Maddie scrunched up her nose. "What?"

"Did Dad's affair cause you to question your relationship with God?"

Maddie grabbed the plates off the table and took them over to the sink. She stood gazing out the window, remembering Jeff's letter she had found in her gram's Bible confessing his thoughts of suicide and God's intervention.

"Mom?"

Turning to face her son, Maddie leaned her back against the sink and crossed her arms over her chest. "No, David. Although that was extremely painful, it did not cause me to question."

"Then what—"

"David, let's change the subject. How did your talk go with the counselor at Forest Hills University?"

David shook his head and took the rest of the dishes over to the sink. "Well, I won't be enrolling for the next several months if I don't want to pay three times more for tuition than a resident would pay. They want my transcripts and hopefully they will let me enroll in May for the fall session."

"I forgot about that." Maddie thought for a moment. "Maybe Nathan could find you a construction job to earn some money to help with your tuition for school."

"That's a good idea. I hadn't thought of that. He has a crew working on the new hospital in Portsmouth. That might be an option."

"That's supposed to be a two-to-three-year project. Still, Portsmouth is more than two hours from here. Maybe he has something closer."

"I'll give him a call."

"Did you call Dr. Adams?"

"No, I didn't see any reason to call her since I won't even be starting school until fall at this rate."

"Yeah, I guess you're right. Will they let you intern here?"

"I don't know, didn't ask yet. And there isn't really any hurry now."

TWENTY-TWO

Nathan woke from a sound sleep, his left leg working a spasm, his head pounding in rhythm with the drum the neighbors were beating. *No, wait, I don't have any neighbors.*

He sat up and squinted at the bedside clock that blinked 3:00 a.m. Nathan stood. The pounding threatened to take him to his knees. He rubbed the back of his neck and his left thigh. Using his cane to help him limp to the bathroom, he swallowed a couple of ibuprofen. He looked at the pale, haggard man in the mirror. He needed to ask the doctor for something stronger. *Really? I thought you didn't want to get hooked on anything. Maybe you are just like your old man.*

Nathan hobbled to the fridge and grabbed a can of soda. Caffeine, maybe that would help stop the beat in his head.

When he woke to his alarm the next morning his headache was gone, but his leg throbbed and felt hot to the touch. He looked over his shoulder at the cane resting in the corner. Maybe that was the problem. He hadn't used his cane yesterday.

Sighing, he limped over and grabbed the stick, eyeing the battered Bible he had pulled out of the trash bin at the road, just before the truck dumped it.

He wasn't sure why he kept the book. At least if Pastor Ben asked about it, he could honestly say it was sitting in his house.

Nathan ran his hand through his hair and looked at the book sitting in the corner on the floor. It was getting him thinking, though. That, and attending church in Carterville.

*   *   *

Nathan limped up the steps to the wide porch of the big house. "Hey, Billy, David," he shouted in the front door, hoping the guys could hear him.

David walked to the porch, hammer in hand, two nails clamped between his pursed lips, Billy close behind.

Nathan gave them the update. "According to Maddie, we have this week to finish all we can and then the project is on hold, indefinitely." He shook his head.

"I know," David mumbled through the nails. "Mom's determined to earn the money since she can't use her investment money."

Billy laughed. "What was that? It sounded like you said, 'Mom took a detour and ate her best pony.'"

David shoved Billy and took the nails out of his mouth.

"Did she find a job?" Nathan heard the skepticism in his own voice, but David just laughed.

"Well, not yet, but you know Mom when she's determined."

"Oh yeah, I know your mother's determination. I wish you'd talk to her about letting me loan her the money. She can pay me back, if she feels the need, when her investments start producing income again."

Billy cocked an eyebrow at the two men. "Guys, you both know that's not gonna happen. Maddie's a proud woman, and this is really important for her to be able to finally do something on her own."

"My dad was way too protective of my mom." David looked around the building. "Actually, I don't think my dad thought she had it in her to accomplish much of anything without his help."

Nathan gave David a lingering frown. "You know he was wrong, though, right? Your mom is one of the most accomplished women I know. Look at all she's done on her own."

"Whoa, hold on. You don't have to convince me. I know my mom is an incredible woman who has always been able to do anything. She just never got any encouragement from my dad. I think he felt more secure knowing she was at home taking care of him and us kids."

"What kind of man thinks like that these days?" Nathan gave David a disgusted look.

"I know." David held up his hands in a defensive posture. "The more I learn about my mom and dad's marriage, the more I realize I really didn't know who they were. I'm definitely getting a better appreciation for my mom since I moved here."

Billy nodded. "It sounds like you admire her too, Nathan."

You're engaged, Nathan. Remember that.

He tried to shrug casually. "I can honestly say Madison Crane is like no other woman I've ever met." He turned away to pick up his tool belt.

The other two snickered and reached for their tools.

"We better get busy so we can get as much finished as possible."

"Hey, Nathan, since I'll need a job after this week, you wouldn't happen to have any construction jobs in the area, would you?" David asked.

"Hey, me too." Billy gave Nathan a hopeful look. "I'm a married man now, you know, and I need a paying job. I may not be keeping my wife at home, but I'm not going to expect her to earn all the money either."

Nathan smiled at his coworkers. "Let me check with my partner, Tim, and Mr. Harper at the hardware store. He pretty much knows what's going on around the area. You could both have a job on the Portsmouth hospital project if you wanted."

"Thanks, Nathan, but if you've got something local that would work better for me. That way I can help Mom with the farm."

"Yeah, me too," Billy added. "With Shauna taking classes online to get her degree, I'd just as soon work local if at all possible." He blushed, then grinned. "We are newlyweds, you know."

"I'll see what I can do, guys. We'll find something closer than Portsmouth."

"Thanks, Nathan," the two said in unison.

TWENTY-THREE

Maddie's tears surprised her.

She missed Alex and Carolyn, but why was she crying now? Maddie wiped the tears with the tail of Jeff's pinstripe shirt she'd worn to paint the walls of the loft. Leaving the wet paintbrush in the roller pan, she went down to the kitchen and poured herself a cup of coffee. Sitting on the porch swing with her right leg folded beneath her, she shook off the memory of rambling around in that huge house in Chicago after Jeff died.

She hadn't thought living alone would cause her sorrow. "Good grief, I'm not really alone. David is here, and so are you two." Maddie nudged the snoozing Rusty with her foot, then looked over her shoulder at the screen door and sighed. David was only here to sleep too. And she never actually got much of a chance to sit and talk with him. She was grateful for the two construction jobs Nathan had found for David, but they did keep him busy.

Glancing at her two companions curled up on the rug spread in front of the swing didn't help with her loneliness. "You two can't carry on a conversation, and that's what I miss, isn't it? Look at me, talking to animals." Maddie brushed away the tears that fell on her lap.

This was ridiculous.

The bell chime on her cell phone startled her. Sniffing away more tears she walked into the kitchen and took her phone from the charger. "Hello?"

"Hey, Maddie. How's it going out there in the wilderness? It's starting to cool off here in New York."

"Oh, Carolyn, it's so good to hear your voice." Maddie choked back a sudden rush of tears. "We're having beautiful spring weather."

"What's wrong, Maddie? You sound like you've been crying."

"This is like déjà vu. Remember after Jeff died? I can't believe it's been almost three years since his heart attack." Maddie gave a nervous laugh. "It is déjà vu, just reversed. Last time it was me crying my eyes out in Chicago and you calling from Jacob's Bend consoling and challenging me."

"I remember that conversation. And look at you, taking the challenge to sell your home and move to Jacob's Bend." Her friend refused to be diverted. "But what's going on? Why have you been crying?"

"That's a good question. I don't know."

"Ah, knowing you, I find that hard to believe. You must have some idea what brought this on."

"Well," admitted Maddie, "I think I'm lonely. But why now?"

"Isn't David still living there?"

"Yes. Or at least he sleeps here."

"Oh. So he's gone most of the time."

Maddie found herself explaining. "He has two jobs now. Nathan found him a renovation job in Carterville and Granny Harper hired him to do some work on her one-bedroom suite there on the farm." She breathed deep. "I'm guessing this is just a preview of what it's going to be like when he goes back to school."

"Probably."

"But that can't be all. Carolyn, I don't understand, why the sadness now?" Maddie swiped away more tears before they could fall.

"I'm only guessing here, but maybe it's because you don't have a lot going on like when you first moved to Jacob's Bend and bought the Riley farm. You were pretty busy, you know."

"I know. I loved all the activity and adventure of doing something so foreign to my former life. And I loved it when Shauna was living here with me. Even though she didn't talk, she was a good listener and someone to share life with. Now that she and Billy are married, I'm lonely." Maddie almost smiled at the self-pity in her voice. *Am I that pathetic?*

"Maybe you need to volunteer somewhere so you can be out around people."

"Maybe. But I don't want to live the rest of my life alone. Though my marriage to Jeff was a struggle, I loved him. I want to love again."

"What does that mean?"

"I don't really know."

"You aren't going out looking for a husband, are you?" Carolyn's voice sounded alarmed. "Like an online dating thing?"

Maddie sniffed. "You know, I've heard of some happy endings with online dating."

"Maddie—"

"No, Carolyn, I'm not planning on hunting, capturing, and hog-tying some man I meet in cyberspace. Still, I don't want to close the door on that part of my life either. Even though I promised myself I'd never get involved with another man after Jeff died."

"What about Pastor Ben? At one time you thought you had feelings for him. That sounded like quite the romantic dinner you two had together in the fall."

Maddie's face flushed at the memory. "Oh my gosh, Carolyn, don't remind me. I practically threw myself at him. And he had to drive through a blizzard when he left here." The mention of the storm caused Maddie to think of another man who had driven out to her home that night. Camping at the foot of his hospital bed for three nights after a near fatal crash on his way back to town had done little to squelch her emotions. Seeing him at death's door caused her to believe her feelings for Nathan were real, until—

"Maddie, are you still there?"

"Yeah. Sorry, Carolyn. I'm here. Just thinking about that night."

"And?"

"And what?"

"What are you thinking? Is Ben the one you want to share your life with?"

"Carolyn, we only had one date."

"But you see him all the time at church activities."

"He hasn't asked me on a real date."

"What about the horseback rides you two have taken?"

"That's not a date. I do enjoy his company. He is thoughtful and kind—"

"And handsome."

"That too. He's very different from Jeff."

"That's for sure. At least the Jeff we knew until the last year of his life."

Maddie thought back to the many changes in her husband before his heart attack and the letter she found in Gram's Bible. "Yeah, well, both Jeffs are gone. And I'm not so sure Ben and I have the same future in mind. I mean, can you see me as a pastor's wife?"

"You might want to give some thought about where you stand with God, Maddie. I know, I know, I've said that to you before, but I don't really think you can honestly go forward without settling that issue."

Jeff's letter flashed through Maddie's mind. "Carolyn, how many times are we going to have this conversation?"

"As many as it takes. Hey, I need to get going. Think about what I said, okay? And you don't have to be lonely. Jesus promises to be with us always."

Maddie raised her brows. "Goodbye, Carolyn."

Maddie glanced at the bookcase where she had moved Gram's Bible to the bottom corner under a stack of old magazines. "Nope, not gonna try that again."

*   *   *

Pastor Ben sat back in his swivel chair and ran his hand through thick, unruly hair. When his hand reached his collar, he realized it was way past time for a trim.

He remembered Maddie's comment to him when they had gone out riding horses last year. *"Your hair looks good."* Maddie had smiled at him from her horse just behind him on the trail. *"Kinda scruffy, hanging over your collar like that."*

Yeah, that was a fun ride, Ben thought. What was it about Madison Crane that caused her to come to mind all the time? She was beautiful, that's for sure. Ben remembered the bounce in her auburn hair when she rode her horse up the trail in front of him. How the waves rested on her shoulders when they stopped to give the horses a breather.

Ben shook his head. It wasn't just that she was beautiful. She was kind. And compassionate. And fun to be with. Why didn't he ask her out on a real date?

You know why, Ben. You are a pastor. A Christian. And you're not sure where she stands with God. Unequally yoked. But that first kiss in her living room after that delicious meal she'd cooked . . . he couldn't get it out of his mind.

He hung his head and ran his hands through his hair. "Lord, I never thought I'd let myself fall in love after the disaster with Samantha. Maddie really is an incredible woman. But am I in love?"

Ben took a deep breath. Maybe he needed to remind himself that she was a member of his congregation, and in his heart he wanted every one of them to know Jesus as their Savior. How could he even think about loving her when he wasn't sure she was a Christian? He shook his head.

Come on, Ben. You just gave a message about being unevenly yoked.

"Okay, enough." Ben straightened up in his chair and opened his sermon notes for the coming service. Time to shift focus and keep first things first.

"Thank You, Lord, for this heart-to-heart talk. I really needed it. Please help me know how to handle this relationship with Maddie. I'm a pastor, and I want to be the man You created me to be. Help me not let my emotions rule my actions. For me, it has to be You first, Lord. Always You first."

TWENTY-FOUR

Maddie loved the view of her land from the cottage porch swing. Especially before the sun came up, savoring the first cup of coffee of the day. Today was no exception. Warmth emanating from Rusty and Sarg resting on either side of her kept the cool breeze at bay as she glanced at the big house across the orchard. Quiet. No hammers in sync, no men laughing at one another's jokes. Just silence.

What was she going to do? David was looking into an internship at Forest Hills University at the veterinary college while he waited out the year to become an Oregon resident. He wouldn't have much time to help with the renovation. Billy would probably take the job in Portsmouth that Nathan offered. And Nathan . . .

Maddie walked inside to fill her cup. Startled when her cell phone rang in the pocket of her jacket, she held her hand to her galloping heart. "Hello? Oh, hi, Mr. Jamison, what can I do for you?" She listened to the low voice rumble across the connection. "You what?"

When the man on the other end of the phone hung up, Maddie dropped into a chair. Mr. Jamison was the second farmer in as many weeks to cancel his lease.

She knew they wouldn't lease the property forever, but she thought they would at least stay until their leases were up.

The phone rang twice after Maddie tapped the number in her contact list on her cell. "Jase, how are you?"

"Hey, Maddie. Doing pretty good. How about you?"

"Well, two of the farmers who have been leasing property from me have decided they are able to make a go of it with the land they own and have asked out of their leases. That means I have a hundred acres available for you to graze more cattle."

"Oh man, that would be great, if only . . ."

"If only what?"

"Well, I'm trying to meet the conditions in my grandfather's will that would allow me to receive my inheritance. I've found a small ranch, and Nathan Carter has offered to loan me the money to buy it. He's also given me a job in the marketing department at his construction company."

"But his office is in Portsmouth. I thought you didn't want to work in an office. I thought you wanted to be outside riding a horse on the range."

Jase laughed. "Yep, that's my plan. Nathan said I could do the work from home in the evenings after I finish punching cattle and raising horses for the day. He understands the need to be out of the office and in the great outdoors."

"I'm sure he does."

"Maddie, I'm sorry to leave you with still more unused land."

"Good grief, I hadn't thought of that."

"Maybe we can work something out."

"No, Jase, you need to move forward with your plans. I'll be fine. I'm glad you are living your dream."

"Well, I wouldn't exactly say I'm living my dream. Yet. It will be some time before that actually happens."

"If there's one thing I've learned in the last few years, it's that you never know what will propel your dream into action. Everything that happens along the way to realizing that dream, good or bad, either breaks you or makes you stronger and even more determined to see it through. Sometimes in the process, the dream takes on a whole new look."

"Sounds like the voice of experience, Maddie."

"Let's just say I'm in the middle of living a dream I never knew was in me. The process has definitely made me stronger and caused me to grow up."

"Grow up?"

"It's a long story."

"Sounds like it would be worth hearing sometime."

"Sure. And I hope it will encourage you in what you have planned. Although, since my husband died, it's been my experience that what you have planned often takes a turn when you least expect it. And not always in the best direction."

"Yeah, like my dad cutting me off."

"That would be a good example. But just as often something better comes along."

It sounded like Jase was either in the saddle or on the road in his car. "Need to get going, Maddie. My horses and cattle will be grazing at Broken Acres for at least another couple of months. It will take that long to finalize the purchase of the ranch."

"Okay, sounds good. Let me know if there is anything I can do to help you in the process."

"Thanks, Maddie, that's kind of you."

*　　*　　*

Maddie thought back to arriving in Jacob's Bend and staying with Alex and Carolyn. The Morenos' transfer to New York. Making a friend of Gael O'Donnell, owner of O'Donnell's Brier, and renting the apartment above her shop. Buying Broken Acres. Yes, leaving Chicago might not have seemed like the best decision at the time, but something better did indeed come along.

But that was then, Maddie realized.

"What am I going to do now?" she asked her sleeping pets. She couldn't find a job that she was qualified for, her investments were frozen, the big house needed to be finished if she was going to rent out rooms and make a living . . . Good grief.

TWENTY-FIVE

"Isaac, I need to finish the renovation of the big house so I can start renting out the rooms."

"Maddie, I thought the leases with the farmers were keeping you afloat."

"Well, yes, they were helping me, but a few of them—truth be known, half of them—have decided they can now make a go of their crops on their own land. Some have bought their own property and plan to expand."

"I don't know what to tell you, Maddie. There are no new developments on the situation with your assets."

"Isaac, can't you light a fire under someone and get them unfrozen?"

"That's not likely to happen any time soon, Maddie."

"Why not?" Maddie's voice took on a louder, assertive edge. She could feel the heat rising up her neck.

"Relax, Maddie."

"Relax? Did you just say relax?"

"You are getting all worked up when there's nothing we can do. Everything on this end is on hold until the investigators finish their probe."

Maddie took a deep breath. "I'm sorry, Isaac. I know it's not your fault. I guess I'll just have to take out another loan. Maybe combine the two into one."

"I wouldn't suggest you do that until things here are settled."

"I really don't have a choice. If I don't make some money soon so I can finish the big house and bring in more income, I could lose everything."

"I would be very careful if I were you. If you default on the loan you could lose everything anyway."

"It sounds like the same outcome either way." Maddie chewed on her lip. "Thanks for your advice. Will you please let me know as soon as my assets are released?"

"If it happens, you'll be the first one I call."

"Thanks, Isaac."

Maddie looked out the window and tried to think of another alternative. Her mind took her to another time. *"Maddie, why won't you let me help you?"* Nathan's offer still made her feel like she was incapable of taking care of herself and her property.

"No. Not him. Not ever."

Maddie shook off Nathan's suggestion to loan her the money she needed to finish the renovation of the big house. Instead, she called the bank and set up an appointment to discuss a consolidation loan, with Broken Acres as collateral.

*   *   *

"Mrs. Crane, am I understanding you to say you want to consolidate the loan you have now by asking the bank to lend you more money for renovation?" The loan officer had a curious look on his face.

"Yes, is that a problem?"

"No, not a problem really. It's just that most people consolidate several loans to get a good interest rate with only one loan rather than three or four with different interest rates. This loan you are requesting is more of a cash-out refinance."

"Uh-huh. And your point?"

"Well, the loan you have now is at an excellent interest rate. If we add fifty thousand dollars, as you've requested, I'm afraid we will need to increase the interest rate."

"By how much?"

"At least two percent."

"Two percent doesn't sound like a lot." Maddie closed her eyes and once again railed at Jeff for not teaching her more about finances. After all, he *was* a financial consultant.

"The other difficulty, from what you are telling me, is that you don't have a steady income."

"That's because some of the farmers who lease my land have terminated their leases."

"Do you have any farmers who will still be leasing your property?"

"No, but I do have two cattle owners who lease over one hundred acres to graze their cattle." Maddie reminded herself that the one leasing a hundred acres had just broken his lease.

"Well, that's something."

"And besides, I'm putting Broken Acres up as collateral for the loan."

"Mrs. Crane, why don't I give you a call after I discuss this with my manager?"

"Is there some kind of problem? Because I'm sure I can find another bank to loan me the money."

"No, no. I don't think there will be any complications. It's just procedure." The loan officer stood and extended his hand. "I will call you in a few days with an answer."

*   *   *

Maddie answered the phone hoping it was the bank with an encouraging answer to her cash-out refinance loan.

"Hi, Maddie."

"Hey, Jase, how's it going? Have you closed escrow on your new place?"

"That won't be happening any time soon."

"What? Why? I thought you were all set to go with Nathan giving you a loan. Did he back out?"

"No, nothing like that. He's a great guy. But someone else bought the property I was interested in. They offered more money if the owners would make it a fast escrow—two weeks fast."

"Wow, I've never heard of property closing escrow that fast. You couldn't offer more money?"

"No, it was getting out of my price range. Like I said, the stipend my grandfather left me and the salary I'm making working for Nathan don't add up to a whole lot."

"Well, I'm sure you're doing your best. It's hard work to keep everything in balance. Good for you."

"Yeah, I have lived a pretty charmed life. I really want to do this on my own, and my grandfather made sure it wouldn't be easy. He knew my dad would make it hard for me in the finance area. The great thing is, my grandfather started out with less than I have. He assured me it could be done." Jase laughed.

"He must have been quite a man, to start with nothing and end up with so much."

"He was a salt-of-the-earth kind of guy, and the money didn't really mean a lot to him. It was a means to an end. The end being the ability to support his family. He would say he wasn't the one who added to his coffers but God, who blessed him beyond his imagination and beyond his capabilities."

"God. He obviously had a lot of insight and ingenuity to be such a success."

"He would say all that came from God too."

Maddie hesitated, and the silence on the line stretched out.

"You don't believe in God, Maddie?"

Even though Jeff's letter once again flashed through her mind, she quickly changed the subject. "So this means you'll still be leasing the one hundred acres from me for your cattle? And good news, I have another hundred acres available for you to expand your herd."

"I will keep the cattle I have there on your property if that still works for you. But expanding the herd will have to wait until I can save some money from my job."

"Oh?"

"That sounds like a question."

"I guess I just assumed since you work for Nathan that he would give you a loan to expand if you needed one."

"He is willing to loan me whatever I need. But I want to keep him as my ace in the hole in case another ranch comes available."

"I see."

Maddie's thoughts continued to churn with plans for Broken Acres. What if the bank manager wouldn't give her the loan? That probably meant no other bank would give her a loan either. Maybe . . .

She would not give Nathan's offer another thought. It was not even an option.

TWENTY-SIX

D avid tramped through the big house, wanting to get some work finished before he had to leave for Forest Hills. But he had left his tool belt sitting on the counter in the kitchen at the cottage.

The veterinary college at Forest Hills University had suggested he apply for a job with a local vet near the university until his Oregon residency became a reality. He only had seven more months, and then he could work part-time and pay the expensive, but not exorbitant, resident tuition fees for the last three years of his veterinary schooling.

Three years. That sounded like a long time. He was so glad the desire to become a vet was back. He'd started to think the one year of veterinary training was just a fantasy and he'd never get back to what he knew God called him to do.

Mom would freak out if I told her that. David laughed to himself. *Why am I so afraid to talk to her about my faith?* David rubbed his hand over his eyes.

The first thing he needed to do when he got to Forest Hills was find a church. He felt like he'd been losing the ground he'd gained the last couple of years in Chicago.

He glanced around the living area Billy, Nathan, and he had worked on the last time they were together in the big house. He liked the open feeling this common area had for people to sit and talk, meet with guests, read a book. Yeah, the massive floor-to-ceiling bookshelves and library setting on the south end of the room would work out great. The huge picture window helped a lot, bringing warm natural light into the room.

David paced off the area where a window seat would be constructed below the three-sided alcove glass windows on the east side of the room. Plenty of room for bookshelves along that back wall.

With his construction career about to be a thing of the past, he grinned, thinking of the conversation he had with his mom months before moving to Jacob's Bend.

"David, remember when you were here last year and you said you loved Jacob's Bend and the area?" his mom had asked.

"Yes?" That familiar longing he had experienced when he stepped on his mom's farm had crept back into his heart.

"Do you think you might consider moving here?"

"Mom—"

"No, David, hear me out. The general contractor on my renovation project for the big house has had a terrible accident and probably won't be able to finish the job. I have a friend here who has been helping Nathan— Mr. Carter—but he's young and I think he needs someone with more experience and maturity to help him out."

"Mom—"

"David, please let me finish. What possible reason could you have for staying there in the city? Everything you could ever want is right here. Well, at least I think it's all here. Would you at least consider coming out and helping me with the renovation? Not to mention I would love to have you here. I miss you."

"Mom, you can stop trying to convince me. I've been trying to tell you, I already made the decision to move to Jacob's Bend last week. I just haven't had a chance to let you know. This works out even better than I thought. Ruth thinks it's a great idea."

"Ruth? You talked to Ruth about this?"

"I wanted to see what she thought. You know how analytical she is and how she can untangle all the pieces and make sense of the pros and cons."

"That's true. She's like your dad that way."

"She was all for my idea."

"David, this makes me so happy. Now, this is a job, you are going to be paid for your work."

"Mom."

"No, David, if you won't agree to be paid I'll just have to find someone else. I mean it."

David had run his fingers through his hair. He did need more money to finance his plans. "Okay, I'll do it. It will help me out with my tuition."

"Tuition?"

"Yeah, after being there and meeting the farmers and hearing your story about how that vet took care of Rusty and Sarg, I'm going back to vet school."

"That's wonderful news. But how?"

"I'm hoping to take online courses."

"That sounds like a perfect plan."

"I thought I could ask the vet there to be a resource. What's her name?"

"Jenny. Dr. Adams. I'm sure she would be happy to help. They are looking for another vet to help in their practice you know."

"One step at a time, Mom. I have to get my degree first."

He was glad he'd run the idea by Ruth. David smiled as he remembered the conversation. She was actually encouraging and so logical. He was glad for the things she'd given him to think about.

David sat on the floor in the middle of the room thinking about the plans his mom had for this house. He pulled his knees up, his strong forearms clasping one another as he stared out the open front door where he knew the night stars would be blazing later in the night sky.

David thought back to a stunning star-filled night in Chicago and the beautiful woman he'd held in his arms. He would never forget that night. Never. They had some fun-filled days doing crazy things. Studying for finals ultimately swallowed up the last days of the semester. Then she was gone. He wondered where she was. She could be anywhere. He shook his head, exasperated. He'd left his heart in Chicago.

The sun was setting when David finally locked up the house. He took a deep breath and also locked his memories away, knowing he would never see her again.

David looked back over his shoulder at the stately house. He wished he could help his mom finish her dream. But Nathan was right, if he was ever going to realize his dream he needed to get back to school and make it happen.

TWENTY-SEVEN

David found that taking courses online to get his degree was a pipe dream. From what the counselor told him, he would have to attend his classes at FHU, *if* he was even accepted.

Connecting with veterinarians in Forest Hills to apply for an internship was the easy part. However, they all told him to contact the VIRMP, Veterinary Internship and Residency Match Program. They matched vets with those wanting internship training. This was the sticky part. He had to fill out mounds of paperwork and then wait until he was either approved or denied. He was hoping for a shortcut to this process. Maybe his mom could talk to her vet friend, Dr. Adams.

"Mom," David hollered into the cottage as the screen door slapped behind him, the ever-present squeak now a family joke. David shook his head and grinned. Sooner or later one of them would remember to add WD-40 to the hinges.

"David, what's wrong?"

"Nothing is wrong. I was just wondering if you could talk to your friend, Dr. Adams, and see if she has any vet connections near the college up north."

"What kind of connections?"

"You know, a vet who needs a smart, strong, industrious student to intern in their practice so he can earn some money to pay for his very expensive veterinary training and possibly have a spare room for him to live in during his three-year term."

"So you are planning on staying up there rather than commuting on the weekends?"

David hung his head. "I've been giving this a lot of thought, Mom. Once I'm an Oregon resident, I can attend Forest Hills University, if I'm accepted. You know there will be a lot of class time and labs and study I have to do in the library. I'll need a job to help pay for my tuition. That doesn't leave a whole lot of time for commuting."

He watched his mom's shoulders slump. "I was afraid this would happen. I knew it was too good to be true."

"What?"

"Your coming here to live, finish your schooling, and have a vet's office nearby."

"Mom, I'm still planning on opening an office near here when I finish school. At least I won't be clear across the country in Chicago. I'll come home for holidays, and you can come up there to visit." David smiled at his mom, trying to let her know everything would work out.

"I'm sorry, David. You didn't pick up and move clear across the country. I did. This is exactly what you need to do. I'm so proud of you for taking on the challenge of going back to school to get your degree. This will be great for you. I'll give Dr. Adams a call tonight and see if she has any suggestions."

David moved toward his mom and slipped his arm around her shoulder. "Mom, I know this is hard. I would like nothing better than to stay right here at Broken Acres and help you finish the big house and see what God has next." He hugged her tight.

His mom looked up at him. "God?"

"Ah, yeah. I went to church while I was in Chicago." He rubbed his chin. "And I kinda liked it."

"You kinda liked it?"

His mom's cell phone chimed.

"Hello, Maddie, it's Nathan." David heard Nathan's voice and felt his mom turn away from him as she spoke.

"What can I do for you?"

David waved goodbye to his mom as he slipped out the door, anxious to get to Granny Harper's to swing a hammer.

TWENTY-EIGHT

"Mrs. Crane, the loan committee has agreed to a cash-out refinance loan for Broken Acres."

Broken Acres . . . broken, hurting people need a place to heal.

The thought echoed again through Maddie's mind as she walked to the picture windows at the front of her cottage and looked over at the big house that sat on a rise across the apple orchard.

"What's that, Mrs. Crane? I didn't hear you."

Maddie started at the voice on the other end of her cell phone. "Oh, ah, that's great. I'm excited to finish the renovation on the big house."

"Big house?"

"Yes, the larger house on the property."

"Okay. Good. You need to know the interest rate on this loan is considerably higher than your original loan. Rates have gone up, and there is a fee to process a new loan."

Maddie shrugged. "Okay, that's fine. Whatever it takes. What will the monthly payment be? I know it will be more, but not that much more, right?" She smiled as she envisioned the big house finished.

"I'm afraid the monthly payment is going to be almost double what you are currently paying."

"Double? Wow." Maddie considered the land she had leased out and the probability that she could find other farmers or cattle owners to occupy the land her renters left vacant.

She had to finish the house. People needed a place where they could heal.

She cleared her throat, trying to swallow the lump that threatened to stop her response. "I'm sure there won't be a problem. I'll make it work."

"There is one other thing I think you should understand, Mrs. Crane."

"Yes?"

"Since you are putting your farm up as collateral for this new loan, if for some reason you are unable to make the payments, you will forfeit the ownership of your farm."

"Forfeit ownership—*lose Broken Acres*—I—"

"That must be made clear before we go forward. Are you certain this new loan is in your best interest?"

"It's what I have to do to finish the big house."

"Okay. As long as you have an understanding of the process should you default."

"Default." Maddie could hear the fear in her voice. "I won't default."

"Great. When can you come into the bank to sign the papers?"

"How about this afternoon?"

"I'll have everything ready."

*   *   *

David sat outside the Forest Hills University administration office, head in hands, frustration and defeat emanating from every part of him. *What am I gonna do now?* Every idea he'd had to make this work was being squashed like ants dodging foot traffic on a busy sidewalk.

"Are you all right, young man?"

David looked up into the concerned eyes of a well-dressed older man who held a weathered, antiquated briefcase in his hand.

"What? Oh, yeah, I'll be fine. Thank you for asking."

"You look like you're lost. Can I point you in the right direction?"

"I wish."

"What was that?"

"Oh, nothing. I'm really not lost in the sense you mean."

The elderly man sat down on the old brick planter seat next to David. He set his briefcase on the ground near his feet, crossed his legs, and criss-crossed his arms over his chest.

David considered the man as he straightened to once again assure the old guy he was fine. He had a scholarly look to him, like maybe he'd been a professor.

David studied the man as he settled reading glasses atop hair more gray than black. A slightly worn tweed sweater vest covered a white long-sleeved shirt. Brown slacks met aged loafers with no socks.

"My name is Harold." The man extended his hand.

"David."

The two regarded each other for a moment until David broke the handshake.

"It's nice to meet you, David. So, if you're not lost in the sense of direction or where to go, how are you lost?"

David took a deep breath and released it slowly. "It's a long story."

"I have plenty of time. My next class doesn't start for another two hours." Harold ran a hand through his thick wavy hair, catching his glasses before they fell to the ground.

David lifted a brow. "Are you a student here?"

Harold chuckled. "No, I'm a substitute teacher. I fill in every once in a while. I'm guessing my wife would like it if it were more frequently. I tend to get underfoot at home."

David smiled. "I'll bet she really likes having you around." He thought about how his mom missed his dad, even though their life together had been anything but ideal until the last year of his dad's life. *I wonder what happened to change Dad so drastically.*

"I'm not so sure about that."

Harold's voice shook David's mind from his dad's transformation.

"Irene is an amazing woman. I tend to spend too much time in her kitchen ruminating and mumbling over the class I'm about to teach. After a while she shoos me out of her domain and directs me to my office. We have a great marriage, but sometimes I think I rely on her kindness and opinion too much. I really ought to give her more space." Harold stared past David.

"Well, I bet she'd be lost without you."

He smiled. "Thank you, but enough about me. What's going on with you?"

David looked into the professor's gentle blue-gray eyes. They reminded him of his grandma Crane's eyes. In a world of dominant Crane men, his grandma Deborah was the kindest woman he'd ever known. "I'll try to condense the story."

Harold leaned back against the weathered brick wall and gave David an encouraging smile.

"I moved here—well, not here, but to a small town about two and a half hours south of here, Jacob's Bend. Have you heard of it?"

Harold shook his head. "No, I haven't."

"Most people haven't. I moved there several months ago from Chicago to help my mom on her farm. She's renovating the larger house on the property to rent out to people who need a safe, comfortable home." David wondered how much he should share about his mom's plans and decided to move on.

"I've always wanted to be a veterinarian, and I attended the University of Illinois at Urbana-Champaign College of Veterinary Medicine for one year. When I dropped out I never thought I'd want to go back and finish."

Harold gave him a questioning look.

"Another long story."

"After I moved to Broken Acres—"

"Broken Acres?"

"That's the name my mom gave her farm." David took a deep breath.

"Let me guess. Another long story?"

"It's my mom's story." David gave an apologetic smile and moved on. "Anyway I realized I needed to wait a year to gain Oregon resident status so I wouldn't be paying a ton of money to attend FHU. Someone mentioned that I could work as an intern for a vet while attending. I wish they would have given me the whole story when I first called." David's shoulders drooped.

"That's not the case. I have to finish my degree before I can intern. I need a job and a place to live so I can attend school here in the fall. From what I understand there's a lot of hands-on training with the classes. It doesn't make sense to live in Jacob's Bend and drive all the way here to go to school. And that's how you found me here shaking my head, wondering how this is ever going to work."

"I see. Sounds like you are quite serious about becoming a veterinarian."

"I am. Even before—" David broke off.

"Before?"

David felt the professor give him a swift glance as he watched a group of students cross campus.

"Never mind. I know, another long story."

"Yeah." David appreciated the reprieve.

David sensed this professor had a caring heart if he would stop to talk to a student slumped on a bench.

"So, David, if there was a way for you to attend here and get your vet's diploma, where would you practice medicine? Do you have an offer from a practice in Chicago?"

"Oh, no. I wouldn't go back there. I'd like to practice here in Oregon." David thought about Dr. Adams. "Actually, my mom knows a vet who has a practice in Jacob's Bend, and I'm hoping I will be able to join their team when I am finished with school."

"So you would practice in Jacob's Bend, then?"

"Yes, I think so. I really want to be near my mom. She's a widow—"

"Oh, I'm sorry." Harold looked down at his feet. "That does make a difference." He glanced at his wristwatch and picked up his briefcase. "Here's my card. I'll be praying for you. If you have any questions or need a listening ear, I'd be happy to help."

David sat up straight. "Thank you, Professor. I *really* appreciate your prayers." David tore a corner off of some paperwork he had received in the admission's office and wrote his phone number on it. "Here's my cell number in case—ah—well, I don't know." David shrugged.

"Maybe we'll see each other when school starts."

"I'd like that."

TWENTY-NINE

"**M**om," David called down from the loft to Maddie, who was standing in the middle of the kitchen.

She walked into the living room, drying her hands on a dish towel, and looked up. "Yes?"

"When are the building materials supposed to arrive so we can get back to work on the big house?"

"Well, they said it might take a week to ten days."

"Why?"

"Why what?"

David jogged down the stairs. "Why is it taking that long? It's Portsmouth. It's not like they have to drive in from two states over."

Maddie tilted her head to the side. "What's got you so riled up?" She looked up at the loft. "And what were you doing in my bedroom?"

David plopped into a straight-backed chair at the kitchen table. "I'm sorry. I'm going stir-crazy with nothing to do. I was looking in the full-length mirror in your room to see if I'm presentable."

"Presentable?"

"Yeah, I'm going back up to Forest Hills to see if I can find a job."

"I'm sorry the internship didn't work out." Maddie had mixed emotions now that she knew David planned to live near FHU. She had thought he could commute, but really that didn't make much sense.

"Me too. But I know God's got something else for me."

Maddie was silent. *God again?*

David looked over at her and squinted, scrunching up his nose. "Mom, remember I told you I started going to church when I was at

Urbana-Champaign? I met these guys in my freshman pathology class, and they invited me to go to a concert with a twenty-something group from their church."

"I remember."

David walked to the cupboard and grabbed a mug for coffee. "The concert was great, and I started attending church with them. It's a massive church, so Sundays were kind of hard to get to know people. But I also went to their Wednesday-night group meeting. Really nice people." He gulped the hot liquid and cleared his throat.

"So you liked this church?" Maddie sat down at the kitchen table, mug in hand.

"I did. You should know what that's like. You attend Pastor Ben's church." He raised an eyebrow and took the seat across from her. "I like Pastor Ben; he's a good teacher."

Maddie buttered the toast she brought with her to the table. "Yes, but that's different."

"How is it different?"

"I originally started attending North Hills to support Angela and Brian Metzger. I met her when I first moved here. She was a new widow and was shy about attending church. So I volunteered to go with her."

"And I think that's great. But you are also involved in helping out in the ministries at North Hills too, right?"

"Yes, Madelyn Simpson is always asking me to help out."

"And you don't want to help out?"

"Of course I want to. I love helping people."

"I know. That's what this farm is all about, right?"

Maddie glanced out the picture window across the orchard to the big house. "Yes, that's what Broken Acres is all about." She breathed deep.

David changed subjects. "So back to my original question. When are we gonna get back to work on the reno?"

"I'll call them today to get an ETA."

"Great. By the way, Mom, are you sure you are going to be able to manage the payments on this new loan? Maybe we should use the money I have saved. I haven't signed up for school yet."

"Oh, no. That money is for your schooling, not Broken Acres." She smiled at her son and placed a gentle touch on his shoulder. "I am excited you're going back to school, David. I'll be fine here as long as the property renters I have hang in there with me until I can fill the rooms in the big house."

David watched her with concern on his face. "Are you sure? You look a little worried. If I put off my schooling a while longer, it shouldn't take us too long to finish the big house. I'd probably only miss the first semester."

"No. Now is your chance to finish school. It will be fine." Maddie poured herself another cup of coffee.

David smiled at his mother, and she felt herself smiling back over the rim of her coffee cup. Even as a little boy David had been protective of her, and since Jeff's death, she'd heard the man-of-the-family note in his voice more frequently. But he needed to live his own life.

I just wish FHU didn't feel so far away, Maddie thought.

*   *   *

George loved traveling in his fifth wheel. Now that it was his home, he relished the freedom and loved not having anything to tie him down. Except now he was on his way to what looked like a permanent job.

But Madison Crane, Maddie, was the nicest lady. This was going to be a pleasure, not a job. He looked to the passenger seat at his longtime companion, Duke, an eight-year-old Australian shepherd he had rescued from the pound. They said he was too rambunctious and hyperactive. George knew running and barking was Duke's nature. God created his kind to herd, for goodness' sake.

Duke lifted his head from between his paws and panted.

"Yeah, you're right, it is about time to stop for a break and let you run a bit." George scratched Duke behind the ear.

*   *   *

Maddie smiled when she heard the deep male voice on the other side of the phone connection. "George. So good to hear from you. Where are you?"

"Oh, 'bout halfway between Chicago and your place, I expect."

"I'm so glad you decided to take me up on my offer to cook for the residents at Broken Acres. Although, like I told you when we talked before you left Chicago, I'm not sure when the job will start or even when the renovation project will be finished."

"That's okay. I was ready for a change and wanted to get out of the freezing winters in Chicago. I've got plenty of money to tide me over."

"I'm sorry to say your apartment in the big house is currently filled with building paraphernalia."

"No problem. I'll stay in my fifth wheel. Is there a place I can park it there on your . . . How many acres do you have again?"

Maddie laughed. "Four hundred and twenty-seven. Most of it was rented out to small crop farmers. I have a couple of cattlemen grazing their cattle right now. There is definitely a place for you to park your fifth wheel with a breathtaking view of farmland, cattle, and mountains. There's a nice level spot next to the big house. Under a huge lovely oak."

"Sounds like heaven, Maddie."

"That's what I think every time I come up over the knoll that overlooks Broken Acres. A little slice of heaven."

"Sounds perfect, although I'm not real sure when I'll be there. Duke and I are enjoying the ride and small towns along the route."

"I know what you mean. There's no hurry, as I said. I do look forward to having you here, George."

"Me too. I love a good adventure, and the change will be good for me and Duke. These old bones could use a change of climate."

Maddie grinned. "I'll see you when I see you."

THIRTY

"Hello, David, it's Professor Taulbee. Can you give me a call when you get a few minutes?"

David listened to the message as he made his way down the long driveway, making a mental note to call Professor Taulbee when he stopped for lunch. He adjusted the volume on his truck's CD player and checked his rearview mirror as he made a left turn onto the highway. An old beat-up car pulled into his mom's driveway. What a rattletrap. Then he realized he'd seen that Olds parked behind the veterinary clinic in Jacob's Bend. He wondered if that was his mom's friend, Dr. Adams. *Mom didn't mention her coming out for a visit.* If he'd known he would have waited to head north. David shrugged.

When he finally hit the outskirts of Forest Hills, David stopped to grab a burger and fries and call Professor Taulbee. "Hi, Professor, how are you?"

"I'm good, David. You?"

"Good here too. What's going on?"

"Well, I'm not sure if I mentioned this when we met that I have a small farm and vet practice a few miles outside of town."

"No, you didn't mention that. Just that you were a sub at the college. You're a veterinarian?"

"I am."

"Wow, that's great. How big is your farm?"

"Oh, it's only about fifty acres."

"Fifty acres? That doesn't sound small to me."

"In the scope of vets and farms in the area, that's quite small."

"Oh, I see."

"David, you remind me a lot of myself when I first started out. Enthusiastic. Determined. Idealistic."

David could feel the heat move up his neck to his face. *Idealistic.* David sighed. *Yep, that's me.* He rubbed the back of his neck with his hand.

"I'd love to be able to invite you out today, but I'm on my way to sub for a night class at the college and Irene is staying the night with a sick friend."

"Anyway, Irene and I had a veterinarian student stay with us, and it was an extremely good experience, all around. Once the ground rules were set." David heard the professor shuffling papers. "He finished school and is now a vet in Iowa, where his family lives."

"That sounds amazing for him," David replied, wondering where this conversation was going.

The professor cleared his throat. "Irene and I talked it over, and we were wondering if you'd be interested in helping out on our farm. We have way too many animals for the two of us to handle alone. There's a nice bedroom and bath above the barn. Your room and board would be included in your salary."

David was speechless. Tears formed in his eyes. He looked up, gulped, and thanked God.

"David?"

"Yes, sir." David sniffed back the tears.

"Did you hear what I said?"

"Yes. Yes, sir, I did."

"What do you think? Irene and I prayed about it for a week and both came up with a yes. Maybe you need time to pray about it?"

David let out the breath he had been holding. "Thank You, God," he said out loud.

It sounded like the professor let out his own breath.

"I just did." David looked up again.

"Well then, what do you say?"

"Just one question."

"Yes?"

"Salary? You said room and board would be included in my salary?"

"Yes, that's right."

"You mean you are going to give me a place to live, food to eat, work I love, and pay me to do it?"

The professor laughed. "Yes, we are. You said you needed a job to help pay for your schooling. We want to be a part of that."

Tears welled up again. "I don't know what to say. This is a total miracle."

"Say yes."

"Yes."

"Wonderful. Irene will be very pleased. Irene is a retired nurse. Did I mention that?""

"No, you didn't. That's a story *I'd* love to hear." David's mind started racing at the future that felt like it had just opened up for him.

"Oh, I'm sure there will be many stories we'll share. How about you give me a call the next time you're headed up this way and we'll have you out to the farm for a look around? See if you feel comfortable on the ole homestead."

"That would be great. Thank you, Professor. I can't tell you how much this means to me."

"It's a win-win for all of us, David."

THIRTY-ONE

Lydia knew she couldn't live this way much longer. Hiding out was taking a toll on her nerves and her health. She needed to get outside, walk in the sun without having to look over her shoulder, fearful of someone recognizing her or pulling out a gun to shoot her.

Remembering that horrible day, Lydia chided herself for letting her face become so familiar. "But how could a simple walk to the store for ice cream turn out so bad? All I wanted was to share a treat with my brother."

Her reflection in the mirror reminded her that she needed to get a job. She was getting thinner by the week, existing on bread and milk, and the little money she had come here with three years ago was almost gone. No one had recognized her yet. Leaving that *safe* house in LA was the best thing she could have done, Lydia was convinced. Living in Jacob's Bend for these last few years had been quiet and peaceful . . . but had also been lonely. She pulled back the curtain at the front window and peeked out. Maybe the gang had forgotten about her. Maybe it was time she showed up in town as Lydia Lopez and gave Witch Hazel some time off.

Spurred on by this radical idea, Lydia hurried to transform back into herself before she lost courage. Old skills moved her fingers as she focused on one task at a time. Hair, makeup, erect posture. No longer stooped old Witch Hazel.

Then, taking a deep breath, Lydia Lopez slipped out the back door of her rented shanty and looked up and down the street. Fear in the form of shivers ran up her back. *I can't do this, I can't. What if someone recognizes me?* She turned to go back into the dark, ugly hovel and pulled up short.

No. She was going. She couldn't live in that cave forever; it was too depressing. She turned toward the street, thinking only about putting one foot in front of the other.

"I can do this."

As Lydia passed the hardware store, she glanced in the window at her reflection. Standing upright to her full five-nine height, she wondered if anyone would recognize her as the weathered old woman everyone knew as Witch Hazel. Without the contacts to make her eyes look dull and filmy, a host of wrinkles, compliments of her makeup skills, a short gray wig, and old lady dresses, surely no one would recognize her.

Lydia's thick, curly black hair hung to her waist. She looked closer at her reflection in the window. *I look twenty-three, not seventy-three.*

As a makeup artist assistant in Los Angeles she had learned several great tips for aging. But now she was dressed as herself, out in public for all to see. Maybe this wasn't such a good idea. What if . . .

No, Lydia, it's time to move on and get a life. She fluffed her hair and checked her makeup. If they found her, they found her. She couldn't live the rest of her life hiding and living in fear.

The plan for her first outing as herself was lunch at the little café in town. One hour max. Five dollars max. She took the first open booth that came available and sat facing the door. Always careful to see who came and went. When she looked up from the menu her eyes locked on the woman in the booth next to hers. The woman was staring at her and smiled in her direction, then went back to her conversation with the young man sitting across from her.

Lydia ducked her head behind the menu. That was the woman who'd knocked on her door. Did she know who she was? No, that was ridiculous. *Get a grip, Lydia.*

Snippets of their conversation drifted to Lydia.

"Mom, I can't tell you how shocked I was when he offered me everything I'd prayed for." The young man's voice sounded almost awestruck.

"That is pretty amazing. When are you going back up there?"

"Well, since the building materials will be here soon, and Billy, Nathan, and I are all available, I thought I'd work on the big house for a couple of weeks, then go up to see Professor Taulbee's farm. I can't believe this is actually happening."

Lydia peeked over her menu to see the woman smile at her son.

"Yep, it's amazing."

Her voice sounds calm, but her eyes look sad, thought Lydia. *I'll bet those green eyes sparkle when she's happy.*

"You said that already. Are you okay, Mom?"

Lydia returned to safety behind her menu as the young man reached across the table to take his mother's hand.

"Sure. Why? I'm very happy for you, David."

Hearing a note of sadness in the woman's voice, Lydia felt strangely sorry for her.

"But——"

"But? No buts."

"Come on, Mom, what's goin' on?"

"Decided what you want?" Lydia lost the redheaded woman's response as the waitress stepped up to her table.

"Um . . ." Lydia glanced again at the menu, realizing she hadn't really been reading it, she had been so distracted by her eavesdropping. *Prices. Check the prices.*

"I'll have a tuna salad, but could I have that on lettuce instead of bread?" Lydia became aware of the redheaded woman's gaze on her again, and fear rose up anew. "Um, and could I get that to go?" As the waitress left, Lydia shrunk back in the booth, putting the young man's head between her and his mother's gaze.

"I know it will be different with me gone," the young man's voice continued. "But you'll have the people who are moving into the big house."

"Yes, I will. Don't worry about me. I'll be fine. Really."

Lydia glanced toward the kitchen.

Where was that salad?

*   *   *

Maddie could see the guilt in David's eyes. Guilt that said he was leaving her alone. "David, please don't feel bad. I lived alone for a long time before you moved out here. I've made a lot of friends, and I'll be busy with the farm and the big house residents. I did it before you arrived, and I'll be fine when you go to Forest Hills. Besides, you'll be coming home to visit occasionally."

She raised her eyebrows at the look on her son's face. "You *will* be coming home on occasion, right?"

"Yes, of course I will, Mom."

"David, uh . . . I feel like I need to explain why I cringe every time you mention, uh . . . God."

David's eyes flashed concern and uncertainty. "I've wondered about that for a long time."

"It isn't that I don't believe there is a God. It's something with your dad. You know how difficult our marriage was. How he sometimes got—"

"Physically abusive?" David frowned.

"Yes." Maddie closed her eyes and shook her head. "Unfortunately, I didn't stand up to him and let it go on too long."

"Mom, that wasn't your fault. Dad had choices, and he made some pretty bad ones when it came to the way he treated you."

Maddie breathed deep, the pain surfacing yet again.

"Mom, we don't have to talk about this. It's over and done. For some reason, the last year of Dad's life was different. He changed."

Maddie ground her teeth, her jaw tight. "Yes, he did. And it wasn't until I found a letter he wrote to me tucked in Gram's old Bible that I understood why."

"What do you mean?" David ran his hand through thick auburn hair, his sea-green eyes anxious.

"I never thought I'd want you to read the letter because it made me so mad and confused. It still makes me angry. But since you keep bringing up God and how He is doing so much for your life, I want you to know this side of your dad and understand his deep pain. See what your God did for him."

"He's not just my God, Mom. He wants you to know how much He loves you and how valuable you are to Him."

Maddie closed her eyes, her heart rate hitting high speeds.

David touched her hand. "Mom, I know Dad hurt you in a lot of ways. I wish I would have been man enough to stand up to him when—"

Tears formed in Maddie's eyes. "No, David. No. I'm so glad you didn't do anything. I never wanted you kids to know what was going on, and I thought I hid it well."

David shook his head.

"I want you to read the letter before you leave for school. Would you want to do that?"

A single tear ran down David's cheek. "Yes. Thank you. I forgave Dad a long time ago. But I'd still like to know what caused the change."

Maddie nodded.

When the woman in the booth next to them stood to leave, Maddie smiled at her and then watched her walk out.

"Why do I feel like I know her?"

"Know who?"

"The Hispanic woman who just left. Do you know her?"

"Sorry, I didn't pay any attention. What makes you think you know her?"

"I'm not sure. Something in her eyes. Almost like fear."

"Fear? What could she possibly be afraid of in Jacob's Bend?"

"I don't know. I wonder if she lives here or is just passing through. I know her from somewhere, I'm sure of it. Those eyes."

*   *   *

Lydia walked as fast as she could toward her shack. She didn't want the redhead to see what direction she was headed or where she ended up. She hadn't sounded like the busybody Lydia had assumed she was when she'd knocked on her door, but her instinctive caution kicked in.

I'll have to be careful to watch for her the next time I'm out.

Taking the long way around, Lydia finally reached her bedraggled shack. She flopped down on the thread-worn couch and let out a breath. That was harder than she'd thought it would be. "But you can do this," Lydia's voice echoed back at her from the barren walls. "You have to do this. Take some time, but you have to look for a job. Maybe in a back room somewhere." She glanced around the dark living room.

"Don't worry, Lydia. Just take it one outing at a time. One day at a time. You *are* going to have a real life again—someday."

THIRTY-TWO

Maddie glanced at the calendar as she reached in the cupboard to pull out a mug. "July 18. Three years. I can't believe it's been three years since Jeff's heart attack." She thought back to that night, remembering every detail like it happened three days ago, not three years.

His last words, *"Maddie, I-I can't."*

Her goodbye to him as the gurney ushered his lifeless body out to the waiting transport vehicle.

The emptiness.

Loneliness.

Excruciating pain.

Lost in the memories, Maddie looked around the small kitchen, dining, and living area of the cottage where she had spent the last year learning what it meant to be a widow on her own with a farm to run. *Widow.* She hated that word.

Who would have thought she would have moved from Chicago all the way across the country to the Pacific Northwest? She shook her head. "What was I thinking?"

Rusty nudged her hand. He looked up at her, panting, eyes full of loving concern and, if she didn't know better, compassion. "Hey, buddy. I'm not saying I don't want to be here or have you and Sarg as companions. But . . ."

The golden retriever gave her hand another nudge. Maddie smiled, bent down, and hugged her faithful friend. "I'm just not sure how I'm going to make the monthly loan payments until my assets are unfrozen." Rusty sat looking into her eyes as if the answer were right there in front of her. "You got any ideas?" She patted his head and ran her hand down his soft back. "I'll figure it out. I have to."

Maddie poured herself a cup of coffee and took it out to the porch swing. Sarg stretched when she sat down next to him. "So, what is your opinion on this dilemma?" Rusty pushed the squeaky screen door open and walked over to sit on the top step of the stairs that lead to the apple orchard. Maddie laughed. "I'm not sure it would feel like home if I oiled those annoying hinges. Nope, need to keep things as they are." She ran her hand across Sarg's white stripe and down his back.

As they are. If things stayed as they were she just might be able to make the payments until the renovation on the big house was finished.

A shiver ran up her back and she looked over her shoulder. Nothing. No one. Shaking her shoulders to ward off the chill, she sipped her coffee.

Once she had some paying residents living there then she could make double payments and do away with the debt once and for all.

The sense of guilt poured into her so fast she couldn't catch her breath. *Breathe Maddie, breathe.* After several deep breaths she looked out over her farm and a shiver ran up her spine again. She looked over at Rusty sleeping peacefully on the top step. She slowly walked over to the screen door and carefully pulled it open just enough to grab the baseball bat she kept inside. Walking to where Rusty slept, bat at her side, ready to club anyone or anything that came at her, she paused when Rusty lifted his head and looked up at her. "It's okay, buddy, if you don't hear anything then I'm pretty sure it's just my imagination."

Why guilt? She was doing everything she could to make this work and keep the farm. What else could she do with all her money frozen? Maybe it wasn't guilt. Maybe it was fear. Standing at the top of the steps, still feeling uneasy, she looked at Rusty for an answer. His drooping eyes let her relax her grip on the bat.

Fear? Fear of not having enough money, like when she was a kid? Fear of being poor? Of mice crawling on her bed? Another shiver went up her back.

Money. Why is everything always about money? She looked over at the big house, unfinished and needing an untold amount of work. Was she dreaming to think she could do this? Dreaming. Maddie slapped her forehead and sat down abruptly next to Rusty, who jumped up, looking at her like she didn't know one end of the bat from the other. Laying the bat on the step below her, she held her head in her hands.

What was wrong with her? Had she forgotten the dream she'd had about all those sad people clinging to pieces of furniture as if their lives depended on it? She remembered Gram's words: *"You can do more than you think you can."*

So why was she worrying about the money? Just because the cost of supplies had gone through the roof and her assets were frozen and she'd used all her savings . . . Maddie pulled on her ear.

The bank had given her a loan. She had the money to go forward. Maddie chewed her bottom lip.

She looked out over her property. All of this was for hurting people who needed a safe place to live. That's why she was doing it. For them. She took a deep breath. She could do this. This was going to work if she had to get two jobs to make those monthly payments. Whether the people who came to Broken Acres were able to pay or not didn't matter. What mattered was that they healed from whatever hardships and pains life had dealt them. She looked over at the big house again. Yeah, this was going to work. With Billy, David, and Nathan working on the renovation, it would be finished in no time.

Once the materials arrived.

Maddie walked to the front door and put the bat back in its permanent home right inside the door. Sitting on the swing she picked up her coffee and took a sip. She scrunched up her nose. It was cold.

She set the cup near the door and then settled on the top step, remembering months ago when she would sit on the porch waiting for Nathan to show up for work at the big house and watching him pull his tool belt and thermos of coffee from his truck looking like he was barely awake. "Nathan," she whispered.

Here it was July and she still didn't know any more than she did in May when Billy told her that Nathan's wedding to Ms. Model-of-the-Year didn't happen. She was probably in Paris or some other exotic place at a photo shoot.

It didn't matter. He was still engaged to *Chelsea*. And he was *definitely* not Maddie's type. "Get that man and his kisses—" Maddie stomped her foot in time to her words. "Out. Of. Your. Head."

Her cell phone chirped in her pocket. Maddie pulled it out, glad for the diversion. "Hey, Carolyn, what's up?"

"What's up with you? I'm just checking in before I head to exercise class."

Maddie looked down at her body lazing on the porch step. "I could use an exercise class. Why don't you and Alex move back here? If you *really* loved me—"

"Okay, enough of the guilt thing. You know there are DVDs you could buy to exercise right there in the comfort of your little cottage." Carolyn chuckled. "What are you doing?"

"Oh, just sitting here talking to the guys about Nathan."

"Nathan?"

Maddie shook her head. She could just imagine her friend's left eyebrow hiked with concern. "Well, I was wondering what happened to postpone his wedding to Ms. Gorgeous."

"When you mentioned that before I thought it was odd."

"Odd? It's pretty obvious to me why it was called off. Those two are completely wrong for each other."

"Really? What makes you say that?"

"She's such a phony, throwing her long, thick blonde locks over her shoulder and posing like she's on camera every time anyone even glances her way. London, New York, Paris. Good grief. Do all fashion models spend every spare minute all over the world? And he's a hands-on contractor who barely takes a trip to the county offices for approval."

Carolyn laughed. "What difference does that make to you?"

"Me? None. No difference at all, just wondering."

"Hmm."

"I've been thinking of ways to make a little extra money to help pay off my renovation loan. Any ideas?"

"Well, you could have bake sales at the church each week."

Maddie held the phone out in front of her, frowning. "You're kidding, right?"

"Yes, Maddie, of course I'm kidding."

Maddie shifted her phone. "Besides, I don't attend North Hills every week."

"What? Why not?" Carolyn's response was stiff, accusing.

"Well—"

"What happened with you and Pastor Ben? I thought you were dating after that cozy dinner last fall."

"No. We are not dating. We . . . we are not anything. He's nice to me in a kind pastor sort of way, but he seems to veer to the other side of the church whenever he sees me."

"Come on, Maddie. I'm sure you're exaggerating."

Maddie glanced at the door leading into the cottage. "Does him not asking me to go horseback riding anymore sound like I'm exaggerating? Does the fact that whenever our eyes connect when he's preaching he quickly looks to the other side of the aisle sound like an exaggeration? Not to mention whenever Madelyn Simpson calls him over to a group I happen to be in he finds a reason to grab a cup of coffee or a doughnut or a child to hold?"

"That doesn't sound like Pastor Ben. I wonder what's happened. He always seemed happy and excited to be with you."

"Honestly, Carolyn, I don't know what I've done to offend him."

"Maddie, I'm sure it's not you."

"Really? Then who else could it be?"

"Maybe it's not a who. Maybe it's a what." Maddie heard car keys jingle. "Maddie, I have to dash. Workout awaits. But I'll call again soon, okay?"

A who? What did that mean? Had Ben meet someone else? Pocketing her phone, Maddie grabbed her coffee cup and headed to the kitchen. "If there was ever a loser in the love department, you're looking at her," she said over her shoulder as Rusty followed her into the house. Glancing toward the living room, at the couch where Ben had kissed her, she sighed.

THIRTY-THREE

"Hey, Nathan," Billy called out from the porch steps where he'd been sitting with David, drinking coffee.

Nathan grabbed his tool belt from the passenger seat of his truck and smiled toward the porch. "Hey, boys. Ready to do this thing?" Nathan strapped on his belt, picked up his thermos from the truck cab, and rubbed his left knee.

Billy watched the general on the project hoist the heavy belt up to his waist only to have it fall back down to his hips. Billy laughed under his breath. Just like all the other guys who wore those heavy belts. Except for a guy named Jordan on the first job he'd worked on. He had to clip suspenders to his belt to keep it on at all, he was so skinny.

Nathan had lost quite a bit of weight since his near fatal car accident. No cane. That was good. Still a slight limp, though.

"You gonna sit there all morning drinking coffee and chewing the fat, or are you two ready to work?" Nathan squinted at them. "That is, unless you're chewing on one of your mom's incredible cinnamon rolls." Nathan glanced over his shoulder to the cottage that sat on a knoll across the orchard.

"Don't I wish." David nodded. "Mom made you guys some of her melt-in-your-mouth cinnamon rolls?"

"Oh yeah, they were amazing. I need to get her to teach Shauna how to make them. My mouth is watering just thinking about those rolls."

Billy looked over at Nathan, who had that look that said he was remembering the offering and the apology note that came with the cinnamon rolls.

"Your mom is something else, David. Nathan, remember how she thought you were talking about her being a squawking female when you were telling me about your parrot?"

"Wait. What?" David smiled.

Nathan looked at the two young men. "Your mom jumps to more conclusions than any woman I know. I could tell you stories."

"I'm listening."

"Oh, no. We need to get some work done here. Still, I wouldn't mind another basket full of those cinnamon rolls."

Billy laughed. "Yeah, me too. Although I'm guessing she made them especially for Nathan, not me."

Nathan's stance stiffened. "What? That's not true. It was a thank-you gift for all our hard work on the big house reno. She definitely wouldn't be doing anything special for me." He looked from David to Billy as they sat silent. "What? She wouldn't. Just watch her body language the next time she's around me, that speaks volumes."

"Body language, huh? You been watching her body language, Nathan?" Billy teased.

David turned to pick up his tool belt.

Nathan shot Billy a menacing glare. "Let's get to work. I've got things to take care of this afternoon."

Billy lowered his voice. "Those things wouldn't have anything to do with your knockout model fiancée, would they?"

"What? Why would you ask that?"

"Well, we . . . ah, I . . . was just wondering why your wedding was postponed. Was Ms. Magazine Cover Queen on a shoot somewhere in Europe?"

"We?" Nathan glanced again across the apple orchard and his face stiffened. Billy followed his glance as Pastor Ben's jeep pulled up.

Nathan cut the conversation short. "Grab some boards, guys, and let's take them inside and get this job done."

*   *   *

Ben inhaled deep and walked to the passenger side of his Jeep. Opening the back door, two arms flew up, begging for release from the car seat. Brian

Metzger chattered like he was leading a group of kids on the playground. Brian broke loose of Ben's hand and ran up the steps to the cottage and knocked on the front door.

"Here, let me help you there, buddy." Ben lifted his hand to knock.

Brian stood, legs apart, hands on his hips, glaring up at Ben. "Don't need help. I knocked."

"Alrighty then. I'll just wait over here by the steps."

Brian nodded like a general whose command had been taken seriously. He rapped on the door once again. "Maddie. Rusty. Sarg. I here."

The door opened quickly, a huge smile on Maddie's face. "Hey there, Brian. I'm so glad you could come out to play with Rusty and Sarg. They don't really have very many playmates out here. Although your buddy, Michael, was out here not too long ago, and he pretty much wore them out."

Brian tilted his head and pursed his lips. "Michael?"

"You know Dr. Adams, the animal doctor? Remember Michael, her little boy?"

Brian's smile of recognition beamed. "Michael. I remember."

"Hi, Maddie," Ben said in a quiet voice.

Ben leaned against the porch post and crossed his arms over his broad chest.

"Oh, hi, Ben. I . . . I appreciate you bringing Brian out. How's Angela doing? I hope she's been drinking lots of fluids and resting. I heard this flu going around is a really bad one."

Why was she talking so fast and breathing so hard? *Maybe she had to run downstairs to answer the door.* Ben pulled his thoughts back to the conversation.

"Yeah, it's been hard on a lot of people this year. Angela is resting. Mrs. Sands will take dinner over tonight and make sure Brian is tucked into bed before she heads home."

"That's great. We have so many caring people in Jacob's Bend."

He smiled at her and took off his cowboy hat to brush his hair back.

Now her face was flushed. *Did I do something?* Ben wondered.

Maddie leaned her shoulder against the doorpost. "Would you like to come in?"

Ben looked over Maddie's shoulder at the cozy home, remembering the last time he went inside; candlelight dinner, delicious food, good company, the kiss. He shook his head. "No, no thanks. I've got to get back to town."

He placed his hat back on, bowed his head, and tipped the brim with his fingers. "Bye, Maddie. See you later, Brian." Ben looked over her shoulder to see Brian trying to wrestle with Rusty.

"Bye," Brian hollered, giggling at his playmate.

"Thanks again for bringing him out. I'll take him home around five if that works."

"Yeah, that's good. Mrs. Sands will be there around four thirty. Thanks again, I know Angela really appreciates you watching him."

"Glad to help."

Ben nodded, then turned and walked to his Jeep.

When he looked up, the door had closed tight. Ben threw his hat on the seat beside him and released a deep breath. He could not let himself think about those beautiful green eyes. Oh, how he would love to touch the soft curls of that auburn hair and kiss her again. *Stop it, Ben. You know this can't work, and you have to stop trying to figure a way around it, no matter how much you care for her.*

Ben closed his eyes. "Lord, I could really use some help here. I'm letting my emotions run away with me . . . again. I do not want to do anything to hinder our relationship or to hurt Maddie. Thank You that Your promises are real. I trust You, Lord. Especially when I can't trust these wayward emotions."

Ben glanced once again at the little cottage where he lost his heart one snowy night.

*   *   *

With the partial shipment of building materials inside the big house, the reno moved forward. Three of the six upstairs bedrooms were just about complete. The other three, along with the three shared baths, still needed a lot of work.

Nathan checked his wristwatch. Two o'clock. "David, Billy," he hollered up the stairs from the front door.

Both stuck their heads out around one of the bedroom doors. "Yeah?" both said simultaneously.

"This day is getting away from me. I have to go. I've got a thing tonight in Carterville. Need to get cleaned up and run a few errands before I head over."

Billy went back to pounding nails. David walked down the stairs giving Nathan a shaky grin as he stood in front of him.

Nathan backed up half a pace. "Yeah? You have a question before I leave?" Nathan looked up to where Billy's hammer kept a steady rhythm.

"Nathan, I just wanted to say . . ." David fumbled with his work gloves as he pulled them off.

"You wanted to say—"

David looked square into his eyes. "I wanted to say that I know you've been attending church in Carterville, and I'm really glad you are searching."

Nathan's eyes grew wider with each word David spoke. "Me, church?" Nathan looked down at his feet. "Whatever gave you that idea?"

"Well, actually, I saw the Bible in your truck the other day and was curious, but decided it was none of my business." David squinted at him, and Nathan tightened his arms across his chest.

Nathan looked up. "And now it's your business?"

"Well." He hesitated again and looked Nathan in the eyes. "Mom and I were in Carterville one Wednesday night and happened to be driving by and I saw you walk into the church, Bible in hand."

Nathan groaned. "Your mom—"

"No, don't worry, she didn't see you. If that matters to you. She was looking my way, talking about the loan she got from the bank to finish this." David waved at the big house.

"I wanted to ask you about that loan business. And also, how did you know about the wedding thing?"

"Well, Jase comes by often to check on his livestock. Not that he volunteered the information. I just asked him how the wedding went and he said, 'It didn't.' That was all the information he would give me. And as far as the loan"—David looked over at the cottage—"you'll have to ask Mom about that."

Nathan shook his head. "You know I offered to loan her the money at no interest to finish this project? She is the most stubborn woman."

"Don't I know it. She wouldn't take my money either. Not that I have even a handful compared to what you have to offer. I think she needs to be the one to tell you her plans."

"Maybe I'll ask her." Thinking of the jeep that pulled up to the house earlier in the day, Nathan shook his head. *Maybe not.*

"Anyway, I just wanted you to know that I'm really glad you are going to church. Changed my life, and I hope it changes yours. I'll be praying for you." David slapped Nathan on the back. "I mean that."

Nathan felt the heat crawl up his neck to his face. He shrugged and scuffed his boot in the dirt. "I'll, ah, see you tomorrow morning. Why don't you guys knock off when you finish framing that bathroom?"

"Will do, boss," Nathan heard David call after him as he opened the door to his truck.

*   *   *

Billy looked up from the two-by-four he was nailing to a floor joist. "So, David, would you like to come over for dinner? Shauna has a friend she has invited over. She's kinda cute."

"Ah, *kinda* cute? What does that mean, anyway?"

"No, she's cute. It's just that I compare every other girl's cuteness to Shauna's beauty."

David raised an eyebrow and laughed. "I would love to meet a *kinda cute* girl, but I'm going to be leaving in a few weeks for Forest Hills, and I don't want to get into any kind of relationship here when I don't even know when I'll be back for a visit."

"Yeah, I know what you mean. But you know, once you meet the *right one* it won't matter how far away you are from each other."

"I know." David stared into the distance, eyes far away, then shrugged. "I already met the right one."

"What? You holding out on me?"

David shook the memory from his mind. "No, nothing like that. We met in Illinois, at college."

"You went to college in Illinois? I thought Forest Hills University was your first take on college."

"No, I got my BS in Carbondale at Southern Illinois University and took one year of veterinary training in Urbana at the College of Veterinary Medicine. That's where we met."

"What happened?"

"That's a long story. The short version is she got busy with finals and didn't have time for me. I guess she graduated and I haven't seen her since." David took a deep breath and let it out slow.

"How do you know she's the right one then?"

David tilted his head to the side. "Billy, how did you know Shauna was the right one?"

"Oh. Yeah. I see what you mean. Maybe you could find her again."

"I already tried. No luck. It's a lost cause." David grabbed a new two-by-four. "It would take a miracle for us to reconnect. I don't think that's going to happen."

David walked across the room and lowered the two-by-four from his shoulder to the floor.

"Maybe when I get close to finishing vet school I'll give some thought to dating again. I just know with classes, homework, and working on Professor Taulbee's farm, there isn't going to be any spare time for girls. Becoming a vet is the most important thing to me right now, with the exception of God."

Billy squinted one eye. "God, huh? I think we've had this conversation before."

"Yeah, and we'll keep having it until you agree to go to church and give God a chance."

"I think we can call it quits for today. What do you say?"

David shrugged. "That sounds good. And hey, thanks, but don't be trying to fix me up with Shauna's *kinda cute* friends, okay?"

"You got it."

THIRTY-FOUR

Maddie looked down at Rusty, curled up beside her chair. Finding a job was hard work. She'd had her eyes open for something, anything, for the past several weeks. And still nothing. The dog's silky tail waved as if in response to her thoughts. Of course, even if there was an opening somewhere, who would ever hire her? She had no experience except as a wife and mother. Maddie sat back hard against the chair and closed her eyes. Her cell phone startled her.

"Hello?"

"Hey, Maddie, it's George."

"Hi, George. How's the trip? Where are you?"

"Oh, since you said there wasn't any hurry, I took a side trip to see the Grand Canyon. That is some sight. Have you been there?"

"No, but I've always wanted to see it. Hope you took lots of pictures."

"I did."

Maddie hesitated to share her uncertain financial state with George, but knew she needed to be honest with him. "George, something has come up that may change our situation here."

"Let me pay the bill for my lunch and I'll head outside so we can talk." George's voice was muffled for a moment. "I usually eat in my fifth wheel, but I was getting a little tired of my own cooking."

"I know what you mean. I feel the same way about mine." Maddie laughed. "I've been looking forward to your cooking."

Minutes later Maddie told George about the extended delay in the renovation project. "So you see, things are somewhat up in the air until they clear up this situation with my investments. However, I did get a loan from the bank and it looks like we'll be able to start working on the big house again. Although, it probably won't be finished and ready for people to move in until some time after you arrive. I'm really sorry, George. I know you left your job at Southside Manor to come out here and cook for the residents, but I won't be able to pay you until—until I don't know when."

"Don't worry about me, Maddie. I was glad to leave Chicago. This will be a new beginning for me. Like I told you before, I've got my social security and pension to live on for as long as need be. This isn't about the money. How about we pray about it and then brainstorm when I get there?"

"Pray?"

"Yeah, you do pray, don't you?"

Maddie hesitated. "Sometimes."

"How about right now?"

Maddie heard fabric rustling and could picture George removing his Chicago Cubs ball cap. "God," came his voice. "We don't know what to do. Yet. Can You give us some ideas to see Maddie through this mess? Thank You, amen."

That was easy, thought Maddie.

Fabric rustled again.

"I guess I'll see you in about a week. I might want to stop and see some more sights along the way."

"Sounds good, George. Take your time and enjoy the journey. See you when I see you."

THIRTY-FIVE

J ase looked out over the range where his cattle gathered to eat. It was happening. His dream was slowly coming true. Searching the valley below, he wondered if his own land waited for him out there somewhere.

He turned at the crunch of gravel beneath vehicle tires. Jase waved at the woman driving the white van with "Hometown Veterinary Clinic" printed on the driver's door.

"Hello, Mr. Worthington, I'm Dr. Adams."

Jase took her extended hand, holding on a bit longer than called for, looking deep into the sensitive, dark-chocolate eyes of the beautiful woman standing before him. She tugged slightly, and he released her hand. "Oh, ah, hi. I'm Jasper Worthington III. Nice to meet you, Dr. Adams." He couldn't take his eyes off her high cheekbones, thick black hair pulled into a braid that fell over her shoulder, and full lips that were smiling at him.

"Oh, I see. Jasper Worthington *the third*." Her eyebrow went up. "That must mean there is a first and a second."

"What?"

"You said you are Jas—"

Jase closed his eyes and shook his head. "I didn't really say that, did I?"

She nodded.

Jase smacked his forehead with his hand. "Let me start over. I'm Jase, that's what people call me.

"Okay, Jase. Where are these ladies that are soon to be mamas? You said you had fifteen head, right?"

"Yeah, yeah. That's right, the vaccinations. The cows are over this way." Jase moved to the open field where his cattle fed.

"Good. You've got them all corralled in one space. That will make this go a lot faster."

Jase wasn't sure he wanted this to go faster. He watched as Dr. Adams moved toward the pregnant cows with poise and a sense of purpose. It sure looked like she knew what she was doing. Brave too. And strong, elbowing those two cows apart to get in between them. This woman knew her stuff. And beautiful to boot. He wondered what her heritage was. Cherokee? Apache? Shoot, he didn't even know what Indian tribes were in this part of the country.

Jase looked out over the land all the way to the majestic mountains in the distance.

"Jase . . . Jase."

Her clear call dug into his distracted thoughts. "Yeah. What do you need? How can I help?"

"Could you bring the black bag sitting on the passenger seat of the van over here?"

"Sure."

Jase grabbed the bag and shot a glance in the side mirror of the van. Hair sticking up on top, stubble on his chin and jaw, dark circles under his eyes from burning the midnight oil to get Nathan caught up on his financials. Jase ran a hand over the top of his head, which did nothing to improve the image in the mirror. Oh brother, he looked like he'd just jumped out of bed, which wasn't too far from the truth. *I think it's time to buy a working cowboy hat.*

"Jase, the bag?"

His head snapped over to the doctor down on her knees patting the flank of a grazing cow. "Yeah, sure, I'm coming."

With the vaccinations complete, Dr. Adams took her equipment back to the van. Jase trailed behind her.

"So, do I write you a check or what? This is all new to me. Raising cattle and horses was my grandfather's life. He taught me a lot, but not everything I'm going to need to know to run my own ranch." He put on his best smile since the rest of him was a total mess.

"No, you don't need to pay me now. We'll mail you a bill, or email it if you prefer."

"Yeah, email would be great. Here's my card with all my information." Jase pushed his hands into the pockets of his jeans. "I was just wondering, why did you want your black bag?"

She smiled and placed his card in her coat pocket. "I wanted the stethoscope to listen to that calf's heartbeat. Just wanted to make sure he starts out healthy. He was born early, wasn't he? All the other mamas have another three to four weeks before calving."

Jase looked over at the calf. "I don't know when he was born. When I bought the cattle he came with his mama. Is he? Healthy, I mean."

"Yes. Strong heartbeat, good loud vocal cords when he's looking for his mama."

Jase rubbed the stubble on his chin with his hand. "Ah, Dr. Adams."

"Jennifer."

"Okay, Jennifer. I know this might sound forward, and trust me, this is so not like me, but I was wondering if you would consider having dinner with me sometime?"

Jennifer frowned.

"Well, ah, I'm new to the area and haven't met a whole lot of people. And I'm really new to this cattle-raising thing. I have a ton of questions. Like, can I call on you to help with the calving? I went through a couple of calving seasons with my grandfather, but that was several years ago. Wouldn't want my lack of expertise to cause problems. I know I need hands-on experience. Thought maybe you could help me out with that."

"I'd be happy to answer any of your questions. You could make an appointment to come by the clinic and we could discuss this further. But dinner?"

"Well, actually, I have to confess, I'd really like to get to know you better."

"Me?" She backed up a step.

"Yes. You."

"Ah, I don't know if that's such a good idea." She looked over her shoulder toward the road.

"Why?"

Jennifer took a deep breath and let it out. Slow. "Jase, you should know upfront that I have a three-year-old son. He means everything to me."

Jase looked down at her left hand. "A son. Wow. What's his name?"

"Michael." She glanced at her hand. "And, no, I'm not married."

Jase gave her a smile that came all the way from his toes. "Well, I'd love to meet Michael sometime too."

THIRTY-SIX

George crested the hill and looked out over the fertile valley below. The Jacob's Bend sign suggested the little town was larger than he had anticipated, almost eighteen hundred residents. The fifteen-hundred-foot elevation was higher than he had expected, but it sure was beautiful. He could see why Maddie fell in love with this place. His trusty dog turned away from the window, his tongue lolling.

He couldn't wait to drive through the little town of Jacob's Bend, his new home. He had lived in the city most of his life, and spending his final years with millions of people he didn't know was not his idea of living the dream. When Maddie asked him to move to Broken Acres and cook for the residents, it had taken him all of two minutes to say yes. What that looked like now, with the renovation of the big house taking so long, was anybody's guess. Still, he was glad he'd made the decision to come.

George took his time driving through town. Picturesque. That's what he would call Jacob's Bend. Like a place out of a novel. The shops were quaint, kept in a way that said these people were proud to be a part of the town. Not a lot of people, just enough to make it comfortable. It actually reminded him somewhat of a quiet little village in the Philippines, near the hospital where he had convalesced. He'd been wounded while running to meet a helicopter during his tour of duty in Vietnam. That village, however, did not hold a candle to this beautiful little town.

George parked on Main Street, outside Lettie's Café. He slowly opened the door, but when he heard the jingle of a bell, alerting the wait-staff that customers had arrived, memories of the Philippines flooded back. That bell sounded just like the little silver bell that hung above the door to let the nurses know a patient needed help. He shook his head and looked into the noisy space before him, half expecting to see Adelle walk up to him with a thermometer in her hand and a smile on her lovely face. It had been love at first sight, at least for George. Long, brown curls bounced across slender shoulders, and hazel eyes sparkled. George had caught sight of the curls when she pushed them under her nurse's cap and asked him how he felt.

Due to his wounds and the pain meds they were giving him, he thought he was delirious and hallucinating when he saw this beauty smiling down at him. One thing he knew for sure, he was going to taste this nurse's lips before he was shipped back into battle.

He could see her as if it were yesterday. His heart leapt when a female voice spoke to him from behind the counter. The present snapped back into focus. He shook his head and smiled at the girl wearing a name tag that said "Kelly."

"Can I help you? Get you some coffee?" She looked at an empty stool at the end of the counter.

"Sure." His voice came out a hoarse whisper. He cleared his throat and took the empty seat. "Yes, thank you. Coffee would be great."

Kelly grabbed the glass coffee decanter and poured a cup. "Just passing though?"

"Ah, actually, no. Me and my sidekick, Duke, just arrived." George threw his thumb over his shoulder, indicating the fifth wheel parked outside the large plate glass window, where his Australian shepherd waited in the passenger seat of his truck.

"We drove from Illinois. Although Duke mostly slept and howled at the moon when it was full."

Kelly gave him a skeptical grin. "So, what brings you all the way out here to Jacob's Bend?"

"A farm called Broken Acres."

"Oh, Maddie's place."

"Yes. Do you know Mrs. Crane?"

"Oh sure. Pretty small town. Everybody knows everybody else." Kelly leaned in to put a pitcher of creamer by his cup. "And their business as well." She shrugged.

George nodded. "Can you give me directions to Broken Acres then?"

Kelly directed him west of town as he sipped his coffee, then asked, "Can I get you something to eat to go with your coffee?"

George realized he'd been eyeing the cinnamon rolls that sat inside a glass pedestal cake plate on the counter and laughed at being caught. "Yeah, could I get one of those cinnamon rolls, heated with butter?"

"Absolutely."

After one last cup of coffee, George picked up his half-eaten cinnamon roll and thermos now full of coffee and moved to the door. On his way out, George gave the café one last glance, thinking of Adelle. He jumped back as he almost ran into a woman coming in the door. "Excuse me, ma'am. Sorry, I didn't see you."

"How could you miss me? There's only one door." She started to move past him.

George frowned, then relaxed. She looked like she was ready to break down and cry. "Yeah, you're right. Again, I'm sorry."

The woman bit her lip and turned back slightly. "No, I'm sorry. I shouldn't have bit your head off."

With that, the older woman walked to the back of the café and sat at a table with a man.

That young man didn't even smile at her when she sat down. She looked old enough to be his mother. George shrugged. *Let it go, George, she doesn't know you from Adam.* "Welcome to Jacob's Bend, George," he said under his breath.

Duke paced from the driver's side to the passenger seat and back when he saw George walk from the café. George patted his head and scooted him over to his side of the cab, offering what was left of his cinnamon roll. "You know, Duke, they looked good enough to eat, but one bite of the dry pastry said otherwise. Looks can be deceiving." He watched Duke lick the icing from his lips with satisfaction. "I could make better than that, don't you think, boy?"

Duke barked in answer to the question. "That's what I thought." George smiled at his buddy. "Let's hit the road and find our new home."

*   *   *

Maddie sat at her kitchen table mulling over a stack of papers that covered the entire wooden top. Head bowed, resting in the palm of her hand, she blew out a burst of air her lungs could hold no longer. "What am I going to do?" She pulled a sheet out from under a pile—a wannabe budget sheet—that had scribbling up, down, and around the margins. Turning the paper around to see the upside-down notations, Maddie threw it over her shoulder.

What possessed her to buy a new truck? What was she thinking? She chided herself. Well, there weren't any frozen assets at the time, and she liked the color. She took her mug to the coffeepot and poured another cup of strong brew.

You liked the color? Good grief. That is the most ridiculous—

A lively tune drew her attention to her cell sitting somewhere beneath the mess of papers. Trying to trace the sound, she tossed more papers to the floor before finding her phone. "Hello?"

"Hey, Maddie, it's George."

"Hey, George. Where are you? Do you have an ETA or are you still livin' the dream, taking your time to see this beautiful country?"

George laughed. "Actually, I'm in Jacob's Bend."

"You are?"

"Yep, just stopped at Lettie's for a cup of coffee. I wanted to get directions to your place. The waitress there gave me general directions, something like, 'Take a left at Toomey's barn.' So I thought I'd call, let you know I'm here and get more specific directions."

"It's pretty easy to find Broken Acres. Just head west on Highway 25 for about six miles, turn left at the old Coca-Cola sign. There's a giant red mailbox at the entrance to the farm. Gate's open. Come on up to the small cottage."

"Great. See you in just a bit. After three months on the road, Duke and I are doggone awful ready to settle."

Thirty-Seven

George couldn't believe his eyes when he looked out over the expanse before him. The impressive mountains in the distance, beautiful green growth everywhere. Two houses sat on either side of what looked like an apple orchard. To the right, a big house that looked like it could house a family of twelve. To the left, a sweet little cottage. Both with inviting porches calling one to come and sit a spell. George saw movement on the porch of the large house and wondered what was going on there. Hadn't Maddie said the reno work was on hold? Duke looked over from the passenger seat and barked twice as if answering the question. George smoothed the Australian shepherd's fur down his back. George grinned when he saw Maddie wave from the cottage porch. Duke jumped into his lap and started barking, no doubt at the golden retriever who stood next to Maddie on the porch.

*   *   *

Maddie stood from the porch swing and gave George a wave. Just as she had done when she first saw Broken Acres, he had stopped his truck at the top of the knoll. She figured he was as dumbfounded at the sight below as she had been. Her phone whistled a lively tune.

"Hello."

"Hi ya, Maddie."

"Granny Harper? Hi. How are you doing? It's been a while." Maddie walked inside to set her coffee cup in the sink.

"It has. It's been too long. I remember the last time we had coffee you mentioned needing a job. Have you found one yet?"

Maddie plopped down on the couch. "No. Unfortunately there aren't a lot of jobs in Jacob's Bend. I think I'm going to need to expand my search parameters." Maddie glanced out the front window. "Especially since I lost another renter. That only leaves Clive Jones with his small herd of cattle and Jasper Worthington. I'll never make my loan payments with only two land parcels rented out."

"Oh my, that doesn't sound good."

"I know. So you got a high-paying, full-time position for me there at your place?" She grinned at the ridiculous idea.

"Actually, it's just about harvest time for the peach orchard, and I thought maybe you might want to help us out."

Maddie sat up straight on the edge of the couch. "Yes. Absolutely. I don't care what you're paying. It's more than the zero dollars I'm making now."

"Before you agree, maybe you should pray about it. I know you have strong muscles and are in good shape, but this up and down ladders and stretching overhead can take a toll on the body. It will take about a week and a half to pick, then I'll need help with canning."

"Granny, you do know I've never done this before, right?"

"Oh, that's not a problem, I'm sure you'll pick it up real quick. And as far as the canning goes, I'll be right there with you in the kitchen, teaching you step by step."

"Like the tomatoes we canned?"

"Sort of. It's a little different with fruit."

"Sounds great. That's a week and a half, plus. That's more paid employment than I have now. And I definitely don't need to pray about it." *Like God is gonna really talk to me.*

"I'll let you know when John says it's time to harvest. Usually about the middle of August, in a couple of weeks."

"Thanks so much for thinking of me, Granny." Maddie walked out to the porch and watched George drive his truck from the top of the knoll that led to her farm.

"You're welcome, honey. It will be good to get together again."

A thought struck Maddie and she grinned into her phone.

"Hey, Granny. Could you use another pair of hands?"

"Sure. You have someone in mind?"

"Yeah. It's a long story, but I invited a friend of mine, a chef from Illinois where I used to live, to come out and cook for the residents who will be living at Broken Acres. I didn't realize at the time that could be some time down the road. He just crested the knoll in his truck, pulling his fifth wheel."

"Bring him along. I'll let John know we've got two pickers."

"Thanks again, Granny. I really appreciate it."

THIRTY-EIGHT

addie put on her oven mitt and delivered the pan from the oven. The sweet, sticky scent of cinnamon coming from baked cookies filled the little cottage. After moving the snickerdoodles onto wax paper to cool, she popped the last batch into the oven and set the timer.

Turning to start cleaning the kitchen, a gentle knock took her to the front door. "Jenny." Maddie looked down into the smiling brown eyes of the little boy who held her visitor's hand. "And Michael."

A grin that could bring sunshine to any room and outstretched arms caused Maddie to pick the little man up and give him a tight squeeze and kiss his forehead. "How's my buddy today?"

Michael held tight to her neck and then squirmed out of her arms to freedom. "Where's Rusty?"

The two women laughed as they watched Rusty trot over, tail wagging, to let the little guy give him a hug around the neck. "I wanna ride Rusty."

"Michael, you know Rusty doesn't like to be ridden like Bridgette does," Jenny reminded him.

"I wanna ride Rusty."

When Michael lifted his leg to straddle the dog, Rusty sank to the floor and turned over on his side. One sigh and he closed his eyes to possibly shut out the dog and pony trick expected of him.

Michael's hurt look melted Maddie's heart. "How about some snickerdoodles?"

"Yum. I like cookies." Michael grinned big and pulled out a chair at the kitchen table to ready himself for the treat.

"Cookies and milk. Just like David, his favorite."

Jenny looked up to the loft and down the hall toward the other bedroom. "Yeah, when am I gonna finally meet this elusive son of yours?"

"I know. Hopefully sooner rather than later. He's leaving for Forest Hills and vet school in a few weeks."

"That's right. He's going to FHU to get his veterinarian's degree. Maybe he'll want to settle down here and we'll have an opening at the clinic when he graduates. I'm sure we'll still be adding to our numbers then. The practice just keeps growing."

Maddie nodded. "So, where are you off to this lovely Friday evening?"

Jenny ducked her head, pink shading her cheeks. "Well, Jasper Worthington asked me out on a date. We're going to dinner in Carterville."

"Jase. He's a nice guy." Maddie lifted an eyebrow. "Handsome too."

"I haven't been on a date in so long I'm not sure I'll know how to act." She looked up at Maddie with a lopsided smile. "He really is handsome, isn't he? That blonde hair tends to find its way over his hazel eyes. His shoulders are so broad he could wrestle any of his steers and win. How does he stay in such good shape if he has a business degree and does Nathan's financials? Doesn't he need to be in an office to do that?"

"That's a good question. Knowing Jase, I'd say he is probably down there punching cows every day." Maddie pointed toward the field Jase rented from her. "Not to mention throwing those bales of hay over the side of his truck to feed his cattle. He said he does the work for Nathan in the evenings at his house."

Maddie watched as Jenny fidgeted with her hands. "Jenny, I'm sure you'll do fine." Maddie looked over at Michael, who had opened the square wooden box next to the fireplace and pulled out a dump truck and tractor and was making mechanical noises only a three-year-old boy would understand. "Was Michael's father the last man you dated?"

"Yeah. After him I was so busy finishing school, joining the practice here, and taking care of Michael, there was no time for anything else."

"I can understand that. Well, I'm glad you are getting out. You deserve to have some fun and find a man who will love and appreciate you."

Jenny ducked her head again. "I'd better get back home and change into something other than doctor's scrubs." Picking up a Spider-Man backpack from the floor, Jenny handed it to Maddie. "Are you sure you want to keep Michael overnight?"

"Oh yeah. It will be fun. That way you don't have to worry about coming all the way out here after your date to pick him up. He would probably already be asleep that late anyway. I'll bring him home tomorrow morning when I come into town to get groceries. I had forgotten how much food David consumes and the fact that hitting the market three to four times a week is the norm when he's around." Maddie smiled at Jenny.

"Well, hopefully I'll be able to meet him before he takes off for Forest Hills. Guess I'd better get going. Come give Mama a hug, Michael."

Jenny picked her son up and ruffled his hair. "Now you be a good boy for Miss Maddie, okay?"

"I be a good boy."

Jenny gave him one last hug and kiss and headed for her car. Maddie turned to her little guest.

"Okay, buddy. I'm fixing your other favorite for dinner. Spaghetti."

"I like sketti," Michael shouted between motor sounds of heavy machinery and the blue pickup truck he ran across the floor.

Maddie pulled coloring books and crayons out of the toy box and set them on the table knowing Michael would likely grow tired of the toys he was playing with in no time.

"Read me a story first."

Maddie squinted at the little guy. "Please."

Michael grinned. "Please read me a story."

A tug on Maddie's leg diverted her attention as Michael solemnly presented the story of a bear to her. Storytime was one of Maddie's favorite things to do with Michael. Not ten minutes into the story of Belvedere the blue bear, Maddie sat the book on the arm of the couch and gently took the sleeping boy from her lap and laid him on the couch, covering him with a lap quilt. Tenderly brushing his thick black hair out of his eyes, she kissed his forehead. "Have a nice nap, buddy."

No sooner had she walked to the linen closet down the hall to get an apron to keep the spaghetti sauce from splattering a not-so-lovely design on her white shirt than she heard David walk in the front door.

David sniffed the air. "Snickerdoodles, yum, my favorite. Mom," he sang out.

"Shh, David." She pointed to the couch.

Too late. Michael opened his eyes, rubbed them, and started crying.

"Well, who do we have here?" David walked over to the couch and sat down next to the little boy. "Hi, I'm David."

Michael looked up at him with deep chocolate eyes, grinned, and looked over at Maddie.

She gave him a nod.

Michael wrapped his arms around David's neck before climbing into his lap.

"Hey." David looked over at his mom. "I think I have a new friend."

Maddie smiled. "David, this is Michael, Dr. Adams's son. Michael, this is my son, David."

"David." Michael mimicked. He brushed David's auburn hair back from his eyes, just as Maddie had done with Michael earlier.

"Thanks, Michael. Hey, were you playing with the truck and tractor?"

"Tractor." Michael climbed down and brought the truck over to David. "Wanna play trucks?"

David smiled big and nodded. "Let me go wash up and we'll make some dirt piles to move with the heavy machinery."

Maddie frowned and David laughed at her expression. "Not real dirt, Mom. You know, like you used to make for us with washcloths and blocks and stuff."

"Oh yeah. I remember. Hey, do you remember the fun forts you, Ruth, and Bracy used to make?"

"Fort?" Michael parroted, excitement radiating from his eyes.

"Yeah, we'll make a fort too, buddy."

By the time dinner was finished and Maddie had cleaned up the dishes, both boys were sacked out on the couch with Michael lying on David's chest, his blankie clutched tight in his right hand, the *Toy Story* DVD playing on the TV.

The entire downstairs looked like a construction site that had blown up, with every toy from the box strewn across the floor. The card-table fort stood strong with the front flap of one of her favorite quilts held open by the baseball bat she kept by the front door.

Maddie quietly put the bat back where it belonged and drew the quilt from the card table. She covered David and Michael with the quilt and ejected the DVD. Brushing the hair back from both their foreheads, she gave each a kiss good night, turned off the lamp on the side table, and headed upstairs to bed. There would be time enough in the morning for the boys to clean up the fun from the night before.

THIRTY-NINE

Maddie gently knocked on the door of the fifth wheel parked on the shady side of the big house. George peeked around the tongue of the trailer. "Good morning, Maddie."

She jumped back at the hearty welcome. Duke sat quietly at George's feet watching the dog Maddie had brought with her. "Oh my goodness, George, you scared the pajiggers out of me."

"Pajiggers, huh?"

She laughed. "One of Granny Harper's words. Love that lady."

"Who is Granny Harper?"

"Oh, you'll meet her soon enough. She has become a dear friend."

"What can I do for you?"

"I thought we ought to let these two guys get acquainted so they can be friends and not adversaries."

"Good idea. Duke is pretty protective of me, but he's also easy to get along with. I've never seen him fight with another dog. Although he has been known to attack a wolf or two."

"Wolves?"

"Yeah, like I said, he's protective."

"Remember the first time we met at Southside Manor in Chicago?"

"I sure do. I think it was like the second time you had come to volunteer. You had been reading to Jonathan, ah, Mr. Richards, and you came running into the cafeteria to get some of that English tea we kept on hand just for him. I thought you were going to pass out when you slipped on the wet floor, fell on your backside, and hit your head."

"I was so embarrassed. What was I thinking, running like that? Thank goodness for Duke. He rushed over and started licking my face. Made me laugh and gave me a neck to hug. Then you handed me one of your incredible orange scones that had just come out of the oven. I was hooked with just one bite. Honestly, George, I think that was my welcome into the family at Southside Manor."

George gave her a gentle smile. "And believe me, you were definitely part of the family. Everyone missed you when you moved clear across the country."

Maddie looked down at Rusty. "I've only had this guy as part of my family for about a year. But I feel like he's always been with me. I don't know what I'd do without him. Rusty is also very protective, but I don't really know how he reacts to other dogs."

"Let's find out. Let go of his collar."

"Are you sure?"

"Yes."

"Okay."

Rusty sat right by her side, his eyes glued to Duke. George gave Duke a scratch behind the ears. "Duke, this is Rusty, Maddie's protector. Now, you two are going to be living on the same property, and we want you to shake paws and be friends."

Maddie giggled.

George looked over at Rusty.

"Yeah, now Rusty"—Maddie made her voice serious—"I know you are protective of me and Duke feels the same way about George, so we need you to be friends and protect everyone who comes to live at Broken Acres. Okay?"

Rusty looked up at Maddie and then walked over and sniffed Duke. The Australian shepherd didn't move a muscle. When Rusty came back and sat at Maddie's feet, Duke walked over and sniffed Rusty. Both looked up at their masters as if to say, "Yeah, we're good."

George grabbed a tennis ball from a bucket that sat by the door of the fifth wheel and threw it with all his might toward the barn. Both dogs raced after the ball, barking the whole way.

"Do you think that's a good idea? Won't they battle for the ball?"

"If my guess is right, this will be like a contest for them. The first one to the ball will be the winner and bring it back. They'll both want another try to be top dog, and this could go on all day. Still, I think this will ultimately become a friendly game for them."

Rusty came trotting back with the ball in his mouth and dropped it at George's feet. Duke came up behind Rusty and sat patiently, waiting for George to throw the ball again. This time he got the jump on Rusty and ended up bringing the prize home.

"See?"

Maddie grinned. "That's amazing. You know a lot about dogs, don't you? I'm so glad they are on friendly terms."

"Me too. I don't think we'll have any problems between them. They're both good-natured dogs. I think they'll be okay together."

Maddie nodded. "George, the other reason I came over was to see if you wanted to help pick peaches at Granny Harper's next week. Since I don't have any work for you to do yet."

"Sure. That sounds good. Is she gonna can some of the peaches too?"

"Yeah. How did you know?"

"I'm a cook, Maddie. I know what happens when you have a whole orchard full of fresh-picked peaches. You can't eat or sell all of them if it's a big orchard, which I suspect it is."

"Yes. I haven't seen it, but from what I understand it's pretty big. She'll pay you a fair wage."

"Do you think she would want some help with the canning? I'm pretty good at that."

"I'm sure she would appreciate it. I'll ask her."

*   *   *

David woke up startled by movement and a heavy weight on his chest. He slowly opened his eyes, somehow instinctively cautious about moving too fast even as his breathing felt constricted.

Looking down, he saw a handsome stock of thick black hair over two beautiful brown eyes looking up at him. A little fist came up and rubbed both eyes clear of sleep.

David smiled, remembering the games of the evening before. "Well, hello, buddy. Did you have a good sleep?"

"Yes, good sleep." Michael smiled big and carefully ran his hand over the stubble on David's chin. Feeling his own chin he gave David a curious glance. He sat up on David's stomach and took his face in both of his small hands. "Pretty."

David grinned and surprisingly felt tears well up. He encased the little guy in a bear hug. Clearing his throat, he heard a voice behind him.

"Good morning, you two."

Michael giggled and held his arms out to Maddie.

David watched his mom pick up the little boy and give him a bear hug of her own.

Michael took her face in his two hands and looked back at David. "Pretty."

"Aw, thank you, Michael. You are very pretty—well, handsome—yourself."

David rubbed his eyes with the back of his hand during their exchange. "Good morning, Mom. What's for breakfast?"

"I'm hungry," Michael said. He squirmed down to the floor, walked over to David, and picked up his hand. "Potty, David. Potty."

"Ah, okay." David glanced at his mom and shrugged. "Sure, little guy, let's go."

Maddie smiled. "I'll start breakfast. Eggs and pancakes?"

"Yes, pancakes," Michael said over his shoulder as he hurried David to the bathroom.

FORTY

David offered to take Michael home on his way to Carterville, but Maddie wanted to give him a bath so his mom didn't have to do it when he got home. She wanted them to have all of Saturday together. She knew how much that meant to Jenny since she only had the weekends to relax and enjoy time with her son. And, she admitted, she wanted to hear how the date had gone.

Jenny said the date went fine. She enjoyed the dinner and Jase's company. They had a good talk and got to know each other a little better.

"Any sparks?" Maddie asked.

Jenny pulled her son into a tight hug, grinning from ear to ear. "I missed you, little guy. Did you have fun at Maddie's?"

"Yes fun. David played trucks. We watched *Toy Story*."

"David?" Jenny glanced up at Maddie, who laughed.

"Yeah, they really did have a good time. The guys played with every truck, tractor, earthmover, and LEGO block in the toy box. The house looked like a construction zone gone awry when they fell asleep on the couch. Michael slept on David's chest all night. I didn't have the heart to wake them up. They looked so cute and comfortable."

"Really?"

"Yes. But they didn't get breakfast until every last LEGO block was in the toy box." Maddie smiled. "They even had fun picking up all the toys. It was a race. The first one at the table got an extra pancake. David's idea. I used to do that with the kids when they were little. It was fun watching them. Who knew two guys could come up with so many different sound effects for machinery?"

"I love LEGOs." Michael smiled.

"Yes, son, you l-o-v-e LEGOs, I know. Thank you so much for having Michael over, Maddie." Jenny hugged him again. "You smell good. Did you have a bath at Maddie's this morning?"

Michael nodded. "With a fire engine."

*   *   *

Monday morning the three men settled their tool belts on their hips and headed inside the big house.

"David, why don't you finish opening the wall from this bedroom into the new bath? Billy, I need to talk to you."

Billy's head shot up and glanced over at Nathan. "Uh, what did I do now?"

Nathan chuckled. "You didn't do anything. But I do have a job offer for you. I know you want to help Maddie finish this job, but I also know that now you are a married man you are looking for permanent employment."

"Yeah. You got something in mind?"

"Well, I do have some connections through my construction company in Portsmouth, and a permanent job is a definite possibility." Nathan slapped Billy on the shoulder.

"There's a new active senior living community on the docket in Portsmouth, and we just won the project. Condos, activity center, dining rooms, golf course, fitness center, aquatic center. The whole nine yards and more. I recommended you to the foreman on the job. He wants to meet with you this week. I told him that I've personally worked with you for several months. That you have a great work ethic and are determined to do the best work possible."

Billy's face shaded pink. "Thanks, Nathan. That's saying a lot coming from you. I really appreciate it."

"I wasn't sure if you were going to go out on your own now that you have your contractor's license or what your plans were."

"I figured I would need to pay my dues and work for somebody else for a while, get my name out there, build a good reputation, before I gave any thought to starting my own company. And there's no one I'd rather work for than you."

"That's smart thinking, Billy, to get some jobs under your belt. If you and the super hit it off, they'll want you to start right away since they are going to break ground next week. The wood and nails won't happen for a while, but there are plenty of other things to do at this stage. And I thought it would be good for you to experience the whole project from day one."

"That would be great. I couldn't ask for a better start in the construction business."

"Okay, here's the super's cell number. Give him a call and set it up."

"Thanks again, Nathan. I won't let you down."

"Believe me, you'll earn every dollar you make. The super is good at what he does and he expects hard work, integrity, and no shortcuts from his people. Which is why I recommended you." Nathan gave Billy a slap on the back. "You and Shauna will be ready in no time to start building your own home."

Nathan could see Billy typing the phone number he had given him into his cell. Billy waved back at his boss as he put the phone to his ear and walked toward the apple orchard.

*   *   *

"Nathan."

"Yeah, David, what's up?"

David looked over the railing down to the first floor. "Can you come upstairs and help me move this part of the wall? It just about came down all in one piece."

"Sure. We can just toss it out the bedroom window."

"Ah, probably not."

"Huh?" Nathan jogged up the stairs. "Oh, wow. It did come down in one piece. Let's saw it into smaller chunks."

"Good idea."

Nathan glanced at where the wall had been. "Man, that's unusual for it to come down like that, I wonder—look up there, near the ceiling. There's a cubbyhole with something lodged in it." Nathan grabbed the ladder and carefully pulled the yellowing paper from its hiding place.

"What is that?"

Nathan shrugged and climbed down the ladder. He opened the paper and began to read aloud.

Dearest E,

Even though your father says he will not give his permission for us to marry because I am poor, I will not give up hope that one day we will be one. I am working to build a home your father will accept and you will be proud to raise our family in. Believe it my love.

I love you,

JH

"Oh my gosh, Bracy would go absolutely berserk if she saw this."

Nathan looked up from the fragile paper. "Your sister?"

"Yeah, she is a fanatic when it comes to historical documents."

"Well, I'm not sure anyone would classify this as a historical document. A love letter maybe."

"Oh, trust me, when she gets her hands on this, she'll not only find out who wrote it and why, but everything there is to know about the family and the story behind the story." David's grin told Nathan more than even his words did.

Nathan laughed. "I can't wait to hear what she finds out."

"She's definitely obsessive when it comes to research, especially historical research."

Nathan examined the page further. "You know, David, it looks like this could have been torn out of a book. Look at the jagged uneven edge."

"Maybe it came from someone's journal."

"Yeah, that could be. Well, we'll let Bracy sleuth it out. I'm looking forward to seeing your sister again. She only stayed for a short time when she was here before."

"Yeah, she's a kick and really smart. Takes after my dad."

"Your mom is pretty doggone smart too, you know."

"I know. I know she is. But I'm talking close to genius level. If Bracy gets anything but an A in any of her classes, she is crushed."

"Well, let's see what she can dig up. When is she coming back out?" Nathan carefully refolded the letter.

"Not really sure when her school takes a break."

Nathan put the letter in his back pocket and turned back to the wall. "Speaking of school, when do you leave?"

"This is my last week here."

"Oh brother."

"What?"

"Billy too. He's going to start work on a project we got the bid on in Portsmouth next week."

David scratched the back of his neck. "That's rough. Can you hire some guys from your company to help you here?"

Nathan ran his hand through his hair, pushing it off his forehead. "I'm not so sure your mom would go for that. Or that she could afford it. They make a lot more than we are making."

"You think?" David snickered his agreement.

"Of course I'd be happy to pay their wages, but you know your mother's stubborn pride." Nathan carefully avoided looking out the upstairs window to the cottage across the apple orchard.

"Yeah. It runs in the family. But I'm learning pride only makes us look good in our own eyes. Everybody else sees a fool. Pride goes before the fall; that's what the Bible says. And I've lived some of that."

"I know what you mean. The pastor in Carterville preached on that last Sunday."

David grinned.

"What?"

"Oh nothing. It's rare I get to talk with another guy about the Bible."

Nathan kicked a pile of the heavy lath and plaster pieces that lay on the floor with the toe of his boot. "Yeah, well, I don't know much about the Bible."

"But you're learning. Every time you go to church. Every time you read the Bible. Every time you talk to someone else who knows Jesus."

Nathan cleared his throat. "We'd better get this plaster wall out the window."

FORTY-ONE

Maddie sat on the top porch step sipping her morning coffee, her right hand smoothing Rusty's soft ears. "I really like the sound of those hammers and power saws. Soon we'll have a place for people to come and heal from life's hard knocks."

She turned from her canine friend to watch the movement at the big house and promptly choked on a sip of coffee. Coughing to catch her breath, she watched the muscular form of a handsome man, dark glasses making his image alluring and seductive—*your contractor*, she sternly told herself—walk slowly toward her. The sight of his navy-blue T-shirt stretched taut across his chest brought the intimate vision of the last time he came to her cottage, and she closed her eyes and took a deep breath.

Shirtless after a morning of heavy work in the unusually hot day, Nathan had come to remove a bat from her cottage. She could still feel the chills that went through her body when he kissed the back of her neck while she held a tennis racket on top of the rodent that had been sleeping on the wall.

When the racket hit the floor, his hands were on her waist, turning her to him. She would never forget the longing in his eyes and her wondering if her eyes had reflected the same need. His kiss had been gentle, though, tentative at first, and had sent her into a lost abyss as she kissed him back with a passion she had never felt before.

Maddie touched her fingertips to her lips. "Nathan."

"Good morning, Maddie."

Her eyes popped open. Cobalt-blue eyes met hers, sunglasses casually set atop his head. She tried to catch her breath and slow down her heartbeat. His tanned biceps reminded her of the lightning bolt that surged through her body when he held her that day.

He frowned. "Are you okay?" Nathan reached out and touched her arm.

She pulled her arm back like a hot poker had touched her, spilling coffee down the front on her pale-green shirt.

"I'm sorry, Maddie, I didn't mean to startle you. Are you okay? Did you burn yourself?" He moved up a step toward the door. "Can I get you a towel or something?"

Maddie offered a shaky smile, trying to collect herself. "I'm fine. The coffee wasn't hot." She looked down at her favorite top. "My shirt wasn't quite as lucky."

He looks helpless, Maddie thought. *Like he wants to help but doesn't know how.*

"So, Nathan." Maddie carefully put her mug down beside her, feeling the coffee-soaked fabric of her top start to cool against her skin. "How was your wedding?" *That was a really stupid question, Maddie. You know it was postponed.*

"Or maybe I should ask, how is married life?" *Stupid, Maddie, stupid.*

Nathan looked at her like she didn't have a clue, which of course she didn't. *Change the subject, Maddie.*

"How's it going over there?" She pointed to the big house.

Again he frowned, moved off the step, and took a deep breath. "That's what I came over to talk to you about. Billy is probably going to be starting a job in Portsmouth next week. One has come up he'd do well at. He could learn a lot and it might help him when he's ready to start his own construction company. And from what I understand, David leaves for school next week."

Fear flashed across Maddie's thoughts, but Nathan quickly continued.

"But I can bring some of my guys over to help me finish the job. There's probably only a couple more material loads to order, right?"

"I don't know. You tell me. I thought you already had enough to finish."

"Ah, no. Actually, I was wondering where you got the list of materials?"

"Well, I kinda listened in on a conversation you three were having and I thought it through and made up a list. I figured I ordered everything you would need to finish. I was pretty happy that it cost so much less than what I had first thought it would."

"Maddie." He shook his head. "Why didn't you come and ask me for a list?"

"I didn't want to bother you."

"Maddie, I'm the super on this project; it's not a bother. It's my job. We need to communicate." Nathan blew out air through his lips. "Okay, how about we work on a list together?"

Maddie squinted, thinking of her options. "That's probably a good idea."

Nathan nodded and rubbed his forehead.

"But I don't want you to hire the men from your company."

"Why did I know you'd say that?" His sigh only stiffened her resolve. "Well, it will be back to just me like it was to begin with, and that will slow things down quite a bit."

She looked over at Rusty, who had pranced down the steps to sit by Nathan's feet, tail wagging, tongue hanging out. Nathan gently petted his head.

Traitor.

Maddie stood up and stepped closer so she could be eye to eye with him. "If there's somewhere else you need to be, go ahead and leave with everyone else."

"Maddie—"

"No, I mean it."

"That's not how I roll. When I start a job, I finish it."

"Okay then, let's figure out what that's going to take."

Nathan looked over her shoulder when Sarg meowed at the screen door.

Maddie opened the squeaky door releasing the cat to take off to the orchard, presumably to his vast litter box.

Maddie picked up her coffee cup and glanced down at her shirt. "But not right now. I need to dry out first."

*   *   *

After planning a time the next day to meet and map out a plan, Nathan headed back to the big house.

His mind took him back to the one time he had been in her little cottage. It was indelibly seared into his mind. The wisps of hair on the back of Maddie's neck, tempting him to drop the kiss he couldn't help but deliver. Her tender lips. The growing need in his body for her. Her arms around his neck, her passionate kiss. Then, like a slap in the face, her pushing him away, rejecting what he desperately wanted to share with her. Now he knew why.

Nathan smoothed the hair on the back of his neck.

In a flash the scene changed to Maddie and Pastor Ben, cozy and kissing in front of a warm fire while snow fell on Nathan outside her window.

Let it go, Nathan. Let it go.

FORTY-TWO

"Want to come to church with me, Mom?" David's question caught her off guard. It was his last Sunday before heading out to Forest Hills, and it looked as if his packing was almost finished.

"Oh, I don't know, David. I haven't been in a few weeks. Too busy out here." *Don't lie, Maddie. You know you just don't want to face Pastor Ben.*

"Come on, Mom, please?"

His fake pouty face made her smile. "Okay, we can go to church."

Maddie sat in the back row behind a very large man and what appeared to be his family. A place she had never sat before in Ben's church. In times past she had sat in the third row so she could hear and see Ben better.

David smiled at her and she smiled back.

"Today we are going to delve into a passage I touched on some time ago but felt compelled to dig deeper. The Amplified translation of 2 Corinthians 6:14 says, 'Do not be unequally yoked with unbelievers [do not make mismated alliances with them or come under a different yoke with them, inconsistent with your faith]. For what partnership have right living and right standing with God with iniquity and lawlessness? Or how can light have fellowship with darkness?'

"Sounds a bit harsh, wouldn't you say?"

*   *   *

Several heads nodded as Ben scanned the congregation.

Then his eyes met David's and stopped. He glanced to David's right. Holding the pulpit in front of him with both hands, Ben tilted his head to see around the man sitting on the aisle in the row in front of David. The man squirmed in his seat, blocking any view of the row behind him.

She was here. Of all the times for her to decide to come back to church, it had to be when he was preaching on this topic? Ben held tight to the pulpit and took a deep breath.

"Let's dissect this verse and see what God has to say. The yoke is a wooden bar or frame that keeps two oxen bound together, going in the same direction, at the same speed, working together to accomplish the same purpose. This verse is talking about two people being mismatched, bound together, such as a business partnership or a marriage." He paused.

"You might ask, what's the big deal? What's the difference? The apostle Paul is making a strong case that for a believer in Jesus Christ to have a binding partnership with an unbeliever is inconsistent with what other scriptures tell us about our faith and walk with Jesus. Believers now have a right standing with God that they didn't have before they received Jesus as their Savior. The Bible is explicitly clear on that subject. There's not enough time this morning to give you all the scriptures that support that truth, and I'd be happy to talk further with any of you privately if you like. Believers are now a part of God's family, as John 1:12 clearly states, with all the benefits and privileges being a part of His family brings."

Ben quickly looked back at David, who was nodding his head and looking over at his mother. Ben remembered another time when Maddie left immediately after the service when he had spoken on forgiveness. Would she leave in the middle of this one?

Ben walked around to the front of the pulpit. "We as believers get to follow God's Word and live according to His commands and plans because we believe He has put them in this book"—he picked his Bible up and held it out in front of him—"to help us maneuver through this life with His good purpose as our guide. Honesty, integrity, faithfulness are just a few ways God would have His children live their lives. And we, as believers, have the Holy Spirit living in us to help us live that life. We'll never get it perfect here, but the Holy Spirit surely does let us know when we're on the wrong path.

"But let's say you're in a business partnership with an unbeliever and he wants to fudge on your tax return so you'll have more money to invest in the business. Or maybe he sees a way to make the competition look bad by telling customers a little lie or two. Can we as believers, in all good conscience, agree with these practices?"

Ben took a deep breath and walked down the steps to stand in the middle aisle. "And in the matter of marriage . . ." Ben walked down the aisle until he could see Maddie, and their eyes locked. "How can a man and woman, one a believer, one an unbeliever, be bound together in body and mind when one knows God is sovereign over their life and the other believes they are in control of every detail of their life? A believer is taught to put the welfare of others before their own"—Ben heard his voice falter slightly and pressed on—"even if their heart breaks when they realize the love they feel is better given from a distance." He turned to go back to his pulpit.

"Is it easy to live according to God's Word?" Ben held up the Bible. "Sometimes it's the most difficult thing you've ever had to do. Is it worth it? Sometimes we wonder. But isn't that where faith comes in? Faith that God sees the beginning from the end? Faith that He knows best? God's best truly does wait on the other side of obedience—even when it's a difficult journey getting there. Let's pray."

*   *   *

Maddie dropped her head and closed her eyes. She felt the tears threaten to fall and determined to fight them back with every ounce of strength she had. She could see the sorrow and resignation in Ben's eyes when they locked onto hers. *So that's why he wasn't coming around.*

She could hold it in no longer when she caught the end of Ben's prayer.

"Father, give us Your divine wisdom in matters of the heart. Be our strength when we want to chuck it all and go our own way. More than anything, Lord, pour out Your lavish love on those who have yet to believe in Your Son, and may they surrender to the truth of who He is. Amen."

Maddie swiped the tears from her cheeks, stood, and walked out the front door.

"Mom." Maddie heard David's voice quietly calling behind her but kept walking until she reached her truck. She popped the locks with her remote and crawled into the driver's seat.

"Mom." David got in on the passenger side.

Maddie sat rigid, staring out the windshield.

"Mom, what's going on? What was that with you and Pastor Ben?"

Maddie studied her hands on the steering wheel until she could control her voice.

"Can we just go home? I really don't want to talk about it."

David's voice was cautiously neutral. "Sure. No problem. Can I just ask one question?"

She looked over at her son, saddened by the worry in his eyes. "Yes, of course."

He looked deep into her eyes. "Do you know what Pastor Ben was saying in there?"

Maddie turned back to the windshield, closed her eyes, and laid her head on the steering wheel.

"I'm afraid I do."

FORTY-THREE

David wished he had more time to help Nathan finish the reno on the big house. Billy was gone, and his mom wouldn't let Nathan hire his own guys. She was so stubborn. He rolled his eyes.

He wished he had more time to talk to her about Pastor Ben's message on Sunday. How could she not want to know Jesus? The gospel was so clear. But it had been a silent ride home on Sunday. *Stubborn. And frustrating.*

Well, one thing he could do before he headed out for school. On his way out of town he would stop at the Hometown Veterinary Clinic. Hopefully he could talk to Dr. Adams about possibly working there when he finished school. That was so far down the road. Would there even be an opening at their office then? Well, at least he could meet the doctors and let them know he was interested in practicing here in Jacob's Bend.

Now that she was alone, it was important that he work near his mom. David checked his watch. He needed to get on the road or he'd miss his appointment with Professor Taulbee. But he had told his mom that he would meet with the vet before he left. Besides, he wanted to tell Dr. Adams what an amazing son she had.

Michael, his little buddy, had definitely grabbed hold of a place in his heart, David realized, and not seeing him for some time would be disappointing. It couldn't be helped. He'd just have to make a point to see him when he came home to visit Mom.

David pulled into the clinic parking lot and jumped out of his car. He checked his watch again. Ten o'clock. Surely she would be here by now.

A young, cheerful receptionist greeted him. "Can I help you?" Her smile grew when she looked up from her desk.

David ran a hand through his hair. "Ah, yeah. Could I talk to Dr. Adams please?"

Patti, or so her name tag said, stood and adjusted her formfitting smock. "I'll go get her." She batted her eyes at him like she had lint in them.

David turned to look out the front windows and shook his head.

He heard a commotion in the back of the clinic and turned to see what was happening. A woman with dark hair twisted up in a clip held a syringe in one hand and was wrestling a large mongrel with the other. David ran to the end of the hall and grabbed the dog with both hands, one around his middle and the other around his muzzle. The woman planted the needle in the dog's hind quarter and then pushed the syringe down. She sat on her heels petting the dog until he slid down on his side on the floor, relaxed, and was out.

"Thank you." She looked over at David.

"Dr. Adams?"

"No, I'm her nursing assistant, Abbey."

David should have known. She was wearing a light blue smock rather than a doctor's white jacket. "You're welcome." He drew his hand along the dog's hind quarter. "He was not happy."

"Yeah, poor guy, he was really scared. Sometimes we need to put them to sleep to even examine them. Dr. Cahn was in another room when he went ballistic. We always have a syringe ready, just in case. Whew."

David looked past Abbey, wondering about Dr. Adams. "Do you know where Dr. Adams might be?"

"In examining room four. You can stick your head in."

"Okay, thanks, Abbey."

"No, thank you for helping with this guy." Abbey and a young man who wore a similar blue smock picked up the dog and together took him into examining room two.

David knocked on door number four. No answer. He could hear something going on in the room, so he cracked the door and said, "Hello."

A guy who was probably an aide, since he was wearing a brown smock, looked up from the floor where he was cleaning up a yellow pool of liquid. "Hi. Can I help you?"

"Yeah, I'm trying to find Dr. Adams."

"Oh, she left a few minutes ago. Emergency out at the Randolph farm."

David blew out the breath he had been holding. "Well, I tried."

"Tried?"

"Nothing. I'll just leave her a note at the front desk."

"Okay."

David asked Patti to leave Dr. Adams a message that he had stopped in to meet her at the request of his mother. "Oh, would you also tell her I really enjoyed spending time with her son? Thanks."

When she was finished writing his dictation, Patti looked up, batting her eyelashes again. "Is there anything else I can help you with?"

"Ah, no. Thank you, though."

FORTY-FOUR

Maddie spotted several people gathered under a large oak tree receiving instructions. "Hey, Granny. Have you got enough people to get these peaches picked before they ripen on the trees?"

Granny laughed. "Oh yes, we have plenty. Too many and they run into each other coming and going. Maddie, you know my son, John, and his wife, Nancy. My grands, Jesse, Jeremiah, and Jonathan—they keep a supply of empty crates on hand to replace the ones that are full. That job keeps them hopping." Granny's eyes went wide when she looked behind Maddie.

Maddie turned around to see George walking up with Duke trotting alongside. "Oh, Granny, this is George, ah . . ." George's grin cut across her train of thought.

"Edwards. George Edwards. Nice to meet you ma'am." George extended a polite hand to Granny and his grin grew.

"Mr. Edwards. I believe we've already met. Well, ran into each other anyway." Granny grinned back at the older man.

Maddie looked from one to the other.

George shrugged. "We literally ran into each other at the café in town. It was my fault, I wasn't looking where I was going."

Granny smiled at the handsome gray-haired man with sparkling eyes. "That's not quite the way I remember it. Thank you for being so kind." A dark shadow ran across her face, and Maddie sent her a questioning glance. "It's nothing, really, Maddie."

"Are you okay, Granny? I've not seen that look on your face before."

"Yes, I'm fine. It's just something I'm working through."

Maddie watched George's smile turn to a grimace. She gave him the *so-are-you-going-to-tell-me-what's-going-on?* look.

George bent down to pat Duke's head. "Okay if Duke hangs out with us? I hate to leave him alone all day."

"Of course. Hi, Duke."

The dog sniffed Granny's hand and then gave it a full lick with his tongue.

Maddie laughed. "I think he likes you."

"Well, shall we get started?" Granny waved her hand toward the orchard.

Maddie looked into the orchard where others were already on ladders and some walking beneath the trees, with what looked like canvas baby carriers hung over their shoulders. They were dropping peaches in the pouch in front as fast as their hands could pick. "Sure. Just tell us where you want us and how to do this and we're on it."

Heading to the row of trees Granny assigned her, Maddie started picking the peaches she could reach from the ground. A funny-looking ladder stood at the end of the row with another woman at the top picking peaches. Maddie couldn't see her face but figured they would eventually meet midway and introduce themselves. Empty crates were positioned on the ground every two to three trees. Granny had instructed them to gently put the peaches in the crates so they didn't get bruised.

George had followed Granny to a far row of trees, and Maddie could hear them talking. "Man, that's a lot of peach trees." George's whistle expressed appreciation for the view in front of him.

"Yes, we have a wonderful orchard. One of the many enterprises my boys have a hand in."

"How many boys do you have?"

"Three. They are all here today. They try to be here for the entire harvest. Sometimes they are called away since Peter is the sheriff and Glenn owns the hardware store in town. I'll introduce you later."

"Okay." Maddie heard George clear his throat. "So, if it's not too forward of me, can I ask what your first name is? I don't really feel comfortable calling you Granny. Especially since I'm probably a lot older than you are."

Maddie grinned.

*   *   *

Granny looked him up and down. He did pose quite a fine figure for a man his age, whatever that was. Wearing a white T-shirt and jeans, she could see toned muscles beneath his deep tan. Granny smiled. "It's Joanna. Joanna Harper."

George extended his hand again, enclosing hers in the warmth of both of his. "Well, very nice to make your acquaintance, Joanna." His eyebrows went up, and he grinned with half his mouth.

Hmm, sassy too. "Nice to meet you—again—George. Shall we get to work?"

"Good idea."

*   *   *

By the time the lunch bell clanged, Maddie's arms and legs felt like over-cooked spaghetti noodles. *I am so out of shape.* She had only filled her pouch and placed the peaches in the crate three times, while the girl on the ladder had made at least six trips to empty her canvas bag. Good thing she wasn't being paid by the bag. She really needed to pick up the pace.

Granny had a full spread set out on makeshift tables of plywood and sawhorses. Part of the agreement was feeding the crew a hearty lunch. The delicious aroma of Granny's home cooking gave Maddie's stomach reason to growl. Summer's farm bounty brought a colorful array of food that made for a sumptuous variety under the orchard trees. To Maddie's thinking, this was the best part of the deal.

After she filled her plate with Granny's delicious fixins Maddie looked around for George so they could sit together to eat their lunch. She glimpsed him coming out of the house, hands full of food, Granny right behind him with her hands just as full.

There looked to be about a dozen people hired to help with the picking. Maddie's scan of the workers stopped abruptly when she saw Nathan Carter at the food table talking to a young woman.

What was he doing here? *I wonder if his fiancée knows he chats it up with other women.*

Nathan looked up and saw her staring. He smiled that heart-melting smile.

Her heart picked up a fast pace, and she could feel the heat run up her neck to her face. *Good grief. Get a grip, Maddie. He's engaged, for Pete's sake.*

She turned around and found a shady spot to sit. The grass was soft and comfortable.

"Hi, Maddie. I'd like you to meet Lydia Lopez. We just met in the food line."

Maddie looked up, and the two women locked eyes. Maddie stood to shake the young woman's hand. "Hi, Lydia. I saw you at the café the other day, didn't I?"

"Hello. Oh, did you?" Her voice was cool. Had Maddie only imagined that flash of—fear—in the dark eyes?

Her curly black hair pulled back in a ponytail made Maddie think of the woman in her row of trees. "Are you working over there in that row on the ladder?"

"I am."

"Me too. You are really good at picking peaches, at least two times faster than I am."

"I've had some experience."

"You have?" Maddie and Nathan said it at the same time.

Lydia shrugged and took a bite of pickle.

"Would you like to sit down in the shade with me?" Maddie broke the silence, her interest in the young woman overriding her caution about spending time with Nathan.

"Sure." Nathan seemed to jump at the chance.

Maddie sighed, instantly regretting the involuntary noise.

"What?" He shrugged and held up one palm.

"Nothing."

Nathan sat while Lydia excused herself to use one of the portable restrooms, and Maddie sat back against the tree trunk.

Maddie kept her eyes on her plate until Nathan spoke up. "I didn't know you were going to help Granny pick peaches."

"That goes for both of us."

"I just love Granny. She is so . . . wise."

"Wise?"

He nodded, a smile growing on his face. "Yeah. She knows exactly who to ask and who to hire. Even though she had an announcement on the bulletin board at the market asking for pickers, she's very picky about who she hires."

"Sounds like you and Granny have become good friends."

"She's great. I know I should be over there working on the reno, but I figured a day or two wouldn't make much difference. Besides, I need to wait for more building supplies to come in. Don't get me wrong, there's plenty to keep me busy until the other supplies arrive." He shot a worried look in Maddie's direction.

"That's good that you still have enough to keep you busy."

Nathan asked his question while looking at the food on his plate, shuffling it around with his fork. "So, why are you here picking peaches?"

Caught off guard, Maddie responded too fast. "Oh, I need the money—the job." She raised her chin slightly, daring him to argue with her.

"You need—" Nathan's head came up fast. "Maddie, please let me help you. Since you wouldn't let me help you with a loan, at least let me help you make the monthly payments until you can get a decent job."

Resenting his pity, Maddie felt her temper flare.

"No." Maddie looked at Nathan's left ring finger. "Does your *fiancée* know you're out here with us peasants picking peaches, meeting with young Hispanic women?" she asked, sarcasm oozing from every word.

Nathan's eyes flashed. Teeth clenched, he looked her square in the eyes. "What is it with you? Do you enjoy raising my blood pressure and making me angry?"

Maddie sat proud.

"Fine." Nathan took a slow breath and released it. "First of all, I'm not married or engaged."

"You're not—"

He held up his left hand. "The wedding was not just postponed; I called it off."

"Oh."

"Second, I don't consider any of these people peasants. I consider them friends. Including you."

"Oh." Maddie bent her head and looked down at her shoes.

"Third, I just met Lydia in the food line, and I was welcoming her to Jacob's Bend. I think she's new here."

Maddie felt her heart drop to her knees. "Oh."

Nathan crossed his arms over his chest. "Is that all you have to say?"

Maddie looked at her plate, her appetite gone. When she looked back up into his incredible blue eyes, shame and guilt streamed through her. All she could say was, "Yes."

Nathan cocked his head in that questioning way he had.

"I'm sorry. Really I am. You'd think I'd learn not to assume about others with all the assumptions others have made about me over the years. I'm sorry, Nathan."

His gaze held a question, but he did not ask it. "It's okay. Assumptions happen with all of us."

"Thank you for being so understanding."

The bell clanged for the workers to start picking again.

Maddie dumped her half-full paper plate in the trash, emotions in turmoil as she picked up her canvas bag and walked back to her row of trees.

FORTY-FIVE

Lydia looked down from the deep foliage surrounding her when she heard someone call her name.

"Lydia."

She moved out from under the thick growth of leaves and peaches and saw the redhead looking up into the tree, her hand shielding her eyes from the sun.

"I didn't mean to scare you off. I'm sorry if I offended you in any way. I'm learning that assumptions and probing questions are not what make a person feel welcome in a new place. Can we start over?"

"Ah, sure," Lydia agreed.

The woman nodded and turned to her end of the row and began picking.

Lydia watched her row mate reach up under the lower leaves of the tree and pick faster than she had before lunch. She wasn't so bad. Still, if Lydia didn't need the money she'd leave right now. She needed to find a new place to live. Maybe someone who was picking had a place to rent. Preferably way out here in the country where no one could track her down. Maybe she could find a job out here. At least she would have work as long as they needed fruit and vegetable pickers. Possibly even into the fall with the grapes.

*   *   *

Maddie thought back to Nathan's words about waiting for building supplies to come in. It would help if she actually ordered the next bunch of supplies. She would do that tomorrow morning before she headed to Granny's. Billy

172

and David were gone and she didn't know how long she'd have Nathan. Good grief, he was not married or even engaged. Maddie chided herself as her thoughts started to wander. *Don't even go there. You two are definitely not meant to be together. You would kill each other.*

But she would not be unequally yoked with him.

Her eyes popped open. She had just told herself that they were not meant to be together. She needed to move on. No matter how lonely she was, Nathan was not the man for her.

When Maddie arrived home that evening, the light on her answering machine was blinking. She really needed to get rid of the landline and that machine and just use her cell. She punched a button that stopped the red light from blinking.

"Hello, Mrs. Crane, this is Devin Chamberlain, bank manager in Jacob's Bend. Could you please give me a call when you receive this message?"

Maddie looked at the clock on the wall. It was six thirty. Too late to call him back tonight. She'd call him in the morning. She wondered what was going on. Gram's words came to her: *"Don't borrow trouble from tomorrow when there is plenty to go around today."*

The next morning Mr. Chamberlain was all politeness and business, asking about her project and the progress she was making.

"As much as I appreciate your kind questions, is there a reason why we are having this conversation?"

The man on the other end of the phone cleared his throat with a slight cough. "Yes, well, Mrs. Crane, I wouldn't normally do this, but you being a widow and—"

"Mr. Chamberlain." Maddie could feel the heat come up her neck.

"Ah, yes. I wanted to inform you that your loan has been purchased, something that often happens. And you will be receiving a notice giving you ninety days to pay off the loan."

Maddie sat down hard on the couch, her mind in a haze.

"Mrs. Crane, are you still there?"

"Who did this? Who bought it and wants it paid off in such a short time? Can they even do that?"

"I assure you, unfortunately, they can and have. As far as who, I'm not at liberty to divulge that information. Privacy act, you know. Besides, they want to remain anonymous."

"But how do I contact them and let them know I can't possibly pay off the loan in ninety days?"

Silence on the other end of the phone.

"Mr. Chamberlain?"

"I'm really sorry about this, Mrs. Crane. We pride ourselves on being a hometown bank here to help our customers prosper in their endeavors. We feel like our customers are more like a big family."

"Then how could you let someone come in and destroy the dreams of one of your family members? Mr. Chamberlain . . . Devin, we've been friends since I moved to Jacob's Bend and I've been faithful in paying on my loan—"

"I know, Maddie. I'm really sorry. This all happened without my knowledge or I would have done everything possible to stop it. But my hands are tied."

Maddie bowed her head, her hand on her forehead. "Isn't there anything I can do? I'm guessing you know I only have one renter leasing my land."

"Yes, well, you could sell off a portion of your land to pay off the loan. Your property is worth a lot more than the loan amount."

"In ninety days?" Panic shouted into the phone.

Devin let out a long breath. "I know."

"Besides, I don't want to sell any of my land."

"I'm sorry, Maddie."

"Yeah, okay. I'll figure something out. I have to. Thank you for letting me know."

*   *   *

When the pickers stopped for lunch the following day, Nathan saw the feisty redhead sitting under the same tree as yesterday barely eating any of her food. Lydia sat a few feet from her, glancing over at Maddie every so often.

"Hey, ladies. Got room for one more?"

Lydia looked up at Nathan, then over at Maddie for her comment.

Maddie didn't even look up.

Lydia shrugged. "Sure. Have a seat."

Nathan kept his eyes on Maddie as he ate his food. Her body language said sad and hopeless. "So, how many crates have you two filled?"

Lydia looked to Maddie.

Maddie lifted her eyes to Nathan. He could tell she was in another place.

"Maddie, are you okay?"

"Huh? Yes. No." She put her elbows on her knees and her head in her hands. "I don't know what I'm going to do. Someone bought my loan from the bank and they want full payment in just a few months. There is no way I can do that since I only have one renter left."

"What? Who bought your loan?"

"I don't know. Mr. Chamberlain at the bank can't give out that information. I'm going to lose Broken Acres." Tears fell through her hands to the ground.

"Not if I can help it."

Sniffing, Maddie wiped away her tears. "No, Nathan. I'm not going to let you bail me out. I need to find a way out myself."

"But, Maddie, how can you—"

"No, I mean it." A lightning storm of frustration, insecurity, and determination spewed from her eyes.

If she had a way to breathe out fire, he was sure she would.

Frustrated, he held his hands up in front of his face, palms out. "Okay, okay. Relax."

"Relax? Are you kidding?"

"Sorry, bad choice of words."

"Ah, Maddie, I know you don't know me very well, but I could use a place to rent." Nathan could see the hope in Lydia's eyes.

"Oh, the renters I'm talking about lease land. They're farmers, cattlemen, and some who raise horses."

Lydia nodded, disappointment visible on her face. "Where do you live?"

"About six miles west of Jacob's Bend. I own 427 acres. Broken Acres."

"Broken Acres?"

Maddie grinned through her tear-reddened eyes. "Yeah, that's what I named my farm. Long story."

Lydia shook her head. "The owners are going to sell the place I'm renting now."

Nathan recognized her posture. *This young woman feels hopeless.*

Maddie spoke up, obviously avoiding Nathan's gaze. "You could stay with me in the cottage and rent the spare bedroom. Now that my son is at Forest Hills University it's kind of lonely out there."

A flood of emotions rushed across Lydia's face.

"What do you think? Would you like to come out and see the place? I can only offer you ninety days." She laughed. "But it might be enough time for you to find something else."

"I couldn't stay in your house."

"Nathan is restoring the big house or you could have lived in one of those rooms."

"Big house?"

"There are two houses on the property," Nathan broke in. "The cottage Maddie lives in and the big house I'm renovating."

"I plan to rent out the rooms in the big house to"—Maddie looked over Lydia's head, as if seeing another time—"hurting and broken people."

Lydia sat up straight. "When you are done with the renovation, I could rent one of those rooms?"

Maddie looked over at Nathan. "Yes, if I can figure out this mess."

"But right now you only have ninety days left to be there," Nathan reminded them both.

Lydia's eyes slowly moved to Nathan.

Maddie ground her teeth, jaw tight. "Not if I can help it."

FORTY-SIX

When her cell phone chimed, Maddie wasn't sure she wanted to talk to anyone. What was she going to do? She couldn't possibly come up with the money to pay off the loan in sixty days. *Unless—*

"Hello."

"Maddie, me girl. How would you be farin' out there on the farm?"

"Gael. It's so good to hear your voice. How was Ireland?"

"Me folks were glad to see me and I them. But I did miss this place and you."

Maddie smiled. "Did you find some new things for O'Donnell's Brier?"

"That I did. Seems I'm always findin' somethin' fun and different for me little shop. You'll be needin' to come over and see the lace curtains I'd be thinkin' would add just the right touch to your livin' room windows."

Maddie closed her eyes. "If I even have those windows much longer."

"What are ya sayin' girl?"

After sharing the news about her loan being sold and the now sixty-day deadline, Maddie wondered aloud, "I'm hoping Isaac has been able to unfreeze my assets."

"Now that would be a sure and certain blessin' then."

"Well, it would certainly help. I've already lost thirty days trying to get another loan. No one"—*except Nathan*—"will give me a loan. My income is not stable enough."

"Oh my. And why would Devin Chamberlain be sellin' your loan in the first place?"

"Good question. Not sure I have an answer."

"Well, I'll be askin' some questions of Mr. Chamberlain when we have dinner this week. There's got to be a way to be fixin' this."

"I hope you're right, Gael."

*   *   *

The next morning Maddie heard a single hammer pounding away over at the big house. It brought back memories of when Nathan first started working on the house all alone, without Billy or David. *What is he doing over there? I thought he couldn't do anything until more supplies were delivered.*

Maddie released her thoughts of Nathan and spent the morning cleaning house. When she sat down on the porch swing to eat her sandwich, she heard a power saw at the house on the other side of the apple orchard. A slight pang of guilt ran across her thoughts. Maybe she'd call him and see if he wanted a sandwich. Maddie picked up her cell to call him. Her phone was dead. "Good grief, Maddie, can't you even remember to charge your phone?" After attaching the phone to the cord plugged into the wall socket, she took a walk over to the big house.

Shading her eyes she looked up to the second floor where the pounding and sawing had come from. "Nathan."

The man stuck his head and shoulders out the upstairs window. Surprise evident on his face, he looked down and grinned. "Yeah?"

His brilliant smile caught her eyes until she realized he was without a shirt, his tan muscles gleaming with sweat from the warm afternoon. She pulled in a deep breath and turned her gaze to the front porch.

"Yeah? Do you need something, Maddie?"

Did she need something? Why did she come over here? *Think, Maddie, think.*

She could hear his boots pounding down the stairs inside, heading her way. When he walked over to her, all she could do was stare and follow his hand when he wiped sweat from his forehead, then down to his well-fitting jeans where he wiped his hand dry.

He frowned. "Everything okay?"

Her heartbeat picked up speed, her breathing coming in short, shallow breaths. *Okay? Okay? I don't think it is. Breathe, Maddie. Breathe.*

"Ah, no, it's not. I've been thinking about my last conversation with my financial consultant. My assets are still frozen."

He shrugged. "And?"

"I know you already know that." She took a quick breath. "Well, I was hoping they would be unfrozen so I could pay off my loan and place another order for supplies."

"And?" He crossed his arms over his well-defined chest.

Maddie puffed her cheeks out with the breath she had been holding. "And they're still frozen."

"You already said that."

She looked deep into his mesmerizing blue eyes. Tears welled up behind her own. "Nathan, I'm going to lose Broken Acres."

Silently, he pulled her into his chest, wrapping his arms around her.

Her tears became a full-on sobbing cry. She wrapped her arms around his waist and laid her head on his chest. She inhaled his scent, salty sweat from hard work, the faint whiff of aftershave, but mostly just him.

Maddie looked up into his eyes that said, "Let me help you," and felt her emotions spiral out of control. Looking up at his six-foot-plus height towering over her, she pulled his head down so his lips met hers.

His lips were gentle, surprisingly so, as she felt again the strength of his arms. She pulled back and ran her hand over his strong shoulders and down to his chest. With a passion she had not felt in a long time—maybe never—she wrapped her arms around his neck and sought his lips again.

Nathan pulled her closer and kissed her like he couldn't get enough of her, his hands caressing her hair that rested on her shoulders.

Her mind was a whirlwind of careless wanderings. *I want this. I want him.*

Suddenly Nathan pulled away. With his hands on her arms, breathing labored, he closed his eyes. He stepped back and ran his hand through his thick hair. "Maddie, we can't do this."

Startled by the sudden change in demeanor, she blinked several times and tried to comprehend what he was saying.

He swallowed and rubbed the stubble on his chin. "Maddie, you do not know how much I want this. How much I want you. But we can't, not like this."

"Why not?" She took a step toward him.

The surprised look in his eyes caught her off guard. "Isn't this what you wanted in the past?"

"I did."

"But . . .?"

He scratched the back of his head. "But." He closed his eyes again.

Maddie crossed her arms over her chest.

When he opened his eyes he looked over at the cottage across the orchard. "And a few months ago I would have picked you up and carried you up to the loft and . . ."

She could feel the hurt and anger growing. "And now?"

"Now I can't do that."

She gave him a laser stare. "Why?"

He looked over her head to the acres spread out beyond. "I can't because . . ." He shook his head. "Maddie, because you are going to lose Broken Acres, you think this will ease the pain?"

Confusion and disappointment filled her eyes.

"Will you please let me help you?"

Maddie gave her head a shake, trying to clear it from his previous words. "Absolutely not."

"But—"

"No. Especially not after . . . after—" She turned and quickly walked back to the cottage. Memories of Jeff flashed through her mind. Rejection had just slapped her hard in the face. Again.

FORTY-SEVEN

Maddie asked Lydia if she needed help moving her things into the cottage. She declined, saying she didn't have much. When she showed up at the door with two suitcases and a duffel, Maddie had to agree.

"I don't want to take advantage of your kindness, Maddie. I've been wondering, have you found a way to keep your property?" She glanced out the large picture windows over at the big house.

"No, not yet, but I'm still trying."

Maddie knew she had to somehow get an extension on her loan, but with the buyer wanting to stay anonymous, she wasn't sure how to go about it.

"Well, in the meantime, if you want any help with renovations, I'm strong and I can help with anything when I'm not picking somewhere."

"Thank you, Lydia. I appreciate that. I know what a hard worker you are. I'll keep that in mind."

*   *   *

Her cell played a cute little tune, and Maddie smiled as her daughter's picture popped up. "Hey, sweetie. How are you?"

"Hey, Mom. I'm good."

"What's going on?"

Bracy cleared her throat and stammered. "Oh . . . so . . . I'm just gonna say it."

Maddie pulled out a kitchen chair and sat. "What's wrong?"

181

"Nothing is wrong. I'm just tired of being clear on the other side of the world from you and David. It's lonely here and—"

"Other side of the world? You're being a little dramatic, don't you think?"

"Well, that's what it feels like."

"I understand. Really I do. But you only have one more year to finish college and then you can move out here." But if she lost Broken Acres . . . No. There was going to be a way to keep it—there had to be.

"That's, ah, that's why I'm calling. I've decided to take a year off and transfer to Forest Hills with David after I get Oregon resident status."

Silence.

"Mom. Mom, are you still there?"

"I'm here."

"So what do you think?"

"Bracy, I get that you're lonely. I've been there. But you have a four-year scholarship to Wheaton. You would give that up?"

"I figure I can get a job and save the money, at least a good portion of it, and I can help you on the farm. Please, Mom. I miss you, and I can't stand being here any longer. I . . . I feel so isolated here."

"That's a funny way of putting it."

"Well, I don't really have anyone here I can talk to. Anyone I can trust."

"Bracy, I have to remind you that you only have one year left."

"Mom, my advisor is the snootiest woman I've ever met. Besides, in the last three years I haven't really made any good friends. They're all into partying. You'd think at a Christian college they would grow up and realize what's important and get their priorities straight. If there's one thing this place has shown me it's that there are phony Christians who put on an act in front of people and then do whatever feels good to them in private. And if you don't join them, they treat you like you've got the plague."

Maddie could hear Bracy suck in a breath like she was going to start in again. "Bracy, I can understand you feeling alone there with David and me on the other side of the map and Ruth in Texas. But it's only one more year. Are you sure this is a good idea?"

"Mom, I want to make a difference in this world. Help other women. Help them know the truth about God."

God again.

"And I want to start now. Please, Mom."

Maddie could just hear Jeff . . . *"She's just like her mother. Determined. Strong-willed."* At least that's how she was when they'd gotten married. Maddie groaned.

"My little rebel. Sounds like you've thought a lot about this. I love that you stand for what is right and good." Maddie thought again about her next statement. "Although if it's like that at Wheaton, I imagine it's a lot more bleak at FHU. It's not a Christian college."

"I know, but I'll have David, and I want to be where my family is. There is nothing for me in Illinois. Please, Mom, try to understand."

"I do understand, and if you feel this strongly about it, I say, come on. We'll figure it out together."

Bracy chuckled. "My mom, the rebel. I wonder where I got it?"

Maddie smiled. "Yeah, I've been called that more than once. It could be worse. You could have my freckles like poor Ruth."

"Funny, Mom."

"But I should let you know, there is some uncertainty about whether or not I'll still own Broken Acres in a few months."

"What?"

"It's a long story, and we can discuss it on our drive back here. I really do think we'll be able to find a way to keep my—our home. So when do you want me to come and help you move out?"

"Well, that's not necessary. Especially since I'm already at the Walters' place staying in that cute little room you told me about with the bed with the yellow comforter and tiny purple flowers that match the curtains. And the purple and lavender pansy wallpaper. They shared how on your drive out to Jacob's Bend they had to pull you out of a muddy ravine in a thunderstorm. You left out some of the best parts when you shared the story."

"What? You're staying at the Walters' home? You are there right now?"

"Yeah, I thought I'd better call you on the first leg of the trip, just in case you were going to take a little more convincing. Mr. and Mrs. Walters are great, and they send their love. I'll be leaving early tomorrow morning. I'm pulling a small U-Haul trailer."

Maddie laughed. "Bracy, you have so much of me in you. You have your Dad's good looks and my adventurous spirit."

"It's been a wonderful trip so far. I love the beauty of the countryside."

"I know, it is beautiful. Be careful. And call me each night when you stop."

"Okay, I will."

"Oh, and stay completely away from Sam's Bar and Grill."

"I don't think you need to worry about that, Mom. I'll call you tomorrow night. Love you."

FORTY-EIGHT

Bracy's jaw dropped when she crested the hill overlooking Jacob's Bend. She pulled to the side of the road at the lookout. Shielding her eyes from the sun with her hand, she couldn't believe the beautiful expanse before her. No wonder her mom and David loved it here. When she came for a quick visit at semester break, it was dark when her mom and she arrived from the airport in Portsmouth and dark when they drove back.

It was breathtaking. She grinned at the feeling she hadn't experienced since before her dad died. A feeling of security, that all was well.

It's home.

Bracy remembered the little shops in town and how everybody knew everybody else, like one big family. Maybe Gael could give her a job? She seemed like a great lady, beautiful inside and out, and Bracy loved her Irish accent. But she'd probably need to make more than Gael could afford to pay. *Oh well, God, You know exactly where I need to work, and I'm excited to see where that is and what kind of job it is.*

The large red chipped mailbox with Broken Acres painted on the side made Bracy smile. When she got out to open the gate, she remembered the long list of things her mom wanted to upgrade on the farm. A solar gate was on the bottom of that list. The hinge on the gate squeaked as she pushed it to the left. After driving through she got out and pulled the gate shut and latched it. Cresting the hill overlooking Broken Acres, the view once again took her breath away. The apple orchard was resplendent with what looked like a bumper crop of red and green apples. Bracy breathed deep. "Home."

*   *   *

"Maddie, I can find another place to rent."

"No, you can't. Lydia, Broken Acres is your home. You aren't going anywhere."

"But Bracy—"

"Listen, as long as you're okay with it, you and Bracy can bunk together. I have a rollaway. I've thought about it, and since you will be sharing with my daughter rather than having your own room, there's no reason for you to pay rent. This is all about family. And you are now a part of our family."

"But—"

"Nope. No buts."

"What about the money you need for the loan?"

"I'll figure it out. Besides, it's not your problem; it's mine."

Lydia cleared her throat. "Family?"

Maddie laughed. "Okay, yes, family. *We'll* figure it out."

Just then a little red four-door sedan with a U-Haul trailer pulled up in front of the cottage.

"Bracy." Maddie ran down the front steps and pulled her daughter into a tight hug. "You're here." She put her hands on her daughter's shoulders and stepped back to look at her.

Bracy smiled. "I'm home, Mom. Home."

"Yes, you are."

Lydia stood on the porch, Rusty at her side.

"Bracy, this is Lydia. She's the one I told you about who has been renting the spare room. You and Lydia will be roommates until—" Maddie looked over at the big house.

"Until?"

Maddie faced Bracy once again. "Until we finish the big house, and then she is going to rent one of the rooms there. She'll be our first resident."

"Hi, Lydia. It's great to meet you. Mom tells me you are a primo peach picker."

Lydia grinned. "Yeah, that's me, primo peach picker. It's really good exercise, up and down the ladder, stretching to get that one peach that is out of reach."

"Wish I could have been here for the harvest."

"Oh, there's plenty of grapes to be harvested come fall."

Maddie hugged Bracy's shoulder. "Well, let's go have some dinner. Your favorite, beef stroganoff."

"Mom, I have missed your stroganoff. Peach cobbler for dessert?"

"Yep."

*   *   *

Adjusting to the time change took Bracy several days. When Sarg landed on her stomach and meowed loudly early one morning, she cracked one eye open and squinted out the side window. "Hey, you. The sun is barely up." The cat's yowl got louder. "Okay, okay. Quiet down, you'll wake Lydia. Let's take a walk to the living room."

Sarg jumped down and ran to the front door, pacing. Bracy gently shut the bedroom door and let the cat out to do his business. Rusty trotted down the stairs from the loft and went to the door. Bracy put her fingers to her lips. "Shh. Don't bark, buddy," she whispered.

Letting him out, she grabbed her sweatshirt from the hook on the wall, punched the on button of the coffee maker, slipped on her tennis shoes, and walked onto the porch to greet the morning. "Absolutely beautiful. Lord, You created quite a pallet of beauty when You made Broken Acres. Thank You for this brand-new day." The quiet beep of the coffee maker took her back to the kitchen.

Mug in hand, she sat on the top step of the porch and watched the cattle that grazed below. A couple of babies chased one another. Setting her cup on the step, she pulled her sweatshirt around her, zipped the front, and headed to the field where the calves played. Closing the heavy gate behind her, she wandered to the middle of the pasture and put her hand out in front of her, calling the little calf. "Come on, don't be afraid, I won't hurt you. I just want to pet you." The calf looked up at her with gentle cow eyes. "Hey, little guy. You are so soft."

A loud snort and scuffling caught her attention. When she looked up, a cow with a full udder pawed the ground and bent her head low. Bracy's eyes grew wide.

All of a sudden an arm wrapped around her from the back and pulled her up on a horse that galloped clear across the field to the gate.

Kicking and screaming, Bracy tried to break loose from the strong hold around her waist. Breathing hard, she could barely release the scream that lodged in her throat.

Whoever had picked her up bent down to open the gate, with one hand securely around her as she sat sideways in the front part of the saddle. The other hand closed the gate behind them just in time, as the mama cow came tearing across the pasture to make sure the intruder had gone.

Bracy's breathing came heavy. Her entire body trembled. She looked the man in the eyes, pushed at his chest, and forced his hand from around her middle. Falling hard to the ground, she closed her eyes and caught her breath.

"Are you all right?" A male voice spoke to her, offering a hand to help her up.

Disoriented and heart beating hard, Bracy looked up into questioning, compassionate hazel eyes. The ground felt wet and cold on her backside.

It's not him. Bracy held her hand to her chest; her heart was racing. She closed her eyes again and held her breath. Now she was lightheaded. She felt faint and told herself to breathe. She didn't have to be afraid. It. Was. Not. Him.

Bracy jumped to her feet, wiping the dirt from her legs and bottom. "I . . . ah. Thank you."

"What were you doing in the pasture? That mama could have trampled you to death if she had reached you. Petting a baby calf is not a good idea."

"No kidding. I think I got that. Everything happened so fast, but it felt like it was happening in slow motion. Whew."

"Yeah, whew is right. Where did you come from?"

She pointed toward the cottage.

"Maddie's?"

"You know my mom?"

"You're Maddie's daughter?"

"Yes. My name is Bracy. Who are you?"

The man climbed back on his horse and offered his hand to her. "Let me take you up to the cottage and then we'll get the introductions out of the way."

"I'll . . . I'll walk."

When they reached the cottage, the man jumped down from his horse. He held the reins in his left hand and touched her shoulder with his right.

Bracy jumped back three steps, eyes wide.

"I'm sorry. Are you hurt?"

"No, I'm not hurt. You just startled me."

"Jase, what's going on? Bracy?" Her mom held a mug of steaming coffee in her hand as she stepped from the porch swing.

"Mom, this guy, this nice man, just rescued me from a not-so-happy mama cow."

"Jase?" Her mom lifted a brow.

"She was petting a calf."

"What?"

"So, you're Jase?" Bracy turned to the flustered man.

"Ah, yeah. Well, actually Jasper Worthington III, but everybody calls me Jase."

Bracy took a deep breath and extended her hand. "Nice to meet you, Jase. Thank you for scooping me up out there."

"I'm glad I came out for an early morning ride to check on the cattle, otherwise . . ."

Bracy shook her head. "I don't want to think about the otherwise. I'm *so* not in the city anymore. I have got a lot to learn about Broken Acres and these animals."

Jase smiled big. His perfect white teeth set in his handsome tanned face caused Bracy to catch her breath.

"Cup of coffee, Jase?" Her mom held up her mug.

"No thanks, Maddie. Need to go finish checking the cattle."

"Okay, we'll see you later. Thanks for saving my girl. Good grief, Bracy, that's something I would have done."

FORTY-NINE

A tall man in a black hoodie smiled as Bracy jogged past him toward her dorm room. She smiled back and gave him a little wave. When she got to the covered bridge, her favorite part of the run, she heard another jogger coming up behind her. She was a little surprised another student was out jogging this late. Never having run at ten in the evening, she didn't see any of the daytime regulars. She should have waited till tomorrow, but it had already been three days. She needed some exercise and some sink time in the lab so she could think through what Professor Harris had lectured on.

Science was definitely not her best subject. Before that thought had a chance to register, a strong arm reached around her waist and a hand clamped over her mouth. Someone picked her up and pulled her, kicking with all her might, into the bushes on the other side of the bridge. He threw her to the ground—

"Bracy. Bracy."

A soft whisper in her ear, a gentle touch on her shoulder. Wide-eyed she sat up, arms fighting off her attacker.

"Bracy, it's me, Lydia."

"W-what? Who's there?"

Bracy glanced around the dark room into tender brown eyes. Lydia sat on the edge of Bracy's rollaway. "Are you okay? You were thrashing and kicking and groaning."

"Huh? Yeah, I'm okay."

"Are you sure? There is terror written all over your face."

She took several deep breaths to slow her heart rate. "Oh, Lydia. Thank you for waking me up. I was having an awful nightmare."

Lydia closed her eyes. "I know what that's like."

"You do?"

"Yeah." Lydia looked to the other side of the room, staring into the dark night.

"What do you have nightmares about?"

Lydia shrugged, scooted over to her bed, and pushed her back up against the wall, her arms hugging pajama-clad knees tight to her chest.

Bracy turned on the lamp that sat on a small table between the two beds. She could feel the terror that lingered from the nightmare.

Lydia turned and looked into Bracy's eyes. "So what's causing your nightmares?"

Bracy rubbed her forehead. Explaining the nightmare was only part of the story. *Can I trust her with this? Maybe if I share it with someone, the nightmares will stop.*

Bracy hesitated, then shook her head. "Okay, you cannot tell anyone, especially Mom. I don't ever want her to know. It . . ." Bracy swallowed hard. "It would kill her. I can't add this to everything else she's going through. Or all the hard stuff she has already gone through."

Lydia nodded. "Okay, deal. I won't say a word."

"My nightmare really happened. I've been reliving it in my dreams for months."

Lydia's eyes went wide.

"I went jogging late one night on campus. I should have waited until the next day, but it had already been three days since I had a chance to run." Bracy closed her eyes tight and began to tremble all over.

"There weren't many people around except for this one guy who had smiled at me as he walked by. When I got to the covered bridge, I thought I heard another jogger coming up behind me. Before I knew what was happening, a powerful arm reached around my waist and a hand clamped over my mouth. He picked me up and pulled me into the bushes on the other side of the bridge." Tears cascaded down Bracy's cheeks. Her breathing accelerated, her heartbeat quickening.

"After he dragged me into the bushes—" she swallowed the lump in her throat and looked down at the floor—"he pinned me to the ground with his body, stuffed something in my mouth, and held a knife to my neck. He ripped my shirt down the front and . . . and . . . told me to lie still or he would kill me."

Bracy's trembling increased. Her hands were cold as ice.

"Oh, Bracy." Lydia reached to take her hands. "You're freezing." Lydia grabbed the quilt off her bed and wrapped it around Bracy's shivering body. "You don't have to tell me the rest."

"I don't know how long I laid there after he ran off." Bracy took a deep breath and shook her head.

"Did you go to the police?"

"No, I was too ashamed. And I knew David would find the guy and kill him. Not to mention what my mom would do. That myth about redheads' tempers is not a myth. At least not with my mom and brother."

"Bracy, I'm so sorry."

She attempted a half-hearted grin at the agony she saw in Lydia's eyes.

"Would you recognize him if you saw him again?"

"No, probably not. It was dark, we were in thick bushes . . ."

"And?" Lydia tipped her head.

"I just now thought of something. Why didn't I think this was weird before now?"

"What?"

"He was wearing dark glasses . . . at night."

"That is weird. Obviously so you wouldn't be able to identify him."

Bracey shivered and let the words tumble out. "The next day I went to the campus nurse to ask questions about pregnancy tests and STDs. She gave me some information, and when I didn't have my cycle the next month I was terrified. But when I took the test it said I wasn't pregnant. I went online to check information about rape. I read that stress from the event could cause the woman's cycle to be abnormal for some time."

"Oh my gosh, Bracy. That waiting must have been horrible. Didn't you tell any of your friends at school?"

"No. I didn't really have any good friends I could trust there. And I was so ashamed." She shrugged. "It's my own fault. I never should have been out there all alone jogging at ten o'clock at night."

"No." Lydia sat up abruptly, her eyes flashing. "It is not your fault, and you've got to stop saying it is. I agree that wasn't the best thing to be doing alone at that hour, but that doesn't give some pervert the right to rape you."

Bracy wrapped the blanket closer.

FIFTY

Bracy closed her eyes and then opened them wide. "Thank you, Lydia. I know that's true, but it's hard to accept."

Lydia nodded and touched Bracy's hand that held the blanket tight.

Bracy wiped her cheeks with the back of her hand. "So, what are your nightmares about? Hopefully nothing like mine."

Lydia gave a wry grin. "Well, mostly they are about gangs and how they're always warring with each other. They're brutal, targeting each other. Seeking retribution. Or so it's called."

Lydia's small frame shivered. Bracy touched her shoulder to give her reassurance and comfort. "Were you in a gang?"

"No." The Hispanic woman held both hands up in front of her. "Thank God."

"Then how do you know about the retribution thing?"

Lydia took a deep breath. Fear settled over her face.

"Bracy, you are the only person I've ever shared this with. You have to promise not to tell another living soul."

Bracy pulled her blanket tighter around her torso and sat on the floor, her back against the rollaway. "I promise."

Lydia joined her on the floor, grabbing a blanket on her way down.

"I used to live in the San Joaquin Valley in California. My brother and I were pickers on the farms there. Lots of produce and lots of poverty. We were poor, but our family was happy. Actually, Mom, Dad, Jose, and I all picked. Mom and Dad wanted my brother and me to go to college, and they saved every bit they could so that dream could become a reality."

"Was your brother, Jose, in a gang then?"

"No." Lydia's eyes blazed. "His dream was to one day own a vineyard. He wanted to go to school to learn viticulture and oenology and become a vintner."

"And did he?"

Lydia bowed her head and pulled the blanket tight around her. "No."

"What happened?"

Lydia slowly lifted her head, her eyes glistening. "He was shot and killed by the leader of one of the gangs."

Bracy sat up and leaned over to touch the other woman's hand. "Oh, Lydia. I'm so sorry."

"I saw it go down. It was late one night. Jose and I went to the little store in our neighborhood for some ice cream. When we walked out of the store, two cars sped into the parking lot, squealing their brakes. We stopped cold. This guy came from somewhere behind us. He started shooting at the guys who jumped out of the cars. I hit the ground, but Jose froze like a deer in the headlights. I knew the leader of the gang, Victor, who was in one of the cars. He shot and killed the guy with the gun, and then he shot Jose."

"Oh, Lydia. That must have been a nightmare."

"It was. It still is."

Bracy nodded. "How did you get out alive?"

"Someone in the store had called the cops and just about the time Victor pointed the gun in my direction, they pulled around the corner, lights flashing, sirens blaring, surrounding Victor and his gang members."

"Wow."

"Yeah." Lydia closed her eyes. "I can still see Jose lying facedown on the ground, blood oozing from his body. The DA asked me to testify against Victor. So I did and they put him away for life, but his buddies, especially his brother who took the gang leader position after Victor went to prison, threatened to track me down. After the trial they put me and my mom and dad in the witness protection program. With my new name, Lydia Lopez—"

"Wait, that's not your real name?"

"No. They moved Mom and Dad to another state, thinking it would be safer if we were separated. I hated to be separated from what family I had left, but I knew it was best for their safety. I don't even know where they are." A tear fell on her blanket. "They moved me to Texas and found me a job in this local theatre group doing makeup. It seems I was a natural."

"Wow."

"But funny things kept happening."

"Funny things?"

"I always felt like I was being watched. Then one day when I was at the market, I saw a car pull up outside and I swear it was Victor's brother with his buddies. The car had a California license plate. So I slipped out the back service entrance, went to my place, packed, and took off. I ended up here in Jacob's Bend, living in this run-down shack in town. I dressed and made myself up to look like an old lady." She smiled. "Actually, the kids called me Witch Hazel."

"You're Witch Hazel? Mom told me about you. She tried every way she knew to help you, she felt so bad for you."

"She did?"

"Yeah."

"I didn't know that. I did see her outside my shack one time and then she came another time to talk to me. I kept trying to get her to leave me alone so no one else would take notice of me."

"You remember what you just said to me? Just because I was out late by myself that didn't give some pervert the right to rape me? Well, what happened to you doesn't give some crazy gang leader the right to keep you in fear hiding out and not having a life."

"True." Lydia hung her head. "It's not how I want to live my life." She looked up. "And I'm guessing you don't want to live the rest of your life afraid of men."

"No, I don't. When Jase grabbed me from behind and rescued me from that mama cow, it took me back. I had a panic attack as soon as I hit the ground when I fought for him to release me."

"I know what you mean. I think it might take some time for both of us to get over those experiences. But maybe together we can help each other. Right?"

"Right." Bracy gave a half grin. "How did you end up at Broken Acres?"

"Your mom."

Bracy smiled at the lovely Hispanic woman sharing her mom's spare-bedroom floor. "My mom. Yep, she's a keeper."

Lydia grinned. "You know, I think she has a sixth sense for people who are hurting and lonely."

"I'd have to agree."

"Sometime after we met, your mom needed a boarder and I needed a place to live. She offered to let me live at Broken Acres. Of course she doesn't know I'm hiding out from Victor's brother." Lydia bent her head and studied her fingers. "Life gets messy, doesn't it?"

"Silence."

"What?" Lydia frowned.

"Sometimes I think silence keeps fear alive. Hiding the truth about what happened to us keeps us in an emotional prison in the same way Victor is in physical prison. We are scared to be honest, truly honest, because we're afraid of what *might* happen." Bracy lifted her hands to air quote the word *might*.

Bracy looked up to see Lydia carefully watching her. She realized she felt a connection to this relative stranger like she hadn't felt since before that terrible night.

"Bracy, you need to tell your mom."

Her comment surprised them both.

Bracy smiled a sideways grin. "I think you should too. Mom needs to know to keep her eyes and ears open for this gang guy."

Lydia nodded. "You're right. But I'm not sure now is the best time with the trouble she's having with the farm and all. We probably ought to be trying to figure out a way to help her."

"Yeah, that's true."

Bracy looked the other woman in the eyes. "Lydia, thanks for listening and not judging. Some would say I was asking for what I got."

"You'll never hear that from these lips. That makes me so angry when people think they understand when they don't have a clue. They've never experienced the shame and the fear, so what gives them the right to judge?"

Bracy nodded.

"Thank you for letting me get this running and hiding thing out in the open." Lydia ran a hand through her thick black hair.

Lydia sat back. "Friends?"

"Absolutely."

The two women reached over at the same time to hug.

Bracy lifted her head and closed her eyes. There had to be an answer to all their problems.

"What are you doing?"

"Praying. Would you like to join me?"

*   *   *

"Hey, Mom."

"David. How's it going? School good?"

"It is. A little harder than I remember. You kind of get out of the lecture and homework mind-set when you take time off."

Maddie laughed.

"I wanted to thank you for putting a copy of Dad's letter in my suitcase. I probably should have read it when you first offered, but I wasn't sure I really wanted to know his dark secrets. But everything makes more sense now. It makes me sad we didn't know what was going on inside of him. And that he didn't feel he could share his thoughts and new faith with us."

"Yes." Maddie breathed deep to push the anger down. How could a few Bible verses make such a drastic change to the man she had known for so many years?

"It's going great living and working on Professor Taulbee's farm," her son's excited voice continued.

"That's great. I'm so glad. You'll be a veterinarian before you know it."

"Well, I still have a few years. So, Mom, what's going on with the farm, the loan, Bracy—?"

"Whoa. Which one do you want me to answer first?"

David laughed his deep, masculine laugh.

"I still have a little time left before the loan has to be paid off. I'm pushing Isaac to get my assets unfrozen."

She heard a buzz on her cell, and when she looked she had a call from a number she didn't recognize.

"Any luck?"

"No, not yet. What's up with you? Are you coming home for Thanksgiving? That is, if we still have a home then."

"Mom, I'm praying for God's intervention. He still does miracles, you know. Okay, stop that."

"What? Stop what?"

"I can see you rolling your eyes."

"You cannot see through this phone."

"Maybe not, but I can see you in my head. That's what you do when you don't agree."

"David—"

"I won't know about Thanksgiving until the week before. Is it okay if I let you know then?"

"Sure, no problem. We'll be here."

After she hung up with David, Maddie called the unknown phone number back. The person on the other end of the line sounded very professional but didn't answer with the name of a business.

"Ah, I received a call from this number. Did you call me by mistake?"

"Is this Madison Crane?"

"Yes."

"I called you intentionally."

"Okay. How can I help you?"

"I just felt you should know that your loan has been paid off."

"My what? Who is this?"

"I—I really would rather not say."

"Paid off by whom?"

"You need to know it's been paid off by someone who wants to remain anonymous."

"How do I know this is real?"

"Let's just say I work fo . . . with the person who bought your loan from the bank and this person's unethical business practices need to stop. I would suggest you contact your friend Elias Jones."

"Elias? What does he have to do with this?"

"That's all I can tell you."

The phone went silent.

FIFTY-ONE

Jasper Worthington II, wealthy businessman and father of Jasper Worthington III, was furious. The plan had been set in motion and would have been completed perfectly if some do-gooder hadn't stepped in.

Broken Acres was set to belong to him in a matter of days, and then Jase would have had no choice but to join him in the family corporate business. Jase would have had to sell his cattle and the few horses he owned and forget his ridiculous plans to own a horse ranch.

But now . . .

*   *   *

Maddie called Nathan's cell and left a message for him to call her back.

What am I going to say when he calls back? Thank you? How dare you? Why would you?

Grateful beyond anything that she was not losing Broken Acres, what Maddie really wanted was to see him in person. Or did she? His rejection clearly told her he wanted nothing to do with her personally. *But then why would he—*

Her phone buzzed in her hand.

"Hello."

"Hi, Maddie. It's Nathan. You called?"

She cleared her throat and wiped joyful tears from her cheek. "Nathan, I don't know where to begin."

"Um, the beginning?"

Maddie knew he was trying to be funny and deflect the attention from himself. "Yes, the beginning."

Her mind ran to the first time she met the man she now owed so much. In a bar and grill she never would have stepped foot in if she didn't need food to stay upright. Little had she known that night was the beginning. Nathan really did care about her and Broken Acres.

"Nathan, I can't thank you enough for what you've done for me. And not just me, but David, Bracy, Lydia, and all the hurting people who will be living—and healing—at Broken Acres."

"Maddie, it's really nothing. I haven't done that much. Although I'd like to do more."

"Oh, but you have. You saved Broken Acres."

"Saved Broken Acres?"

His voice questioned, still deflecting.

"Yes. Thank you for paying off the loan. I know it's supposed to be anonymous and no one told me it was you, but I know it was. Thank you doesn't seem to say everything in my heart. That said, I want to start making payments so I can pay you back."

"Wait, Maddie. The loan is paid off?"

Maddie held her cell out in front of her and frowned. "Yes."

"I wish I could say it was me. I *really* do. But you made it perfectly clear if I did anything regarding the loan, I'd never see you again. And I did not want the wrath of Madison Crane causing me nightmares."

"I said that?"

"Yeah, you did. And knowing your temper and stubborn streak, I wasn't going to take that chance."

"But who—"

"I don't know. But that's great news, right?"

Maddie sat down on the couch. "It is great news, but I need to find out who did this so I can pay them back."

"That might take a little digging, but I'll bet we can get to the bottom of this."

"*We?*"

"Yeah. You don't think it was an accident I was the one you called, do you?"

"Well."

"Maddie, I know you don't want to admit it, but God's hand is all over this."

"God's hand? You see God in this? Nathan, I never thought I'd hear anything like that from you."

He let out a long breath. "I never thought anything like that would ever come from my mouth either. But God is teaching me a lot."

If he's waiting for a response, he's not going to get one, thought Maddie. She was glad when he changed the subject.

"So, how did you find out the loan was paid off if some anonymous entity bought the loan from the bank?"

"Someone called and told me. Now that I think of it, this is getting a little weird."

"You think? Who called you?"

"That's just it, I don't know. Do you think it was a prank?"

"I don't know. Did they say anything else?"

"This person did say Elias was somehow involved."

"Elias at the county?"

"Yeah."

"Okay, then that's where we'll start."

"There's that *we* again."

"That's right, and it's gonna stay that way."

Maddie felt a grin spread across her face. She was actually relieved Nathan had offered to help. Who would have thought she and Nathan could work together without their tempers flaring?

*   *   *

When they arrived at the county offices in Carterville, Elias was gone from the building on his lunch hour. "We might as well go have lunch while we wait. I'm starving." Nathan patted his stomach.

Maddie merely raised her eyebrow. He'd seen her give David the same look.

At the Carterville Café, Nathan grinned behind his water glass as he watched every move Maddie made. Her probing green eyes scanned the menu, seeming to dissect every item. He'd seen those gentle eyes flash almost black, hands waving the air in an effort to let loose her pent-up anger more than once. The wrath of Madison Crane. Unfortunately, his own temper had gone over the top each time.

Strong yet delicate hands held the menu, reminding him of how she held his bare shoulders tight when he kissed her. His blood warmed at the memory even now.

"What's good here?" Maddie caught him staring and frowned. "What?"

"Oh nothing." He smiled.

She tried again. "Is there something you really like to eat here?"

"BLT, fries, chocolate shake. They serve thick smoked bacon, raised locally."

"That sounds great." She closed her menu and took a sip of water. Nathan's gaze broke away from her as the young waitress took their orders and winked at Nathan as she turned to walk away with their menus.

He smiled after the cute girl, gauging her age to be midtwenties. He shook his head.

"Friend of yours?"

Nathan's face shaded pink and he took a swallow of his water. "No. Never saw her before."

"Well, she definitely saw you."

One side of his mouth pulled into a grin. "Jealous?"

Maddie gave her head a definite shake. "Hardly." She glanced over at the girl calling out their order.

I guess I was hoping for a yes, he thought, then chided himself for being a fool.

Maddie moved the conversation in a different direction. "Carterville is named after your grandfather, right?"

"Great-grandfather. He helped establish the town after he came out here looking for land to raise cattle. If you drive out in the country you can see acres and acres where cattle barons used to graze their cattle."

"Used to? Don't they still raise cattle around here?" She waved her hand as if covering the entire area.

"The land pretty much stands empty these days. There was a terrible drought in the early days, and most of the grazing cattle didn't survive. My great-grandfather's land ran along a healthy creek. He offered his water to the other ranchers, but it wasn't enough. Not many survived. My great-grandfather could see the future was in growing the town, so he invested the money he had saved in bringing new businesses and people in by way of his stage line. When the railroad became an option, he negotiated to have lines run near the town. Farmers came in after the drought and legally took over the land deserted by many of the cattle ranchers. Their crops did well in the fertile land where the cows had grazed. Together with my great-grandfather, they came up with clever ways to get water to the crops, digging more and deeper wells and irrigation trenches from the creek. Long story short, people were thankful to my great-grandfather for bringing in new business and giving others a chance at a new beginning. So they named the town after him. He had a large family, ten children. My maternal grandfather came from that lineage."

"Your maternal grandfather. What about your father's father?"

A dark shadow passed over Nathan's face. "My father's dad made his money in the lumber business. My father lost it all drinking and gambling."

Maddie's pained look of surprise caught him off guard as he heard her voice change. "Tell me about your father."

"Maddie, I don't think—"

"Why do you hate him so? Why is there anger in your eyes when you talk about him?" Her green eyes probed his.

"Okay, if you want to know, I'll give you a brief summary of my dad's existence. My father was an abusive drunk who could not get over the fact that he was never good enough."

Maddie frowned.

Nathan took a deep breath. "From what I've pieced together, when he was young he thought he owned the world. Well, at least the small part of the world that held his father's lumber business. I guess my grandpa's lumber business was considered a great asset in those days, offering jobs and incentives for many of the residents in the surrounding areas. My mom said Dad was arrogant, bragging he could do anything and have any woman he wanted."

"Sometimes having everything is the worst thing a person can have." Maddie's painful expression gave him pause.

"Yeah, well, it definitely was for my dad."

"Didn't he work at the lumber mill?"

"If you could call it that. He put on gloves, went out into the forest where the men were felling the huge trees, sat on his truck's tailgate, and shouted orders at the men. Needless to say, there was no love lost between the men and my dad."

"You said he was an abusive drunk. When did that start?"

Nathan ran his hands through his thick brown hair. "The way that started is another story. Better forgotten."

Maddie tipped her head, eyes questioning.

"No, really, trust me on this. Anyway, being that arrogant, I-can-have-any-woman-I-want kind of guy—" Nathan shook the chill from his shoulders and pushed it down his back. *That was me.* He shot a disgusted, almost sad look over at Maddie.

"Nathan, are you okay?" Maddie touched his hand that lay on the table.

He looked up at her and saw intense sorrow reflected in her eyes.

"Yeah, I'm fine." Nathan tried not to react to her touch by pulling away from the fragile connection, but the subject made it hard. "One of my dad's rich buddies challenged him to ask my mom on a date. She said yes, and unfortunately on their first date, I was conceived. Mom won't tell me how that all went down."

"Ah, do you think . . . ?"

Nathan waved off her question. "But the expression on her face when it came up the one time I asked was . . . I don't know, fear, shame, disappointment? Anyway, when the doctor confirmed she was pregnant, my grandfather made my dad marry her."

"Oh."

"Yeah. When his drinking got worse, so did the abuse. One time I got between him and my mom. He shouted in my face that it was Mom's fault he had lost the lumber business. If she hadn't gotten pregnant, he would be rich now. He said I was a mistake, and it was as much my fault as my mom's."

"Nathan, I'm so sorry. Did it ever get better?"

"No. Only worse."

"Did you have any siblings or good friends to help you?"

"My brother, Sammy, died in an accident while he was at boot camp. He was eighteen years old." Nathan stared out the picture window, his heart's fierce pounding causing him to close his eyes and pray.

*   *   *

Maddie could see deep anger consuming him. The veins in his neck bulging, the red flush running from his neck to his face as his hands clenched.

Nathan let out a ragged sigh and sat back in his seat. "Mom was pregnant with my sister when my dad lost his temper and pushed her so hard she tripped and fell. She went into early labor and Desiree was stillborn. That sent my dad to skid row where he died a miserable drunk."

No wonder this man's temper ruled his emotions. *I can't imagine having to live though all that.* Maddie's heart ached for him.

"I always swore I would never drink or let my temper get the better of me." Nathan closed his eyes and shook his head. "I really messed that up."

Maddie remembered Nathan, drunk and offensive at the bar on her trip to Jacob's Bend. She desperately wanted to forget the whole thing, but couldn't. Listening to him share about his abusive, alcoholic father and the horrible life he and his mother had lived, she knew the drunk she encountered that night was not the same man she was sitting across the table from now. This man had made something of his life.

"But Nathan, you own a multimillion-dollar construction company. That wasn't from your dad. You made that happen."

"Co-owner. My partner, Tim O'Leary . . . I believe you met him at the hospital."

Maddie nodded but said nothing.

"Tim is the brains behind it all. I just started building. Creating something from nothing helped me see all the spiteful, degrading names my dad called me were not true. Pounding nails with a hammer was a good release for the anger that swelled inside of me. Tim made the business into a thriving operation. I'm not in the trenches much these days, although I'd rather be there than in the boardroom. That's Tim's domain, not mine."

The waitress brought their food and gave Nathan a big smile, asking him if she could get him anything else.

"No, thanks. I'm good." Nathan looked down at his plate.

It took both hands for him to pick up half his sandwich. Maddie watched his eyes grow wide as he stifled a laugh watching her do the same. "You are gonna love this."

Maddie could barely get her mouth around the triple-layer sandwich. "This is really good," she mumbled. Setting the sandwich on her plate, Maddie covered her mouth with her hand while she chewed.

Nathan had taken three bites to her one. He nodded, his mouth full.

Maddie continued to tackle the sandwich, then paused for a drink of water. "But, Nathan, you are in the trenches at Broken Acres."

"Yeah." He let out what sounded like a frustrated breath. "Speaking of. I could finish the job a lot faster if I could get some help out there. But you won't let me hire any of my guys, remember?"

"Nathan, you took on the job all by yourself when we first discussed it. How did that even happen? Your company is in Portsmouth, right? How did you end up here?"

Nathan rubbed his chin. "It's a long story I'm sure you wouldn't be interested in hearing."

"Try me." Maddie reached for a fry and dipped it in ketchup.

Nathan checked his watch. "Elias is probably back from lunch. Are you finished eating?" He looked at her half-eaten sandwich and fries. His plate was empty of everything except the rind from the orange slice the cook added to the plate for color. "Or maybe you want to finish."

"No, I'm finished. Maybe I could get a box for the sandwich."

"Sure." He waved the waitress over. She seemed happy enough to help Maddie leave.

FIFTY-TWO

Elias smiled big when he saw Maddie walk in the door. "Well, now, look who's come to grace these here offices."

Maddie shook his hand and smiled back. "Hi, Elias. How are you? How's Abigail?"

"We're doin' mighty fine. Me and the missus took a drivin' trip back to the ole homestead in Kentucky. Didn't much feel like home no more. Not many of our folks stayed there. All scattered 'bout the US. Nope, this here is our home, and we're mighty glad to be back."

"It's good to see you. Been quite a while."

"Yup." The older man adjusted his thick dark-rimmed glasses and glanced over the rims at Nathan with a wary squint.

"What can I do for ya?"

Maddie looked over at Nathan. He nodded.

"Well, Elias, I had to take out another loan to finish the renovation on the big house. Did you happen to hear about that?" She gave him a hopeful grin.

He crossed his arms over his chest. "Ah, yeah."

"It seems *everybody* knows about my loan." Maddie rolled her eyes. "It looks like someone anonymously paid it off, and I'm trying to find out who it is so I can pay them back."

He looked over at Nathan. "Ah, yeah?"

Maddie looked over Elias's shoulder at the photo hanging on the wall of his prize-winning pig that brought about their friendship. She remembered the first time she met him and how she'd realized the way to friendship with the man was by admiring his pig.

"Elias, I received an anonymous call that you might know who paid off my loan. And since you know everything that happens in this county, I thought maybe you could help me out."

Elias ran his hand over the top of his graying flattop. "Now, Maddie, even if I did know, and I'm not sayin' I do, I couldn't give out that there information. It's confidential." A frown creased his forehead. "I guess who-ever it is has their reasons for wantin' to keep it anonymous."

She shook her head. Glancing at the papers sitting on the counter, an idea came to her.

"Elias, just suppose these papers lying here were confidential, would there be a problem if I happened to see"—she looked down at the top sheet of paper—"Jimmy Brown's name staring back at me?"

Elias glanced at the name on the page and quickly turned the sheet upside down. "Now, Maddie."

Maddie gave him the best pouty face she had.

Nathan looked from one to the other. "Listen, Elias, there are ways of finding out who paid off the loan." He mirrored Elias's crossed arms over his chest.

Elias dropped his arms to his sides. He bent his head and peeked over the top of his glasses. "Well then, I guess you'd best be lookin' into them ways, 'cause you ain't gettin' nothin' from me."

Maddie took a deep breath and let it out slowly, ready to lay into the stubborn Kentucky pig farmer. She was interrupted, though, when Nathan touched her elbow and suggested they try another plan.

Outside the county offices Maddie fumed, pacing, hands flying. "Why is this so hard? I mean, I'm grateful someone saved my farm, but still . . . I need to find out who it is and pay them back. I don't want to be indebted to anyone."

Nathan stopped the grin that had already started in his eyes.

"What?" Maddie threw up her hands.

His grin grew. "Oh nothing."

"No, what?"

"I'm glad I got you out of there before you unleashed the wrath of Madison Crane on poor Elias. It's not a pretty sight when you are on the receiving end of that anger."

She closed her eyes and took a deep breath. "I only unleash my wrath on annoying, obnoxious drunks who think I ought to follow them home."

Nathan hung his head and rubbed his chin. He looked her in the eyes. "Are you ever going to forgive me for the one time I drank and made a fool of myself?"

"One time?"

He frowned. "Okay, the first time was that night. The second was the last time I'll ever touch any kind of alcohol." He ran his hand down his left leg.

"I hope so. You almost died."

He closed his eyes, and Maddie wondered what he was seeing. Her sitting in a chair at the foot of his bed, head on her arms, sleeping? Or Chelsea storming in to take control?

Nathan's chagrinned words recalled her to the present. "Don't remind me. I'll never do something that stupid again."

Maddie's tone softened. "I'm glad."

Nathan moved toward her, and Maddie felt her legs go weak and her heart rate double.

"Maddie."

He was close enough to touch her shoulders.

Maddie felt like she might pass out from lack of oxygen right there on the steps of the county offices. Her legs certainly weren't making it easy for her to walk away.

"Maddie, are you ever going to forgive me?" His voice was almost a whisper.

"I . . . ah."

He shifted his eyes to her lips and leaned in. Maddie pulled back and almost tumbled down the steps behind her. Letting out the breath she had been holding, she held out her hand. "I forgive you, Nathan. Friends?"

He took her hand. "If that's what you want."

Maddie tried to smile, but her lips wouldn't cooperate. What was wrong with her body? "You said there were other ways to find out who paid off my loan." Finally, her brain was working.

He was looking deep into her eyes again. *Think, Maddie.*

She turned away and started down the steps toward her truck.

"Yes, there are, if you'll allow me to let the legal department in my office check into it. I'm sure they can get the information you're looking for."

"It looks like I don't have a choice."

He raised his eyebrows with a look that said, "Really?"

"I'm sorry. Yes, I would appreciate it if you could find out for me."

*   *   *

Maddie couldn't wait any longer. Three days was long enough for Nathan's legal department to get the information she needed. She had to know.

She called and left a message on Elias's line at the county. "Hi, Elias, thought I'd drop by and check on the permits for the renovation, see if they need to be renewed." Maddie knew they were still good for another three weeks, but she wanted to see if she could talk Elias into giving her some information about who paid off the loan. The thought hit her like an early morning wake-up call. *Why would he have that information anyway?*

Maddie stood at the foot of the steps that led to the county offices and in particular, Elias's office. She blew out the breath she had been holding and walked into the building. Elias was not at his desk. She shook her head, frustrated. Her eyes landed on the scatter of papers on the counter. She recognized a name. Jase. He must have been trying to buy another ranch.

Maddie casually moved the papers on top to get a glimpse at Jase's paperwork. *This is sneaky, Maddie. It's really none of your business.* There for all the world to see was the deed of trust to a parcel number she recognized right away. The Riley farm. Broken Acres. It had been her name that occupied that parcel number and deed of trust not too long ago.

So it was Jase. But how could he do that? Where did he get the money? And why would he pay off the $120,000 loan on Broken Acres?

Disappointed and confused, Maddie whispered, "I think Jase and I need to have a little talk."

Fifty-Three

Having everyone gathered in the big house dining room and the delicious smells of Thanksgiving dinner warmed Maddie almost as much as having the people she cared about sharing the memorable event. The ten-foot table was dwarfed in the large room they had opened up by taking out the wall between the dining room and the parlor. Three empty chairs would soon be occupied by David and his two landlords, Professor Taulbee and his wife, Irene. They were running late and would arrive just in time for dessert. There was enough food to feed three times the dozen plus who would grace the table. Everyone brought their favorite dish, and George, Maddie's soon-to-be chef, and Granny Harper cooked the turkey and stuffing in Granny's kitchen.

George being the elder male of the group sat at the head of the table sharpening the knife he would use to carve the thirty-pound golden-brown tom that sat before him. Granny sat to his right, Michael and Michael's mom, Jenny, to his left. Jase pulled out Bracy's chair and sat between her and Jenny. Lydia and Maddie filled in the opposite side of the table.

Maddie frowned when she saw Nathan grin at his name on the place card at the seat next to hers.

Maddie glanced at Nathan's place card and then across the table at Bracy, who seemed to be having a difficult time suppressing the giggle that Maddie knew was just below the surface. When she squinted at her daughter, Bracy shrugged.

Maddie noticed that Bracy had strategically placed Professor Taulbee next to her probably so she could pick his brain about Forest Hills University. She wanted as much information as she could get about spending her last year there to receive a journalism degree. Her goal was to go into investigative journalism, investigating mysterious stories that needed solving.

Maddie's eyes continued around the table. Irene would flank Nathan, with Billy and Shauna finishing one side of the table, while David would hold up the last place next to his new friend, Professor T.

Nathan pulled out Maddie's chair, ushered her into her seat, and took his own.

Maddie breathed a deep, satisfied breath and looked at George, who was tapping his fork against his water glass. He looked down the table at all present, landing his gaze on her. "Maddie, would you mind if I give thanks?"

Maddie looked uncomfortably around the table at all the smiles. "Ah, yeah, sure."

George took Granny's hand, giving her a smile, and then Michael's. Everyone took the hand on either side and bowed their heads.

Maddie's hand, warm and clammy, rested in Nathan's. She opened her eyes to see his response while George prayed. George thanked God for everyone by name and the bounty that sat before them. He gave God praise for the blessing of the year they had and the plans He had yet to unfold. Nathan nodded ever so slightly, seeming to agree with all George was saying.

Who was this man who was so careful about his choice of words, stopping when it seemed evident he wanted to let go with a curse word? This man who no longer wanted her but whose hand sat warmly wrapped around hers?

A flashback of a few weeks ago came to mind when Maddie practically surrendered herself to him and he suddenly stopped the passionate kisses and held her at arm's length. Who was *this* Nathan, and what had caused the major change in not only his actions but his character?

George asked for a safe trip for David and the Taulbees and smiled big when everyone joined him in saying, "Amen."

Everyone chattered while passing the food. Maddie smiled at those sitting around the table, thankful for each one, knowing they were as close as any family she'd ever known. It brought pure joy to hear Shauna talking about her studies. The trauma of the many deaths in her family and not being able to speak for almost a year had lifted when she said "I do" to Billy during their wedding ceremony.

This time together flooded Maddie's heart with thanksgiving and hope for a bright future along with memories of times past. They were making a memory now, sitting around the table with full stomachs, in no hurry to clear the table, wash dishes, put leftovers away, sharing all the year had held and what the future might have in store.

Billy leaned back in his chair, stretched, and moaned. "That was the best Thanksgiving dinner I've ever had. What's for dessert?"

Everyone laughed.

"What? It's been at least two hours since we ate dinner. We've been sitting here gabbing for at least that long."

"More like forty-five minutes." Shauna laughed and kissed his cheek.

He smiled big at his bride. "I love your laugh." And he captured her lips right there in front of everyone.

Maddie pushed back her chair. "I'll get dessert."

Jenny stood. "No, let me. I think both my legs have fallen asleep along with my son. Here, hold Michael?"

"I'd love to."

Jenny brought out the dessert plates—paper, a Crane family tradition—and went back to bring the first offering of myriad dessert choices.

The front door opened, waking Michael. He rubbed his eyes and raised his arms, ready for the jostling and tickling he'd receive. "DD."

"Hey, buddy." David picked the little guy up from Maddie's lap and threw him in the air. His giggle made everyone laugh with him.

Maddie glanced at the two and tipped her head. Funny, they both had that same one-sided grin.

"Mom, everybody, this is Dr. Harold Taulbee and his wife, Irene. They've been kind enough to adopt me, give me a place to live and a job working on their farm—"

David glanced over at the door that lead to the kitchen and froze as Jenny walked out of the kitchen.

Jenny dropped the pie she held in her hands.

"Jay R?" David whispered, just barely loud enough for everyone to hear.

A dozen pairs of eyes bounced back and forth as the two spoke more with body language than words.

Maddie stared from one to the other.

"You two know each other?"

"Mommy." Michael stretched his arms out to Jenny.

David looked from Michael to Jay R. "You're Michael's mom?"

"Ah . . . yes."

Michael squirmed out of David's arms to the floor and ran to his mother's open arms, stepping firmly into the spilled pie.

"Michael . . ." Jenny tried to scoop her son off the sticky mess, and Maddie jumped up to help, reaching for his apple-sugared socks.

Jenny looked up at Maddie, tears spilling from her eyes. "Oh, my gosh, Maddie." Jenny mouthed to Maddie—*the pizza guy.*

Maddie's hand flew to her mouth, and her eyes went wide as a light went on in her mind. "Oh. Oh!"

Jenny's story of how she fell in love with this guy in college who delivered pizza, the only man she had dated there, caused tears to well up in Maddie's eyes as she looked from Jenny to Michael to David. Jenny had told her she was sad and disappointed that she would never see him again.

Shauna moved to Maddie's side and put an arm around her shoulder. She pointed to the floor. "Let me clean this up."

Maddie stared through Shauna and looked over at Dr. and Mrs. Taulbee as George stepped forward into the awkward silence to greet them. "You must be starving. Can I get you something to eat?"

FIFTY-FOUR

Maddie pushed the porch swing with her foot. The gentle sway had rocked Michael to sleep in her arms, wrapped in the quilt she had made him. Maddie gazed at him in awe.

A grandson. I have a grandson. Chills ran down her arms as she pulled him into a tight hug. Everyone else at the table had been as shocked as she when the reality of Michael's parentage came to light, and she had suggested that David take Jenny for a walk. "That makes Jenny, my . . . my . . . Oh my, what is she?" Maddie looked over at the big house where David and Jenny were still sitting on the porch steps long after everyone else had left. The Taulbees were now settled in the suite off the kitchen, where Billy once slept. They had cleared out all the building supplies that had been stored in there during the reno and turned it into a comfortable guest suite for the Taulbees.

Maddie smiled at the sleeping boy in her arms, recalling the look on her son's face as he and Jenny had walked out the door.

My daughter-in-law? Well, maybe not yet, but . . .

*   *   *

"I can't believe you're here, sitting next to me." David's eyes were glued to Jay R, who was leaning against the porch post. He knew it now with certainty—this was the only woman he had ever loved.

Jenny walked over and sat down next to him. She gave him a quick smile. "David, I can't believe you are here and your mom is one of my best friends. How did that happen anyway?"

David grinned and with absolute assurance said, "God."

"What?"

"That's how this happened. God made a way for us to find each other again. Can you think of another explanation since we didn't have a clue what our real names were, where we lived, or how to locate each other?" David rested his forearms on his legs and bent his head. He ran his fingers through his hair as he shook his head. "Michael is my son." He blinked away his own tears when he saw tears in her eyes. "I can't believe it."

"Well, it's true. You're the only man I've ever been with." Jenny sat up straight, her voice defensive.

"No. I didn't mean it like that." He smiled and took her hands in his. "I mean I love that little guy. Since the first time I met him here at Mom's I've loved being with him, telling him stories, playing games and dump trucks with him. He's a great kid. You've done an amazing job raising him." He took a deep breath. "I just wish I could have been with you through the pregnancy and delivery and helped in raising him."

Jenny's eyes softened. "It's not too late."

David's head popped up, feeling hope spring inside. "Really?"

"Of course. You're his father. He needs a dad."

"Did you try to find me when you found out you were pregnant?" David wanted to know, no, needed to know. "I tried to find you, Jay R—I guess I'm going to have to get used to calling you Jenny, huh? I tried, but no one knew who you were or where you went. Where did you go?"

Jenny's gaze dropped to her hands. She took a couple of deep breaths then looked him in the eyes. "At first, no, I did not try to find you."

"Really?" He could feel the frustration and hurt well up inside. "Why? Didn't you think that I—"

Jenny held up her hand. "There was so much to do to get ready for finals. So I could finish my final year. I had to do well, David. My dream had always been to be a vet—"

"No kidding." David flinched at the sarcasm that stung through his words.

"I know it was your dream too. I'm sorry. After school was over I did try to find you."

"Why did you try then?"

Jenny reached up and pinned a loose strand of hair behind her ear. "My sister wouldn't let it go. She said you had a right to know."

"I think she was right." He stood and walked to the orchard and back.

"Please, David, sit." The anguish on her face cooled his temper. He sat.

"I tried every place we had ever been, but no one knew who you were or where you went. Even the pizza place said they'd never heard of you."

"Ah." He grinned ruefully. "I was delivering pizza on a dare from a friend when I met you. When we started dating and decided to play that game." David shook his head. "I can't believe we did that. I thought it was fun, intriguing. Until I fell in love with you and we—"

"Yeah, I know." Jenny closed her eyes.

"I never worked at the pizza place."

"I found that out. I didn't know where else to look after canvassing the whole campus."

"Okay, I can understand that."

"Then my sister called and told me about the position here in Jacob's Bend. I thought it would be a good idea to have a fresh start. Besides, my sister lives here. She's the librarian, you know."

"No, I didn't know that. I'd like to meet her and tell her thanks for encouraging you to find me."

Jenny nodded.

David locked eyes with her. "Jay R, sorry, Jenny."

"Jay R was the first thing that ran through my head. My full name is Jennifer Ruth Veronica Adams."

David nodded his understanding. "Jenny, we have a son, and I want to be a part of his life." He took her hands into his and gently touched her cheek with the back of his fingers. "And I want to be a part of your life too. I feel like we've wasted so much time. I've never loved another woman. You are the first and you'll be the last."

Jenny leaned her cheek into his hand. "David, we hardly knew each other back then. The fairy-tale game we played didn't really leave any room for us to tell each other our life story or where we came from, our background, our heritage."

David opened his mouth to speak.

She pressed her finger to his lips. "I've never felt about anyone else the way I feel about you. Is it love?" She gave him a half grin. "I don't know."

David caught his breath.

"But I would sure like to find out. Honestly, I've missed you. Do you think we could start as friends and *parents* and see what happens?"

"I know what will happen on my end. I already love our son, and I know what I feel for you is deeper than anything I've ever felt. I think it's permanent. The love has not diminished over the years, and when I saw you holding that pie in the doorway, I knew it had only grown stronger."

"Oh my gosh, the pie." She laughed.

Her laughter dazzled him.

"But if that's what it takes to make you see how much I care for both you and Michael and that I want us to be a family, then that's what we'll do. Although I'm not sure how long I can keep my feelings, and hands, in check." He raised an eyebrow. "Even now it's hard to keep my hands off you."

She leaned in and gave him a peck on the cheek. "We can do this, David. If it's meant to be, it will all happen as it should. Not in the heat of passion. That didn't exactly work out great for us last time." She wrinkled her nose. "Okay?"

"Okay." David took a deep breath and blew it out. "One more thing. Do you think it would be all right if Michael called me Dad?" He tipped his head to the side and smiled, knowing he probably looked goofy with excitement over the idea.

"Of course he can call you Dad. After all, that's who you are."

His smile spread across his face and up to his eyes. "The thing is, he might have a difficult time calling me Dad. How do we make it easy for him?"

"We'll just start by telling him you're his dad and then see how he reacts. How does that sound?"

He took her hand and helped her up. "Let's go see my son."

"Our son?"

"Yeah. Our son." His smile lit up the dark night.

FIFTY-FIVE

Maddie stretched as she walked into the kitchen and pressed the button on the coffee maker.

She walked over to open the blinds in the living room and remembered David was asleep on the couch. She picked up the blanket he had kicked off during the night from the floor and covered him to his shoulders. Maddie gently moved his hair from his forehead and smiled. Watching him sleep reminded her of Michael in her arms on the porch swing. *They look so much alike. Why did I never see it before?*

Michael did have his mother's American Indian heritage, with his thick jet-black hair and deep chocolate eyes. Yet at times she remembered seeing David's mischievous sparkle in those eyes.

David is a father. The coffeepot beeped, and she pulled out four mugs from the cupboard. Everyone would no doubt want coffee when they woke up.

Sitting in the comfy wingback chair she had repurposed with denim postscript fabric that sat next to the couch, Maddie pulled her legs up under her, sipped creamy coffee, and watched her son. "You are going to be an amazing father, David," she breathed into her cup.

David's eyes blinked open. He turned on his back and stretched until his feet hung off the armrest of the couch. "Hey, Mom."

"Hey, yourself. Did you sleep well?"

"Oh yeah, once my head hit the pillow it was all over."

"Just like your dad."

"Yeah? Dad always seemed so restless. I guess I thought he probably slept restless too."

"Nope. It took him all of sixty seconds to fall asleep, and he slept soundly all night. He did wake up awfully early, though."

David clasped his hands behind his head and smiled.

"What?"

"Oh, Jenny."

She smiled. "Yes, Jenny."

He looked his mom in the eyes. "She's incredible."

"Jenny is a wonderful woman and mom."

"And Michael, what a terrific little guy. I already love him. He's . . . he's my son."

"Now, that is incredible. David, you know I love Jenny very much. And Michael. I still can't believe I'm a grandma."

"You?" He sat up and threw the blanket back on the floor. "I need coffee."

"It's all ready. Grab a cup and join me on the porch." Maddie grabbed the blanket David had let fall to the floor and pulled her sweater from one of the hooks on the wall near the front door.

David nodded and ran his hand through his hair.

The minute Maddie unlocked the front door, Sarg and Rusty ran to meet her. Rusty's tail wagged so fast and hard she thought he might knock Sarg in the head. Instead, Sarg meowed and wound himself through her legs. "Okay, okay, there, go. Run free."

When the screen door played its squeaky rhapsody, David scratched his head. "Mom, we need to oil that thing."

"Yeah, I know. Later."

They sat side by side on the porch swing, taking in the view of the farm. Maddie piled the blanket on their laps. "So, what were you saying about Jenny?"

He grinned again. "She said Michael is the same as Dad and me. Hits the pillow and is out all night but wakes up about five thirty or six."

"Of course he does. Like father, like son."

"Mom, you know, even before I knew he was my son, I loved him."

Maddie gave him a quick hug. "I know. So what happens now?"

"Good question. Jenny says she wants me to be a part of Michal's life and she's going to tell him I'm his dad. We were going to tell him yesterday, but he was asleep when we came back from the big house."

"What about you and Jenny?"

"Well, we didn't get to know each other much when we first met. We never should have played that game."

Maddie shrugged. "So what does your getting to know each other look like?"

"We date."

Professor Taulbee and Irene appeared in the orchard and waved. Maddie and David waved back.

Maddie turned back to David. "Living two and a half hours from each other? How does that work?"

"We don't know exactly. But we both know we don't want to date anyone else."

"Are you going back with the Taulbees? I know your sister was hoping to drive up and check out the school."

"Yeah, I'm leaving with Professor T. and Irene, I need to get back to school. I plan to come home on weekends, if it's okay with you, unless I have a ton of homework or hands-on training. Jenny said she and Michael could come up to Forest Hills too. If it's okay with Professor T. and Irene. Of course, she would sleep in their spare bedroom."

"Good morning, you two," Irene said with a bright smile.

"Quite an eventful day yesterday." Professor T. smiled at David.

"Eventful? That's an understatement, sir."

The screen door squealed again as Lydia and Bracy stepped out onto the porch holding steaming cups of coffee. Maddie smiled when Lydia asked Mr. and Mrs. Taulbee if they wanted coffee. As she swung back through the door, David jumped up and offered his seat on the swing to Irene and joined Professor T. on the step.

"What a beautiful morning." Maddie watched Bracy breathe deep.

Everyone nodded looking out over the landscape of Maddie's farm.

"It's like this every morning." Maddie's face shone pure joy.

FIFTY-SIX

Nathan parked his new truck on the side of the barn where George had parked his fifth wheel before he moved it to Granny Harper's property. Since there wasn't much for him to do at Broken Acres right now, George took a job with Granny's son, John, on the family farm. The fifth wheel was the perfect place for him to live while working there on the Harper property.

Nathan shaded his eyes to look over at the cottage as Rusty came running to him, tail wagging, and licked his hand. Nathan crouched down to eye level with the friendly golden retriever, ruffled the fur around his neck, and let him lick his cheek. "Hey, buddy. Glad to see you too, but it's only been a day since I saw you." He glanced at the cottage porch. People sat everywhere sipping from their mugs.

"Now that's a sweet sight, isn't it?" Rusty barked once as if to say, "Yep." Nathan stood, and Rusty led the way on the path through the orchard, the branches heavy with fall apples.

David walked over to meet Nathan halfway.

"How's it goin', Dad?" Nathan grabbed David's hand and gave it a hearty shake.

David's face shaded red and then his whole face lit up. "It's goin' great. I'm actually excited about being Michael's father. I know being a dad comes with a lot of responsibility. Even though I'm not sure what that means with us."

Nathan slapped the young man on the shoulder. "God will show you."

"Yeah. What? God?"

Nathan lifted his sunglasses from his eyes to his head. Not only did he give David a big smile and a nod, but he gave him a big brother hug as well. "Yep, God. I'm learning a lot about Him these days."

"Nathan, that's great. You said you had been attending a church in Carterville. Are you still going there?"

"Yeah. It's a pretty big church, and that's fine with me. I can get lost in the crowd. I've been going to a Bible study on Wednesday nights too."

"You are really serious, aren't you?"

He glanced over at Maddie sitting on the swing chatting with Irene.

David followed his eyes. "Yeah, I know. But don't give up on her."

Nathan's head snapped back to David. "Oh, I'll never give up on her. Although being near her is getting more difficult all the time."

"How's that?"

Nathan thought twice about sharing his feelings and temptations with Maddie's son. Even though he and David were friends he still felt uncomfortable talking to the young man about his mother in those terms.

"Oh, you know. Her temper. Her sarcasm. I never know if she's going to be sweet or sour."

"Is she still giving you a hard time?"

"More than you know."

Maddie waved from the porch, calling the two men over.

"Good morning, Nathan." Maddie smiled down at him from the porch as he and David approached.

Nathan felt his heart rate double. *I think I'd rather have her sarcasm.* He closed his eyes and took a couple of deep breaths to slow his heart rate down.

"Would you like some coffee? Lydia just made a fresh pot."

"Sure. Yeah." He rubbed the back of his neck. "That would be great."

"We're waiting for the catering service to bring breakfast."

He squinted at her. "Catering service?"

"George and Granny. They said since we have so many people here today they would make breakfast at Granny's and bring it over."

"Sounds good. I can only imagine what those two will come up with. They are both really good cooks. Whatever it is, you can bet it's gonna be incredible."

As Maddie walked into the house to pour Nathan a cup of coffee, he watched every step she took, every movement.

David shoved him with his shoulder. "Man, you've got it bad," the young man whispered. "Seems to me, from what Mom has said and your reaction when you are around her, that you two have a love-hate relationship."

Nathan felt his cheeks warm. "You ought to know, lover boy. Jenny is an amazing catch."

"Ah, you don't have to tell me that. I knew it the minute I met her. But our relationship is totally a love relationship." David gave Nathan a knowing glance.

Nathan turned as Maddie returned with a fresh cup of coffee. As he reached for the mug, their fingers touched, and he pulled his hand back, spilling coffee on his hand and the ground.

"Ouch, that's hot."

Maddie's green eyes sparkled at him. "Ah, yeah, it's coffee." She leaned in to look at his hand. "Are you okay? Did you burn yourself?"

"No, I'm fine. Just fine." Nathan heard David chuckle under his breath and shot him a dirty look.

*   *   *

Coffee mugs in hand, Nathan and Maddie walked toward the orchard. "So, what do you hear from your oldest daughter? Ruth, isn't it?"

Maddie shook her head. "Ruth. Dear Ruth. She's such a worrier. She's worried about David finishing school and Bracy waiting the year to get resident status. About me owning Broken Acres and what I'm going to do with so much land. I don't know what she'll say when she hears about Michael. She loves kids, and I think she'd like to start a family. But she's feeling kind of lonely there in Texas. Her husband's family lives in England, and I don't think they have plans to move to the US."

"Why doesn't she move here?"

Maddie stopped.

"What?" Nathan looked back over his shoulder to see Maddie looking at him like he just found the answer to global warming.

"Nathan, that's a great idea. I'd love to have a closer relationship with Ruth. She's a lot like her father, very responsible, levelheaded, knows what she wants and how to get it. Why not? With David and Bracy here, why shouldn't I ask if she and Matt would consider moving here? But then, Matt's job. Hmm that could be a problem."

Maddie shaded her face as she looked out over her property, and Nathan found himself staring at the picture she made against the rolling hills. Her eyes caught his staring at her.

Maddie continued. "I've always been completely the opposite. Neither one of them could ever understand my take-it-as-it-comes, no-big-deal personality."

"I love that about you." Nathan watched her smile abruptly change to a look of shock and . . . caution. *Well*, he thought, *I believe it, so why not say it?*

"You love . . . " She cleared her throat. "You love what about me?"

"That you don't hesitate to follow your dreams. That you follow your heart. You care about hurting people and will do whatever it takes to help them." He took two steps toward her, his eyes locked on hers, daring her to believe him, to trust him.

"I love that knowing you has changed how I see people." He took another step. "I love your temper and how you make me angry." *God, what am I doing?* he prayed silently. *I'm going to scare her off.*

Maddie stepped back and crossed her arms. "You *love* my temper? That's odd. I would have thought by your reactions to my temper it would be high on your 'things to change in Maddie' list. Now you're saying you *like* it?" Maddie turned away from him and kicked a clump of dried grass, whispering something.

"What did you say? I couldn't hear you." Nathan stepped closer again, so close he could reach out and touch her. *Easy, Nathan. Don't rush her.*

Her head slowly came up, and she searched his face before looking off into the distance again. "Oh, nothing. It really doesn't matter."

"Maddie." He studied her beautiful profile looking over the horizon. "Tell me what's on your mind."

"For years I was compliant and Jeff was the one with the temper. I was frightened of what he would do if I let mine loose. I'm afraid my temper, well, actually stuffing my anger, has gotten me in a lot of trouble. So every time I blow up it makes me wonder who I really am."

Nathan reached for her hand, gently taking it in his own and feeling it tremble in his grasp. "God made you who you are, Maddie. You have great value to Him. I'm just learning what all that means, and I can tell you it's real and it's true. He is helping me curb my temper. I'm trying to let Him handle my frustrations." He released her hand and walked over to one of the apple trees, reaching for a low-hanging apple as he continued. "You of all people know what my temper looks like."

"God? When did all this God stuff happen with you? I don't remember any constraints when you hit on me or when you were drunk."

"You're right. Drunk and obnoxious do not demonstrate who God is." Nathan admitted, flinching at the memories. "Neither does trying to take advantage of a frightened woman."

Maddie was watching him closely now, and Nathan hurried on before he lost what he needed to say. "Actually, after I got out of the hospital, after the accident, I found a package Pastor Ben had left in my room when I was in the coma. It turned out to be a Bible. I threw it in the trash." Maddie's eyes widened slightly, and he held up a hand. "I pulled it back out to read it. I'm glad I did."

"But I've never seen you at church."

"No, I've been going to a church in Carterville. I'm learning a lot about The Three, as the pastor calls them."

"The Three?"

"Yeah, you know, Father, Son, and Holy Spirit."

"And that's what is changing you?"

Maddie's question hung in the air between them, interrupted as her cell vibrated and she turned away. "Hello? Oh, hi, George."

Nathan watched her move away and sighed.

It can change you, too, Maddie. Only in the best ways.

FIFTY-SEVEN

"Hey, Maddie." George switched his cell phone to his left ear as he watched Duke run free with the farm dogs, yipping at the feet of cows in the field, doing what God created him to do. "Since you aren't ready to start back working on the big house, I thought I'd stay at the Harpers a little longer and help John on the farm with some cleanup and repairs."

"Of course. That sounds good, George." Maddie assured him. "I know Granny will appreciate it. She's concerned John has taken on too much with his brothers busy with their own careers."

"Yeah, she told me. I'm happy to help. I like to keep busy. Let me know when you are ready to move into the big house and I'll be there to help."

"By the way, thank you for the delicious brunch this afternoon. You and Granny should open a restaurant."

George laughed. "I don't think that is going to happen. Talk to you soon."

"Duke," George whistled, and the dog halted his herding the cows and looked up. "Duke, come on boy."

Duke ran clear across the pasture and stopped, panting at George's feet. "Good boy." George bent down and stroked the dog's head and back. Duke looked up when the screen door slapped shut.

Duke whined, and George released him to go say good morning to Joanna. He didn't like calling her Granny like everyone else did. He called her by her given name. "Good morning, Joanna."

Joanna walked over to his fifth wheel, Duke circling her as she walked. "Good morning, George. Did you have breakfast yet?"

"I did. Had some toast and coffee."

Joanna nodded. "Me too. After the breakfast we prepared and took over to Maddie's, I'm just about out of food. I need to go into town and do some shopping."

"Want some company?"

"Sure, that would be nice."

*　　*　　*

After thanking God for the bountiful supper, Granny looked up and saw John, who sat at the other end of the table, glance from his wife, Nancy, back to her. She wondered if he had something on his mind. She knew that look on her son's face.

"Pass the green beans, Jeremiah."

She frowned. "Did I hear a please attached to that request?"

John shook his head. "Please pass the green beans."

"What is wrong with you, John? It's not like you to be so short with the kids. Maybe you need to do a little humble dish washing. It's been a while."

John hung his head and rubbed his chin. He placed his hand on his son's shoulder. "I'm sorry, Jer. Granny's right, I've been short and unkind to all of you lately." He looked around the table at his loved ones. "Forgive me?"

Everyone talked at once, excusing and forgiving him and gladly receiving him back into the family's loving graces.

While Nancy got the boys ready for bed, Granny dried the dishes while John washed by hand. No fancy dishwasher tonight.

"You want to tell me what's bothering you?"

John scrubbed and rinsed the casserole dish and handed it to her. "You seem awful cozy with George."

"Cozy? George and I are friends."

John fervently scrubbed the roasting pan. "Don't get me wrong I think he's a nice guy, hard worker, but, Mom, are you sure you want another husband?"

"Husband? No." Her hands paused drying the green bean pan and she stared at her son. "Why would you ask me that?"

"Well, you've let George cook in your kitchen more than once, and that's unheard of. It's rare that even Nancy uses the kitchen."

"Does she want to cook the meals? I thought we had this all figured out and everybody was okay with the distribution of chores around the farm. I'm happy to relinquish the kitchen if Nancy wants to cook."

"No, she hasn't said anything at all about cooking. It's just so odd to see you and a man in the kitchen together."

She slung the towel onto her shoulder, crossed her arms over her chest, and turned to face him.

"John, George is an incredible cook. He could be a chef in a fine restaurant if he chose to. But he prefers cooking good, healthy, down-home dishes. We have cooking in common along with many other things. We enjoy each other's company. I get lonely here all by myself."

"Lonely?"

Granny could tell by his startled look the word took John by surprise. "Son, you're busy on the farm; Nancy has her part-time job as an aide at the school, not to mention head of the school's PTA. The boys are either in school or helping around here with chores. You all are very loving and careful to make sure I don't do too much. That leaves me alone and unproductive most of the time."

"Unproductive? You? Mom, you've never had an unproductive day in your life. You're always busy doing something, helping someone."

Granny studied her son. "John, what are you afraid of? Don't you like George?"

"Yes, of course I like him. He's really a great guy, it's just . . . I don't know. You and George seem a little old to be having a romantic encounter."

"Old?" The heat moving up her neck must have told John he had used the wrong word. "You know how I feel about that word. You are only as old as you allow yourself to think. My body may be seventy years old, but inside I'm still thirty-five. And who said you can't fall in love at our age?"

John was speechless. Almost. "Love?"

"I'm not saying I'm falling in love with George, but if I did I would expect you to honor and respect my choices and decisions." She countered her stern words with a gentle touch to his cheek.

"John, everyone needs someone to care for and someone to care for them. It might be George; it might never be anyone. It doesn't mean I love your dad any less."

John looked up, tears in his eyes. "I don't want you to move away. I love knowing you're here and you're safe."

"Move away. Why would I move away?"

"If you marry George he'll probably want you to move back to Illinois with him or—"

"Whoa, hold on. First of all, George and I are just friends. That's all. And if by some chance our relationship turns into something more than that, George is not moving back to Chicago. He is staying right here in Jacob's Bend to help Maddie with her place, do the cooking for the residents of the big house."

"So then what's he doing living here in his fifth wheel?"

"He's been helping you. Where else should he be? There's not much for him to do at Broken Acres right now. At least until they continue with the renovation work. And you said yourself you needed a hand around here catching up on all the things that have gone by the wayside."

John gave his mother a lopsided grin. "Yeah, I did. And honestly, George is a godsend. He never seems to wear down and is good at everything I throw at him."

Granny nodded. "So he can stay?"

"Of course, Mom. Will you just keep me informed if this becomes something deeper than friendship?"

She chuckled and shook her head. "Don't worry, son, I'm not going anywhere. But it's nice to know I'd be missed if I did decide to leave."

"Was there ever any doubt?"

"I guess not. But it's nice to hear it sometimes."

FIFTY-EIGHT

Bracy parked her car on the street and checked her hair and lipstick in the rearview mirror. She locked the doors and headed to Lettie's Café at the end of the block to meet Jase for lunch. She wasn't sure if this was a date or if he wanted to explore Jacob's Bend with her like he had mentioned. Besides, she wasn't looking for a relationship.

Fluffing her short blonde hair, she stopped to glance in the Harper's Hardware picture window to make sure she looked okay.

Loud voices caused her to peek around the corner into the alley. Jase stood toe to toe with a well-dressed man old enough to be his father.

"Are you crazy? What were you thinking, Jase? I refuse to bail you out of this mess."

"Mess? I'm not in any kind of mess. I'm glad I did it, and I'd do it all over again if I had the chance."

"How can you say that?"

"Easy. Every decision I make apart from you gives me more freedom than I've ever had."

"Freedom? Oh, you'll have freedom, all right. Freedom to fail. Freedom to live a life of poverty."

"Listen, Dad, I'm twenty-five years old and no longer accountable to you. I've done almost everything Grandpa stipulated in the terms of his will."

"*Almost* is the operative word. You don't have your own start-up ranch, and squandering your investments and all your savings to bail out some insecure, inconsequential, ridiculously inept woman so she won't lose her farm is not going to help you reach that stipulation any time soon."

Bracy wondered what Jase's father was talking about. He used all his money to bail someone out of a financial mess? Could Jase be the anonymous person who bought her mom's loan? Why would he do that? She could see Jase was about to lose it. The bulging veins in his neck, his accelerated breathing, and the color that seemed to move quickly up his face didn't bode well for the conversation.

"Jase."

Both men turned to Bracy as she walked to Jase and kissed his cheek.

His startled look said he was surprised but not unhappy with her greeting.

"I thought I heard your voice down here on my way to Lettie's. Are we still on for lunch?" She looked the older man in the eyes and saw only haughty anger.

"Oh, ah, Bracy, this is my father, Jasper Worthington."

Bracy extended her hand. The man looked down at her hand and over to his son.

"This is not over, Jase."

"It is for me, Dad."

Jase folded Bracy's hand over his arm and walked her out of the alley.

His arm was hot and his face still had a trace of the anger he obviously had not completely let loose on his father.

"Are you okay?" Bracy gave him a concerned look.

He smiled at her and opened the door to Lettie's. "I am now. Thank you for rescuing me."

"Turnabout is fair play after you rescued me from that mama cow. Now we're even. Although I'm not sure which of us was in more danger." Bracy was relieved to see Jase laugh.

They sat in a booth at the back of the café. Bracy watched Jase's anger ebb as the waitress brought menus and took their drink orders.

When they were alone again, Jase apologized for the scene she'd walked into. "This could have turned out worse than the cow encounter. My dad is bullheaded beyond reason. Beyond anything you could imagine. He does not give up until he gets what he wants."

"And what does he want?"

"Me." Jase looked down at the table at his folded hands.

"Jase, what did your dad mean when he said you had squandered your investments and savings to bail someone out?"

Jase looked her in the eyes, his face flush. "It doesn't really matter."

"I think it does. That is quite a noble thing to do."

Jase chuckled. "I wouldn't call it noble."

"I would. Can I ask you . . . was he talking about my mom's situation? Are you the anonymous person who bought her loan?"

"Why would you think that?"

"She told us that someone had *bailed* her out."

He grinned. "Even if I did, I'm not sure it's going to make a difference, at least when it comes to my future. I don't know how this is all going to play out. My dad is not going to give up trying to pull strings to get me where he wants me."

"What does that mean?"

"He wants me under his thumb. He's got these grandiose plans for my future, to be part of his corporate world. That is not me, and I'm done with him telling me how to live."

"Okay."

"Sorry. I shouldn't be unloading all this on you."

"No, I stuck my foot in when I walked into that alley."

Jase nodded. "Maybe I ought to explain. My grandfather was the best man I've ever known. Down-to-earth. Loving, yet strong. He started with nothing and grew his holdings into the empire my dad controls. My grandpa always liked being outdoors on his land, doing what he loved, ranching. God's country, he called it. My dad hated it."

"Oh."

"I spent most of my time with my grandpa. He was my hero." Jase bowed his head, and his voice broke.

Bracy gently touched his clasped hands that rested on the table. "I'm sorry this is so hard for you. What happened to your grandfather?"

A grin appeared on Jase's face. "He died the way he wanted, in the saddle. Well, standing next to his horse at a cattle roundup. One of the mama cows didn't like the guys branding her baby and got away from the cowboy who was watching her. She picked up my grandpa and tossed him in the air like a rag doll and then stomped him to death."

"Oh, Jase, I'm so sorry. That's awful. You . . . you weren't there to see it, were you?"

The deep sadness in his eyes branded Bracy's heart. "No, I was away at college, my last year. He and I were going to start a new ranch, only this one would be a horse ranch. I'm starting fresh with cows and a few horses to get the capital I need to grow a breeding horse ranch."

"Sounds exciting."

"It will be," Jase acknowledged. "My grandpa left several stipulations in his will for me to accomplish before I would receive my inheritance. One was to start from scratch like he did with basically nothing and build my small place into a thriving working ranch."

"Wow, that's quite a job."

"Yeah, he was like that. I'm excited to get started. I had a bid in on the perfect place until my dad bought it out from under me." His nostrils flared.

"Why?"

"Because he thinks with all his money he can spoil every chance I have to fulfill my grandpa's terms and live out my dream. He wants me to work for him in the family corporate business." He shook his head. "There is no way I could stay cooped up in an office or a boardroom. I have to be out on the land. Attending four years of college confirmed being confined inside four walls was definitely not for me."

"How are you going to make that dream a reality?"

"I'm really not sure. But trust me, it is going to happen."

"Your father said you were in a financial mess. What's that all about?"

Jase shook his head. "My father is the one who bought Maddie's loan from the bank for Broken Acres and called in the loan."

What a mean man. He must be miserable and very unhappy. "Why would he do that?"

"To once again control me. All my cattle and horses are grazing on Broken Acres land. If he owned it he could do what he wanted with my leased land. It was just time to stop him. And besides, he was about to ruin your mom's life. I couldn't let him do that."

"So, if I understand what you're saying, you've used *all* of your resources to pay off Mom's loan."

He nodded.

"So that means *you* now own Mom's farm?"

"I do."

Bracy frowned. "How does that make you different from your father?"

"Bracy, I don't want to own Broken Acres. I just wanted to show my father he can't manipulate everyone and have everything he wants just because he's rich. I plan to somehow make a way for your mom to pay back the loan, without interest."

"And how does that work exactly?"

Jase closed his eyes and pressed his eyelids with his fingers. "I'm not quite sure."

Bracy laughed. "Ah, maybe you could just sit down with her and tell her the truth."

"Now, that's an interesting idea. Yeah, I could do that. I don't want her to be all gushy with gratitude and feel like she owes me. She doesn't. In all honesty, I did it as much for myself as for her. To free me once and for all from my father and his unrealistic expectations."

"Freedom comes with a price."

"What does that mean? I'm fine with using my investments and savings to help your mom . . . and myself."

Bracy could tell by the questioning look on Jase's face that he didn't know what to make of the somber expression she was giving him.

"Silence is not the best way to accomplish your goals. Believe me, I've tried that." Bracy shook her head. "I know my mom. She believes open, honest transparency is the best way to live, and I know she would appreciate that from you."

"You're right. From the first time I met your mom, I could see she was a woman of integrity. She would not appreciate someone keeping secrets."

Bracy tipped her head and raised a brow.

"She also might not be happy to know that part of it was using her to get at my dad." Jase picked up a menu, obviously wanting to end the conversation. "Hey, I'm starving. How about you?"

Bracy opened her menu. "Yes, absolutely. Lettie's special burger with everything, fries, strawberry shake—"

"Whoa, you are hungry."

"Yeah, I get that way when there's stress involved."

"Are you stressed?"

Her face lit up from the handsome smile that came her way. "Not anymore."

FIFTY-NINE

Ruth picked up her cell phone for the fourth time and stared at her mother's number. *Okay, I need to do this.*
She'll think you're weak. No, she'll know you're weak.
I don't care, I need to talk to my family. If only Dad were still alive. He understood me. Although I'm not sure even he would have understood this.
Oh, he would have, but no one else will.

"Stop it. I'm not listening to your lies anymore." Ruth hit her mom's speed dial.

"Hi, Mom."

"Hi, sweetie. How are you? Seems like weeks and weeks since we've talked. How's Matthew?"

"Oh, he's doing fine. Busy with work. You know how that is."

Maddie chuckled. "I sure do."

"Mom, I was thinking of coming out for a visit."

"That would be great, Ruth. I was just thinking that the other day. When were you thinking of flying out?"

"Well, actually, I think I'm going to drive. See all the sights and states I've never seen between here and there."

"Can Matt take that much time off work?"

Silence.

"Ruth?"

"Ah, Matt has to work, so I'm coming by myself."

"What's going on? Is everything okay with you and Matt?" Ruth heard the frown in her mother's voice.

"Mom, you are such a worrier."

"Me? Isn't that like the pot calling the kettle black?"

"Okay, I'm the worrier in the family."

"You think?"

Silence.

"Ruth? Are you okay?"

Ruth sniffed and rubbed the tears from her cheeks. "Mom, I . . . "

"Are you crying?"

"Mom, I just need to be with my family."

"This is so not like you. You always plan every detail with purpose, like your—"

"I know, like Dad. This time I'm being spontaneous. Like you."

"You know Bracy said that same thing. That she needed to be with her family. Is there something you're not telling me? Do *all* my kids have secrets they are keeping from me?"

"What does that mean?"

"Well, I hadn't planned to tell you on the phone, but David has a girl-friend . . . and a son."

"What? When did that happen?"

"So, he hasn't told you yet?"

"No."

"Well, I won't steal his thunder. I'll let him tell you the story. But David is a father and you are an aunt."

"Oh wow. I need to get outside my bubble and stay in touch with my family. I am such a loser."

"Ruth, I can't believe you said that. You are *not* a loser. You are incredible, going to school, entertaining Matt's clients . . ."

"Thanks, Mom. Okay, I get it. I'm calling my brother after this call."

Maddie took a deep breath. "And then there's Bracy."

Ruth could hear the pain in her mother's voice. "She told you? I'm glad. I've been after her for months to share what that . . . that . . . evil man did. I wish she had reported it to the police so they could put him away for life."

"Yes, she told me. All I could do was hold her as we cried together. I was so angry, I wanted to hop a plane and track that pervert down. Someday he will be caught. I'm so glad she is living here now."

Ruth sucked in a deep breath.

"What about you? Are you okay? Please tell me what's going on. I'm concerned about you."

Silence.

"Ruth."

"Mom, what if I just want to go on an adventure like you did when you drove out there?"

"But you're not me. And you have a husband."

Ruth gave a heavy sigh. "Mom, just tell me if it's okay for me to come out and see everyone."

"Of course. Anytime. Always."

"Great. Thank you. I'll leave tomorrow and see you in about four days."

"Okay, sounds good. You *are* planning on traveling only during the day, right? And you will call me and check in every night when you're safe in your motel room?"

"That sounds like something I'd say."

"Ah, you did. Just before I left Chicago."

"That's right, I did. How funny."

"I love you, Ruth. Please be safe."

"Thanks, Mom. I love you too."

*   *   *

Maddie rummaged through her photos and pulled out Ruth and Matt's wedding album. She looked closely at Ruth's face in each picture. Not only did she not smile, but she had a look of what Maddie could only call distress.

How had she never noticed that before? With a sinking heart, Maddie realized that Ruth and Matt stood a good six inches apart in every photo. She also realized there was not a single picture of the two kissing. Come to think of it, the kiss at the altar never happened. Ruth had dropped her bouquet, and after she picked it up they immediately walked down the aisle to the reception area. With only David as best man and Bracy as maid of honor, the pictures had all been taken in the reception room. Maddie thumbed through the pictures again looking for anything else she missed.

What was going on? She didn't like her kids keeping secrets from her. *I thought we had a good, close relationship.* Maddie shook her head.

Did the kids feel that way about her? Had she been totally honest with them? Maddie hung her head.

This was going to stop, right here, right now. "I pledge to be open and honest with all my kids and my friends. No hiding the ugly parts of my life or the ugly side of me. I wish it wasn't true, but I do have a prideful, selfish side. How can I ever change that?" She looked up. "Can you help me out here, Gram?"

*   *   *

"Maddie, me girl."

"Gael, how are you? I've been meaning to come into town for a sip and a visit, as you call it."

Laughter on the other end of the phone lifted Maddie's spirits.

"Well, you'd be doin' me a favor if ya come in for a visit. I'm wonderin' if ya might consider takin' a job?"

"A job? What kind of job?"

"Workin' in me store. I'll not be havin' a lot of extra money to be payin' ya at first, but when me second store starts payin' its way—"

"Second store?"

"Yes. I'm thinkin' we need that sip and a visit to be talkin' this over. Oh, and, Maddie, me girl, I talked to Mr. Chamberlain from the bank at dinner a bit ago and he said that sellin' of your loan took place right under his nose and he didn't even know it. I was for givin' him a piece of me mind, but that poor man was so crestfallen, I didn't have the heart. Can ya come to the store tomorrow for tea and scones, Maddie girl?"

"Sure, I'd love a break and some time to talk about a job. I want to tell you all the news. I am not going to lose Broken Acres. And what is this between you and Mr. Chamberlain?"

"Saints be praised. Your farm is safe. I look forward to hearin' all about that. And, this is not about *me* havin' dinner with the fine man. Sure and I'll be seein' ya at nine. That gives us plenty o' time to chat before the openin' of the store."

SIXTY

After the Wednesday night Bible study Nathan asked the pastor of the church he attended in Carterville if he could sit in the sanctuary to process some of his thoughts. Sitting in the front pew he looked around at the Bible verses painted on the walls.

"For God so loved . . ."

"I am the way, and the truth, and the life . . ."

"If anyone wishes to come after Me . . ."

"Blessed are those who are invited to the marriage supper of the Lamb . . ."

"God, You call us over and over. Looking back I can see that so clearly now. You kept calling me until I gave in and said yes. You never gave up on me. Please, God, don't give up on Maddie."

Nathan hung his head, held it in his hands, and whispered, "God, I'm new at this Christian stuff, and I thank You for never turning Your back on me. I know I don't deserve to ask You for anything with the life I've lived." He looked up at the cross that hung on the wall behind the pulpit.

"Thank You, Jesus, for Your sacrifice for me. Me. A loser if ever there was one."

Nathan wiped the tears from his face. "What I felt for Chelsea was about as far from love as it could be. Lust, yes; love, no. I think I was trying to fill the emptiness I felt with a person. What a blueprint for disaster. God, I think I'm in love with Maddie. Ah, You know, Madison Crane." He looked up again.

"Keeping my hands off her is getting harder and harder. And the pastor said in his sermon that some guy named Paul said we need to stay pure when it comes to sex. You know I have not been good at doing that. But I didn't know."

He looked up to the beamed ceiling. "The pastor said we are supposed to wait until we get married to another Christian to have sex. Is that even possible? But what if the other person isn't a Christian? What happens there? Maddie's kids believe in You. But she is pretty clear that she's not one of Your flock. Is that right? The pastor said something about sheep. I am getting this all messed up."

Nathan rubbed his forehead. "I have to confess, I am not pure. I've probably done everything the Bible says you are not supposed to do. But I want to change that. Be the man You want me to be. Can You help me out here?"

He closed his eyes and shook his head. "Could You please, God . . . don't give up on Maddie? And keep me strong when I'm around her. This is really hard." Nathan looked up again at the cross.

"What You did was harder."

*   *   *

"Bracy, Lydia, dinner is ready," Maddie called out the front window.

The two girls came in, passing through the squeaky screen door without even a second look at it. There was comfort now in the everyday sound.

"When does Ruth get here?"

"She should arrive in the next day or two. Bracy, pass the carrots please."

"Maddie, I wanted to talk to you about Ruth."

"What about her, Lydia?"

"Well, she and Bracy ought to share the spare bedroom—"

"No." Both Maddie and Bracy said in unison.

"Ruth can stay in the suite off the kitchen in the big house now that we've cleaned it up and made it livable. The Taulbees said they felt very comfortable in the suite."

"Oh, I wouldn't feel good about that. I could stay there while she's here."

"Now, Lydia, you are as much a part of this family as Ruth is."

Lydia's face shaded red. "Thank you, Maddie, that's very kind of you, but—"

"No buts. Besides, I have a feeling Ruth may need a place where she can have some alone time."

Bracy looked up from her plate. "Why's that?"

"I don't know exactly. Just a feeling. I think it will be good for her to have her own space."

"If you change your mind, you let me know and I'll move my stuff."

"Lydia, it will be fine, really."

Bracy smiled big. "Besides, I like having you as my roommate."

Lydia's eyes smiled. "Was your sister ever your roommate?"

"No, thank God."

"How come?"

"She is very . . ." Bracy glanced at her mom and shrugged.

"Organized?"

"That's a nice way of putting it."

*   *   *

Nathan walked up the steps of the cottage to the porch and reached out to knock on the screen door when he heard singing through the open window. He leaned against the support post of the porch, his arms crossed, right ankle resting on his left, captivated by the melodious sound coming from the woman's lips. Memories of the first time he knocked on that door came flooding back. One of the many arguments and loss of temper both he and Maddie had experienced early on.

When quiet humming replaced the singing, Nathan stepped forward and knocked lightly on the screen.

Maddie came to the door wiping her hands on a towel. "Nathan."

He squinted to see her face better through the screen. It looked like her cheeks were tinted a little pink. "Are you baking?"

"Baking? No."

Nathan's curiosity pressed him on.

"Did I catch you in the middle of something?" Was she embarrassed?

"No. No, just washing dishes. Would you like to come in?"

He could feel his own cheeks warm. "No, thank you. I just found out it was Jase who paid off your loan. Sorry my legal department couldn't get that information quicker. Did Jase tell you?"

"Well, not originally."

"Huh?"

"I, ah, got tired of waiting for your legal department and went to see Elias again."

"And when did you do that?"

"Well, actually, three days after our first visit."

"Aha."

"Now, don't get angry. I found the information I needed sitting right there on the counter while Elias was away from his desk."

"Really?"

"Don't give me that look. It's not like I was rummaging through his files. It really doesn't matter how I found out. Jase and I had a talk about his plans, now that he owns my loan on Broken Acres."

"And?"

"And, he has no intention of keeping it. His father was the one who originally bought it and he planned to foreclose." Maddie shivered.

"Okay." Nathan held his hands out palms up.

"It's kind of an involved story."

"I'd like to hear it."

Maddie blew out a frustrated breath. "Well, Jase wanted to be free of his father's tight hold on his life since he would have owned the land Jase had his cattle on. So he took all of his savings and investments and paid off the loan. That means he owns Broken Acres." Maddie grimaced.

"Jase has no desire to own Broken Acres, he's simply a good guy trying to help a friend and show his father he is determined to live his life his own way. I've already started making payments and plan to find a way to buy Broken Acres back from Jase."

"Yeah, that's pretty much what my legal department found out. So how are you going to buy back the farm?"

"I haven't quite figured out all the details yet. But Jase and I have a plan to partner up so the stipulations of his grandfather's will can be met. Since he now owns a farm, well, he calls it a ranch, as his grandfather wanted, he can go on to the next phase. So we'll keep the arrangement like this until he has met all his grandfather's requirements. I've got a sign up at the market looking for farmers to lease parcels on Broken Acres, and Gael O'Donnell has hired me to work in her shop. I get to work with the customers, help with inventory, and she's going to teach me how to keep her books. She's thinking of opening another shop in Carterville. I would manage O'Donnell's Brier in Jacob's Bend while she manages her new store. So I'll be able to pay Jase monthly, and eventually, I'll figure out a way to borrow the money to pay off the loan."

"It sounds like you've got this all figured out. Are you sure I can't—"

"Absolutely not."

Nathan turned and faced the big house. He breathed deep to clear the agitation that was building. "I actually stopped by to say I won't be able to work on the big house—"

"What? Why not?" A frown replaced her sheepish grin.

"My partner, Tim, is taking a month-long honeymoon to travel around Europe. I have to run the company from our corporate office in Portsmouth."

Maddie ran a hand over her forehead and pushed silky waves that fell in her eyes away from her face. "A month. What am I going to do?"

"Maddie, if you'll let me finish?"

She looked into his deep blue eyes through the screen. "Okay."

"I know you didn't want to hire any of my guys to help me with the renovation, but I have some seasoned, experienced construction workers who have been with me for years. I'm considering one who could work on the reno while I'm gone, now that the rest of the materials have been ordered."

"But, Nathan, I can't afford anyone from your construction crew."

He laughed. "But you can afford their boss?"

"Oh, that. We had an agreement before I knew you owned a million-dollar construction company."

"That's true. And I plan to honor that by making up the difference for the salary of the man I want to replace me—on the job—for a month." He wanted to be sure she didn't replace him for anything else.

"Nathan, I don't know. I don't feel good about it."

"About what?"

"About you paying his salary."

"Only part of it. You'll still be paying him what we agreed upon. You will still be in charge."

Maddie caught her lip between her teeth as she looked over at the big house. "Okay. I really don't have much of a choice. But only for a month, right?"

"Right. Absolutely. For sure."

SIXTY-ONE

R uth walked out of the lovely little suite off the kitchen and ran squarely into a guy carrying a sheet of drywall. White powder sprinkled her hair along with her Vera Wang top and designer jeans. "What are you doing?" she blurted out, brushing the powder from her clothes.

The man stuck his head around the side of the drywall. "What are you doing in here? Who are you?"

"I could ask you the same thing."

"But I asked first."

"This is my mother's farm, her house. I'm staying in the cook's suite." She pointed toward the kitchen.

"Oh."

"Oh? That's all you have to say? You've ruined my entire outfit." She glanced down at her top and pants.

The man looked her up and down with a sly frown. "You don't look ruined to me, lady."

She could feel the heat rising to her neck. "Who are you, anyway?"

"Name's Sampson. Jared Sampson." He set the piece of drywall down, the muscles in his arms bulging from the weight, and offered his gloved hand.

"Well, Mr. Sampson, I'll be sure to send you the dry-cleaning bill."

Ruth stomped toward the cottage, the squeaky slam of the screen door mirroring her mood.

*   *   *

"Mom, who is that guy over at the big house?"

"Oh, that's Jared Sampson."

"I got his name, and a dusting of drywall powder." She fanned her clothes for her mom to see. "What is he doing over there? I thought a man named Nathan was doing the reno."

"He was. His partner is on his honeymoon, a month-long honeymoon. Nathan had to return to their corporate office to run the company in Tim's absence. So he sent Jared to work on the big house."

"Well, *Jared* needs to learn some manners. He totally powdered me with drywall dust."

"That's not a very good way to begin your stay here."

Ruth shook her head and looked over at the coffee maker.

"Help yourself and then join me on the porch swing."

Ruth savored the coffee with both hands around the cup, taking in the warmth. "Mom, you need to oil that screen door."

Maddie smiled. "I don't even hear the squeak anymore."

The swing moved gently as the ladies sipped their coffee. The warmth of the coffee and the peace of the scene spread through Ruth as she looked around. The trees of the orchard seemed content in their soil. Beside her, her mom watched a scattering of birds wing through the morning sky. Rusty and Sarg slept just outside the reach of the screen door, should it open.

"Those two are so cute. You'd think they grew up together here on the farm."

Maddie nodded. "Sometimes they can get on each other's nerves and snap at one another. But mostly they're pals."

Muffled hammering caused Ruth to look over at the big house, and she caught her mom's green eyes full of concern, watching her.

"Okay, tell me what's going on, Ruth, and don't try to hide behind nice talk."

A single tear fell on Ruth's lap. "Oh, Mom, I'm afraid I made a terrible mistake."

"What kind of mistake?"

"Matt."

"What about Matt?"

Ruth looked her mom in the eyes and lowered her gaze to the coffee cup in her hands. She knew even though her mom was a patient woman, she would only wait so long to hear Ruth's story, and then there would be questions. Lots of questions.

"My marriage to Matt is a farce."

Ruth let the sentence hang in the morning air for a moment. How to explain?

"When I first met Matt, he asked me out on a date. During dinner he offered me a business proposition. Since Matt is from England and was here on a job visa, he could only stay for a short period of time before having to return home. He wanted to live and work here permanently." She squinted at her mom. "He said if I would marry him, in name only, he would put me through college, pay for all my schooling. Since I wanted to be a doctor and didn't have the money to finish all eight years of medical school, I thought it was a good plan. Matt gets the US citizenship he wants and I get a doctor's degree."

Her mom's face showed shock and concern. "Ruth, I knew you wanted to train to be a medical assistant of some sort, but I never knew you wanted to be a doctor."

"It just kind of evolved from assistant, to nurse, to doctor. I, ah, kinda feel like God is leading me this way."

"God?" *What is going on with my kids?*

"Yes, God. I hadn't given Him much attention for several years. When the reality of what we had done hit me I was guilt-ridden and overwhelmed. I decided to start attending a church in Texas. You know, there is one on almost every street corner. Anyway, God and I are on good terms now. I know it wasn't His idea or plan for us to live this lie. Yet for some reason God continues to love and encourage me."

"Hmm."

Ruth shook her head. "Anyway, becoming a DO was a dream I never knew I had."

"DO?"

"Doctor of osteopathic medicine. They are trained to ask questions to get a good understanding of a patient's lifestyle, which can impact their condition. DOs take a more natural approach to treatment, but they can prescribe medications if necessary."

"Ruth, I think it sounds like a great field to get into. But this is not the way to do it."

"I know that now, Mom. Matt is a great guy. He's always felt like another brother to me. I thought we could help each other out."

"Ruth."

"I know. Believe me, I know."

"What does Matt's family say about this?"

"That's the thing. He doesn't have any family in England. He was raised in an orphanage and always dreamed of being an engineer and working in the US. He worked his way through college and then after graduation he was offered the job with Dad's firm."

"So what are you going to do?" Maddie's concerned expression only deepened Ruth's sense of guilt.

"After we got married I helped Matt fit into the corporate scene as his devoted wife. I had learned a lot growing up watching you help Dad become a success."

Maddie breathed deep and shook her head. "And from what David has told me, you also watched and heard our tumultuous relationship. I'm sorry you kids had to go through that. I thought we were hiding it from all three of you."

"Mom, that's all in the past."

"I know. But I feel so bad that those years of ab—" Maddie swung her head around and looked Ruth in the eyes.

"Abuse?"

"I'm so sorry if you've been scarred in any way."

"Mom, we are all okay. Sometimes I have flashbacks, but I just tell myself that was a long time ago and things are different now. They are better."

"Yes, they are."

"Anyway, not long after you moved out here, I went back to school. I finished what was left of my general ed. at the junior college. I have worked hard toward getting my BS degree. I still have another year of school to make that a reality. Matt has been great. He's not only paid for everything, he has been my biggest encourager. And now I'm looking at several more years of osteopathic medical school and two years of residency with hands-on training. But I don't want to look at more years of marriage to Matt."

"Does Matt know how you feel?"

"He knows I've never been happy with the fake marriage. He's set to take the naturalization test to become a citizen next month. Once he takes the oath of allegiance and becomes a US citizen, we can get a divorce."

Maddie cringed. "You don't feel anything for him, Ruth?"

"I feel toward him like I do David, like a brother. There are definitely no romantic feelings on either side." Ruth hesitated, then continued. "Actually, he met a girl and wants to date her, but he can't tell her what's going on until he receives his citizenship papers."

"Has he been kind to you?"

"Matt is the gentlest, kindest man I've ever met. He treats me like a kid sister."

"That's good."

"Mom, I know it was dishonest to marry Matt, but he has nothing and no one to go back to in England. Here he has a good job and friends, and we are as close as he's ever had to a family."

"He's always been like a son to me. And I'm pretty sure David and Bracy think of him as a brother. We all love Matt." Ruth could almost hear her mother's thoughts reeling, but the next question was surprisingly simple. "What will you do now?"

"Matt will still pay for my schooling after we're divorced. He's not the kind of guy to break a promise. Even an expensive one." Ruth gave a rueful laugh.

Maddie shook her head. "This sounds so unfair to Matt, Ruth. How is he with all this?"

"We both knew from the beginning this is how it would end; we just weren't sure how long it would take. The United States government says we have to be married and living together for a minimum of three years. It often takes a lot longer, which is why we have been married almost four and a half years. They have been good years, really, Mom. Matt has been busy building his career, and I've been busy making school a priority." Ruth took Maddie's hands in hers.

"Mom, I love Matt like a brother, and I know he cares about me in the same way." Ruth smiled. "It's been like having David as a roommate all this time. But I miss my family. I want to be with all of you."

Her mother's arms pulled Ruth into a tight hug. "Of course. But how will that work? You have to live here a year to claim residency to attend a university."

"I know, and I told Matt he could use that money from the year I'm out of school for himself, buy a house, take an extended vacation, whatever. You know what he said?"

"What?" Maddie looked skeptical.

Ruth teared up. "He said he would pay the out-of-state cost, and if I didn't agree he would just put the money away to pay for med school."

"Oh my goodness, Ruth. What an amazing man of integrity. Can he afford the out-of-state tuition?"

"He says he can. Mr. Birnbaum, from Dad's firm, thinks the sun rises and sets on Matt. He is grooming him to take his position as CEO. Matt seems to instinctively know a good investment from a bad one. It seems like Mr. B. gives him a raise every quarter. Not to mention his commissions are through the roof. Mom, trust me when I say that Matt makes a lot of money."

"I'm so glad for Matt."

Ruth nodded. "Some woman is going to get a real treasure when he falls in love." Ruth turned to look at her mother, surprised that the next question seemed so hard. "Mom, what do you think? Can I come home?"

Tears filled her mother's eyes. She held out her arms, and Ruth snuggled into her warm and familiar embrace with a smile. "Welcome home, sweetheart. I will love having all my chicks under my wings."

Ruth pushed back and squinted at her mother.

"Okay, let me rephrase that. I will love having you all nearby."

"It can't happen soon enough for me. I never thought I'd be homesick for a place I barely know. But this place, this farm, definitely feels like home."

SIXTY-TWO

Granny Harper knew just about every family in the valley. As well as every farmer, orchard grower, and vineyard owner.

"Granny, thank you for putting me in touch with your neighbors. I needed the work and the money."

"Lydia, you are one of the most efficient and hardworking women I've ever met. I wish John had enough work around here to keep you on full time." With Lydia's lovely bronze complexion, Granny couldn't tell if the woman was blushing, but the look in Lydia's eyes told her she felt encouraged.

"Thank you. My father was big on work ethic and going beyond what was expected. It feels good to know I've done a good job."

"Good? I'd say exemplary is more like it."

Lydia bent her head and tucked her chin into her chest.

Now Granny knew for sure Lydia was blushing. "So, Lydia, have you had any experience working in vineyards?"

Lydia's head shot up. "Oh yes. It was my favorite picker's job."

"I'd say you are much more than a picker, Lydia. You have a love for all growing things. I watched how carefully, but quickly, you brought the fruits and vegetables to your canvas pouch."

"I love the scent of the raw earth. I'm amazed at how it gives forth such beautiful and tasty crops."

"That would be God's doing."

Lydia smiled.

"So, my friend Tony owns a vineyard on the other side of the valley." Granny waved her arm toward the east. "He's looking for reliable people to help prune his vines. He had a very good harvest this year."

Lydia's eyes lit up. "I'm your girl." Lydia's troubled gaze settled on Granny's fields.

"Are you okay, Lydia?" The elder woman gave her a gentle touch on the shoulder.

"Oh, ah, yeah. I was just thinking about my brother. He always wanted to be a vintner."

"Is that right? Is he working at a vineyard somewhere?"

Lydia took a deep breath. "No, he died a few years ago."

"Oh, Lydia, I'm so sorry." Granny had a sense Lydia did not want to talk about her loss.

"So you have some experience then, trimming the vines? I understand there is a precise science in pruning each vine."

Lydia gave a half smile. "I have a little experience. But I would very much like to learn more."

"Well, Tony's your man. His award-winning vineyard has been handed down from his grandfather to his father to him and probably a few generations before that. Tony learned everything at his grandfather and father's knees. Legend has it his great-grandfather brought the first rootstock from Italy. Strong, vibrant stock."

"Really? Wow, that's amazing. Yes, I would love to help prune Tony's vines."

"Here's Tony's phone number. Tell him you are the Lydia I told him about."

Blushing again. "Thank you, Granny."

*   *   *

Lydia thought back to her brother's dream to be a vintner and how his life was cut short by an arrogant, bloodthirsty gang boss. "Jose, you would love it here in Jacob's Bend. Good, rich, fertile soil. Nice people." It felt like home.

A deep male voice spoke into her ear.

"Hello."

"Oh, ah, hello. Is this Tony?"

"Yes. Who is this?"

"This is Lydia Lopez. I think Granny Harper mentioned me to you?"

"Oh yeah. Hi, Lydia. Granny tells me you're a good, hard worker. Have you done any work with grape vines?"

"Yes, some. More with fruit and vegetable picking."

"Well, I can always use a good worker. The crop this November was excellent. The wine from these grapes ought to be one of the best we've had. I usually give my workers a few weeks off and let the vines rest after we pick. We normally start pruning after the holidays. We'll begin next week. Why don't you plan on coming out to the farm next Monday unless someone calls and tells you otherwise?"

"Okay. Great. Thanks, Tony."

*   *   *

Lydia stood on the knoll overlooking Broken Acres. Home. Family. Maddie had said so. A new beginning.

If this was going to be her home, she needed to leave the past where it belonged. She needed to quit hiding and live her life, instead of living like a mole burrowing below the ground in the dark. If they came, they came.

"I have a family now. A family." Lydia grinned and stepped to the other side of the knoll and walked the short distance . . . home.

SIXTY-THREE

S trolling through the town graveyard, Maddie sat on the first bench she came to. She kept trying to make sense of her jumbled thoughts. That only made them collide and shatter into a dozen more.

Why was everything so hard? Why couldn't at least one thing turn out the way she had planned? All she wanted was to do something, one thing, on her own. To show people she could accomplish something.

No, Maddie, you want Jeff to know you are able to set a goal and finish it without his help. To prove him wrong. But he's gone. And death certainly terminates dreams.

She opened her eyes and glanced at the monuments that stood before her. Headstones. Lost lives. Lost dreams. Who were they? Did these people make an impact on the loved ones in their lives, or like her, were they failures?

Failure. That pretty much summed up her life. After Jeff's heart attack, as she tried to cope with the aloneness and took on all the challenges of being a widow, she had no idea what she was doing, as was evidenced by where she found herself now.

Swiping stubborn tears with the back of her hand, she walked among the headstones reading the epitaphs. "Dearly Loved Sister. Patient Caring Friend. Beloved Wife." She couldn't help but wonder if she was any of those things. Or would her legacy be "failure to realize her destiny"? Destiny. What exactly was she set apart to accomplish? Because whatever it was, she was failing terribly in the process to get there.

Maddie stopped at the Goldberg family plot and sat on the half wall that encased it. She looked up. "Why am I here? My life has no meaning. I keep messing up so badly I can't imagine why You ever gave me life." She hit her forehead with her hand.

Good grief. Who was she talking to? Obviously not God, at least not a God who cared or helped people through life like Pastor Ben kept saying. His God didn't care two cents about her.

She closed her eyes tight. Suddenly long-ago life events flashed through her mind. Her and Carolyn playing together as kids. High school and college together. Standing up at each other's weddings. Life with Jeff. David, Ruth, Bracy. Jeff's death. Selling the Chicago house and most of their possessions and moving to Jacob's Bend where Carolyn and Alex lived. Lived. But no longer. They were back east in New York. She shook her head.

Pastor Ben's words tore at her heart. *"You are loved with an everlasting love. God cares for you like no one else ever could. He promises never to leave or forsake you. Believe it. Because God never lies."*

Could that be true? Did the God her gram loved and talked about really love her?

The last few lines of a poem she had read came to mind.

Quiet emptiness invades my mind.

Silence—everywhere—silence.

Forgotten.

Aloneness.

That was her life. Sure, there were people all around her, but in reality, inside she felt all alone.

A flock of geese flew overhead.

"When I see geese fly overhead, Mads, it reminds me that God hears me and I hear Him. It always seems to happen just after I've asked Him about something important in my life."

Maddie looked up. "Gram, how did you hear God?"

"You are never alone, Mads. God is always with you. Give Him a chance to show you how much He loves and forgives. Talk to Him. Tell Him your heart. God is listening."

"Gram, all the wise words you left me with. I wish I could believe like you did. Like the kids do. Like Jeff did." Maddie hung her head. "Even Nathan . . ."

"Talk to Him, Mads. God is listening."

*   *   *

Maddie walked along the neatly trimmed path reading the headstones.

"'Help us, O God . . . forgive our sins for Your name's sake.' Psalm 79:9"

He loves and forgives. Ben's message on forgiveness reminded Maddie of her anger with Jeff. Her pride became a priority over forgiving Jeff for his abuse.

Maddie breathed in the cool, crisp air and dug her hands into the back pockets of her jeans. She pulled a crinkled piece of paper from her pocket and remembered having taken the letter from Gram's Bible to make a copy for David. What was it Jeff had said?

I knew deep inside me I had found the one thing, Person, rather, who could take away my guilt. I cried like a baby and told God every sin I could remember and desperately asked Him to forgive me.

More geese flew overhead.

Maddie closed her eyes. "God, I'm beginning to think that You might be real."

She opened her eyes and stared down at the letter. She could see it. In the people around her. In her son and daughters. In the way things had fallen into place. In the protection and provision that had made it possible for her to keep Broken Acres.

Maddie's heart raced. "Michael," she whispered. "Oh my gosh. God, You gave me a precious grandson." She couldn't hold her guilt in any longer.

"God, it's not that I need to forgive others." She felt her cheeks. Hot. Wet.

Maddie looked up. "*I* need forgiveness. I need *Your* forgiveness."

Many Heartfelt Thanks

As my dear friend says, "One does not write a book alone." This is especially true with the Jacob's Bend series. In *Broken Acres* my characters tried more than once to direct their part in the story, with little success. However, in *Splintered Lives* they took literary license and pretty much told me situations in their lives I had no idea they had experienced. They had me apologizing for the unfortunate events they had to suffer. Events that continually surprised me throughout the story. Hopefully they surprised you too.

First and foremost, immense gratitude to The Three for walking through every chapter, scene, paragraph and word to bring this book to life. Without my Father, Jesus, and the Holy Spirit, there would not be a *Splintered Lives*. Truly, I simply have the privilege of holding the pen.

Tremendous, profound thanks to Val Coulman, who went through this book with a magnifying glass of literary insights; checking grammar, show don't tell, character development, and plot flow.

Julie Monroe, you are a godsend. Your editing has made this book a much more cohesive read and has made the author look like she knows what she is doing. Thank you. No, really . . . thank you!

It always amazes me how beta readers see things so differently, each pointing out exactly what is needed for the story to be what it ought to be. Thank you barely expresses how grateful I am for each of you. Roblynn Chance, Sue Cunningham, Alisha Geyer, and Kristi VanDuker, you all deserve so much more than a simple thank you. This story would not be what it is without your inspiring suggestions, ideas, and most important, prayers.

Sarah O'Neal, cover designer extraordinaire. Your cover design is once again magnificent. Thank you for always being willing to brainstorm when I give you a not-so-right picture that just won't work. And for seeing the possibilities of the one that will.

Janis Rubus, your photography always leaves me jaw-dropped. You capture the scene and the personality of this author so well. Thank you for your honesty and suggestions for another beautiful cover. Once again, thank you for your treasured friendship and listening ear.

Thank you, Dan Wright and Dave Sheets of Fitting Words Publishing Services and your talented team, for taking a chance on this newbie and for taking time to teach me what this *next level* is all about.

Words fail thinking of the time and love that went into the sketches of the Broken Acres farm. Kristi VanDuker, immense thankfulness goes out to you for your stunning work.

Thank you to Jared Brumble for his extensive banking experience in explaining the foreclosure process.

And to you, dear reader, you make it pure pleasure to put pen to paper and tell the story of characters I hope you will adopt into your heart. That you will weep when they weep and laugh when they laugh. May they capture your heart as they have mine.